to Irene I [...] (£2.00)

D0459501

# *The* HOLDING

# The HOLDING

## MERILYN SIMONDS

M&S

**National Library of Canada Cataloguing in Publication**

Simonds, Merilyn, 1949-
The holding / Merilyn Simonds.

ISBN 0-7710-8065-4

I. Title.

PS8587.I46H65 2004     C813'.54     C2003-906716-5

We acknowledge the financial support of the Government of Canada through the Book Publishing Industry Development Program and that of the Government of Ontario through the Ontario Media Development Corporation's Ontario Book Initiative. We further acknowledge the support of the Canada Council for the Arts and the Ontario Arts Council for our publishing program.

This is a work of fiction. Names, characters, places, and incidents either are the products of the author's imagination or are used fictitiously.

Typeset in Centaur by M&S, Toronto
Printed and bound in Canada

This book is printed on acid-free paper that is 100% recycled, ancient-forest friendly (100% post-consumer recycled)

McClelland & Stewart Ltd.
*The Canadian Publishers*
481 University Avenue
Toronto, Ontario
M5G 2E9
www.mcclelland.com

1 2 3 4 5     08 07 06 05 04

# *The* HOLDING

# MARGARET

*Summer 1859*

*I am a woman Alone in all the wide World.*

*Until today I had three Brothers, William Wallace, Robert Bruce, Harry Douglas, named for good Scots heroes, every one. Margaret the Queen, they called me. Now the Queen has taken her Revenge.*

---

Margaret pauses, regretting the baldness of the last sentence. But it won't do to start crossing out. As it is, she has but a few pages at the back of the old book on which to tell her story. The task nearly overwhelms her. If only she could put it on paper as it exists in her mind, years recollected as a single moment – the seawall at Pittenweem, the Madawaska hills, the crossing, the clearing, Ewan, all one.

But time and space rule the page, force her to chip at the round stone of memory, choosing this bit, discarding that, so much overlooked, abandoned as she rearranges the fragments to make a path from then to now, from there to here where she sits on a stump within view of the cabin, the plates of rabbit stew unwashed on the table, sauce congealing on her brothers' lips.

There's just time to make this record, leave something of herself behind, then she'll find her way out.

That was how it ended, but where does it begin?

Pittenweem. A small child on her knees, coarse grass pressing crosshatches into her skin. She is pushing a little boat around a puddle, a boat she fashioned from a scrap of paper she found blowing down the wynd. She wore it like a cap as she rambled the brae, looking down upon the cottages that clung like gannets' nests to the cliff at the heel of the bay. Coming across the puddle, she removed the hat and kissed it, setting it on the water, keeping it steady with one hand until she spied the brown lugsail, her father's boat, the *Mairead*, moving out through the Firth of Forth, pursuing the herring, the silver darlings, into the perilous North Sea.

Seven times she circles the boat around, not sunwise but the other way, withershins, her eyes never off the dark sailcloth though it shrinks to the size of a pocket handkerchief, an envelope, a stamp. Then she stops, and as if impatient with her game or with a puddle so circumscribed, she strikes the paper sail, capsizing the little craft.

The child hears her name called and turns to see her mother running through the gorse, the flowers a shifting golden flame against the dark sky of the woman's skirts.

The mother scolds the girl as she pulls her to her feet. Have you no thought for your father and brothers? Come, bring this wee Fifie to safe harbour.

And she stretches her daughter's hand, forces her fingers to the sagging sail, but the child will not take hold. The two of them stand, their backs to the sea, wind fingering their red-black curls, mother and daughter, alike as two leaves on one tree, each stubborn as the other.

The mother relents first. With her own hand she sets the boat right and guides it to the shore, lifting it into her apron pocket. You're an odd one Margaret Jannet, with your tempers and your stares. Whatever shall become of you?

We will leave this place, she says, the words told to her so often they come to her as memory.

The wind, like a gossip, is everywhere. It fusses with their hair as they stand on the braehead and it writhes through the village kirkyard, too.

Margaret is older now, as tall as her mother. Her bedgown jacket, printed with blue heart's-ease, billows gently at her chest and her layered petticoats, the topmost one drawn back as an apron, give the appearance of widening hips, though by the slimness of her hands it is clear she is still a girl. She stands with her mother before the family marker, a plain grey stone like all the rest, inscribed already with too many names. Sophia, Robert Roy, and James Henry, all lost to the cholera, the babies Isobel and Bride, dead even as they entered the world, and the most recent, Angus Stewart, lost at sea when Margaret was only seven. For him, the weight of stone holds nothing down.

*You ask too much of me*, her mother whispers, although her father is nowhere near.

A sway of dark skirt, and Margaret leans to glimpse a woman slipping between the graves. She follows, for she has seen her before, though always at a distance, gathering simples on the brae or seaweed on the tidal rocks, pausing by the kirk tower or at the lip of the seawall, gazing down at the water that worries the stones, one hand fixed on the last bollard as if she were tethered to it. There is something odd about her clothes, the old-fashioned white cloth she wears under her head-square, the rough weave of her skirt. Odder still is her bearing, something furtive in her posture despite her frame, which is sturdy, and her glance, which is compelling, defiance in her eye. Margaret has followed her down the wynds from High Street to the Shore but she loses her every time, once by St. Fillan's sea-cave, once in the knot of fishermen that gathers at an upper turn to stare across the roof-tops, taking measure of the weather as it moves across the Firth. The old woman is an incomer, a stranger to the village who seems to pass unnoticed by everyone but her.

She pursues her now between the obelisks and the monuments until at last she has her trapped. The old woman turns to face her, a slight smile on her lips, as though this was her intention, the two of them alone in a crease of wall where the grass grows high and the markers are laid flat as if to make certain the dead keep to their place. The old woman regards Margaret with encouragement, a promise in her gaze, but before the girl can think to ask who she is or what she wants, the woman takes a step back and dissolves through the stones.

But that is not where the story starts, in childish games or faintly smiling ghosts. It begins, like birth, in blood.

*My name is Margaret Jannet and I come from Pittenweem, where the mother of my mother's mother's mother, Jannet Cornfoot, died condemned a Witch.*

The tide is turning, the sea withdrawing into itself, allowing its bones to show. Soon the men on the seawall will slip the ropes from the bollards and the emigrant ship, the *Deirdre*, will sail out to sea, past the May Isle, which in that troubled light of early spring seems to hover above the Firth.

Margaret leans on the ship's rail, watching the ribs of stone rise, then the water shifts, the sunlight darkens, and the old woman rises, too. A rope is tethered around her body. It stretches from the bowsprit of the *Deirdre* to a clutch of men on the seawall who are hauling on the rope mightily, pulling the woman up, her neck, her arms, her chest exposed, and Margaret thinks, they're saving her!, but the men let slip the rope and the woman sinks under the waves, out of sight so long Margaret believes she surely must be drowned. Then the men set to work and haul her up again, spluttering.

The villagers gathered on the shore jostle, pressing forward for a better view, the fishermen careful not to wet their feet though the women boldly wade into the seawater, rucking up their skirts, mindless of their modesty, their fish-hawking voices chanting a shrill chorus, though Margaret can't make out the words.

Only one man is brave enough or fool enough to step into the sea. A sailor tosses him the rope and he strains against the tide, dragging the woman's body out onto the rising stones, stones that Margaret has crouched over nearly every day of her life, picking whelks and winkles to bait her father's lines, gathering sea-moss for carrageen jelly when her brothers' throats were raw.

She looks away, to the passengers milling behind her on the deck. They move as in a dream, oblivious.

The woman's clothes are torn from her body, which lies broken and bruised upon the stones, parts splayed at odd angles, swollen beyond their natural form, breasts blackened by fire, her belly sieving fluid from a thousand pinpricked holes.

The sight stays the mob, and in that fresh moment of silence, Margaret thinks she hears the woman breathe, hears a faint rasp of words, though whether they beg for mercy or pray for death she can't be sure. The woman's whispers stir the rabble as a breeze stirs fallen leaves, and they move about uncertainly. Then a shout gives them purpose, and they part for a brace of men bearing a door like the Ark of the Covenant high above their heads.

The men hurl the door onto the broken body, and as if waiting for that signal, the horde scatters along the shore, prying up boulders in a frenzy, casting them down upon the door, stone on stone on wood on bone, a pummelling like thunder, like rapid cannonfire, while the man who walked in the sea, the man dressed all in black, lifts his face to the heavens, singing,

> In the name of Jesus
> In the name of Jesus
>     we have the victory
> In the name of Jesus
>     demons will have to flee

His words are drowned in the rumble of a sledge drawn along the shore. The driver whips the oxen, prodding them onto the stones, onto the door pressed onto the woman, driving the beasts forward, yanking them back, whipping them forward again. The others, worn out with their labours, content themselves with taunts — what good your simples and your charms now, Jannet Cornfoot? — until no more blood seeps among the stones.

Margaret bows her head to her hands, her fingers taut against her temples, her pulse a reassurance, a blessing, a curse.

The weather for the most part is fair, with a right wind that pushes the *Deirdre* through the green galleries of the sea. At times, the breeze is so light that the water seems scarcely interrupted by the ship's keel. At others, it stops altogether and the sails collapse with a rustle and a sigh. Then the ship drifts for hours, purposeless, expectant. The passengers hush their conversations and their movements, in the belief that by keeping very still they might entice the wind to fill the sails with its breath. The fisher-folk among them set to whistling softly, luring breezes with wordless, tuneless ditties, while above them on the deck, the crew, for the same reason, hurl knives into the mast from as great a dis-tance as they dare.

Once, the wind in its whimsy whirls around to blow from the south, driving the *Deirdre*, unwilling, toward the top of the world and then, as if to make them lose their bearings altogether, it spins the ship like a child in a game of blind man's buff and blows them back from whence they came.

At best, the passage across the Atlantic takes a fortnight, but they are at the mercy of the wind and the sea. Toward the end of the third week, after a period of eerie calm, Margaret watches a stiff breeze making for them, its progress a spreading stain upon the waves. By nightfall, all the sea is aboil. The captain kilts up the sails' folds in preparation for the gale, but still the wind drives them into a landscape of liquid mountains, whipping the ship up steep slopes one minute, propelling it down into black chasms the next. Seawater spews across the decks, spilling through cracks in the timbered flanks. The ropes and yards howl as the wind tugs at the sheets, and when the ship meets a wave head-on, it moans like a sailor punched in the ribs.

I saw the new mune late yestreen
Wi' the auld moon in her arms,

An ever an alake, my friend
'Tis a token o' deidly storms,

                          her father sings as his family
huddles in the lower of their two berths, their arms wrapped
around each other's waists to keep themselves from tumbling into
the puddles spreading over the floor.

The hedge of household goods the emigrants constructed in
the passageway, shaping snug dens of privacy between the rows
of berths, splits apart. Trunks and barrels, boxes and kists, creels
and sculls topple, skittering bow to stern, port to starboard,
until the baggage is so strewn and mixed that it will take days of
calm for each family to recover its own. And when they do, there
will be curses and deep-hearted sighs, for if they were foolish
enough to pack a China teapot or a looking glass, it will be
smashed to smithereens, and the cloth satchels and pasteboard
boxes will be soaked with seawater and worse, for urine and
faeces slop from the privacy buckets and the floorboards are
slick with sickness.

Almost no one is immune to the *Deirdre*'s mad tossing. Not
those who dose themselves with whisky mixed with mustard, or
Quires powders, or drops of laudanum. Not those who hold at
arm's length a tumbler half-filled with water, concentrating
with all their power on keeping the liquid level. Though the
MacBaynes, sipping a tea that Margaret's mother makes from
peppermint leaves and crushed cloves, suffer less than the others.

The passengers are battened below deck for days while the storm wears itself out, but Margaret is never afraid. She has lived all her life by the sea, and she knows how capricious it can be, how swiftly it can change from nourishing mother to the she-devil that hides fish and drowns brothers and sons. Being accustomed to a danger lessens its operation on the mind, and so Margaret's thoughts are left clear, although the threat itself is not removed, nor the knowledge of it, and caution installs itself in some deep place from whence it can reach out to touch the heart in unsuspected ways.

They sit in utter darkness, the lanterns put out lest they capsize in the ship's roll and set them all afire. They sit listening to the wind, to the waves, to the creaking timbers, to the heave and thud of the little vessel, straining for the first signal that the storm is ending, the first sign of their salvation or their doom.

One by one, they tire of listening. Just as the cradle-rocking of forward motion became the normal way of things, so the desperate roll grows commonplace. Robert Bruce ventures first, teaching his sturdy limbs to move about in the dark, hanging on to the ends of berths, timing his progress to the pitch of the deck, a few broad strides as the ship pauses at the centre of its pendulum, then running uphill or down as the *Deirdre* leans into the next wave, hopping over the sickly waste that swills across the floor.

When the less afflicted among them take out their whistles, their pipes, and fiddles to play the songs of home, songs of a calmer sea, Robert Bruce pulls his dour older brother to his feet, and soon all three MacBayne boys are beating the rhythm with their heavy boots on the hollow wooden floor, the movements of William Wallace economically precise, Robert Bruce perspiring copiously with his exertions, while young Harry Douglas flails about like a drunkard, his fervent dance steps deranged by the mad tossing of the sea. Even Margaret's mother hums along as her husband sings,

> When haddocks leave the Firth of Forth, and mussels leave
> the shore,
> When oysters climb up Berwick Law, we'll go to sea no
> more.
> — No more — we'll go to sea no more.

What saves Margaret is not the music, but the trees. Curled against the hull in the darkness, she inhales the final breaths of the stalwart logs that last made the crossing in that hold, torn from their home-soil to furnish masts for English ships. The Bush, the Backwoods, the Pineries — those words mean nothing to her yet, and although Fife was named for its forests, they fell so long before her time that she grew up knowing trees only in isolation or in poor huddled clumps: the pears in their neighbour's dooryard, the sycamores that straggled down the road out of Pittenweem. She could no more imagine a forest than she could forget the sea.

Still, she catches the scent of pine and savours it, picks at the shiny amber tears that course down the wall, rolls the sticky residue between her fingers, sniffing it, laying it on her tongue. The taste is pungent, mysterious. She plucks a new piece every night, believing that if she holds it in her cheek until morning, she'll dream the secrets of the place her father would have them call home.

*My father was a Fife fisherman, but he never loved the Sea. He was a Highland man, and his Heart ached for unfettered Hills. So we set sail for the wilds of Canada to live as God intended, as Lairds of the Lakes and Forests.*

Because she is slight and still all but a girl, Margaret can go wherever she pleases. When the hatches are opened and the emigrants driven from the hull — for the sake of their health, the captain declares — she huddles against a bulwark in the part of the ship reserved for those who have paid first-class passage, out of sight of the ladies and gentlemen who stroll the deck or assemble their chairs to rest under rugs in the sun, dipping their pens in silver inkwells, committing their thoughts and observations to leather-bound journals.

From her lookout, Margaret sees spouting black whales big as Jonah's leviathan and shoals of dolphins and porpoises, leaping and turning summersets, crossing back and forth before the bow. If her brothers are near, she might cry out, Grampus on the port side!, but she never shouts the word, Porpoise!, as some of the ladies and gentlemen do. Just as she never cuts her nails on Sunday or starts to knit a gansey on Friday, for she takes it as given that no enterprise will succeed if commenced on that ominous day. In the morning, when she rises from her berth, she puts her right shoe on first, and when a bad smell flares her nostrils, she spits. She never wears green, the colour of the faeries, and she always ties a red thread, the conquering colour, somewhere on her person. And although she left her piece of charmed witchwood hanging by her cottage bed, she said nothing, understanding how unlucky it is to turn back once a journey is begun. She knows these things the way one knows to breathe, with the same unthinking certainty. That these well-bred men and women, raised with all of life's advantages, do not think to take similar precautions is an astonishment to her.

The birds she saw during the first few days at sea were the same as those that kept her company on the red cliffs at Pittenweem – noddys and bawks, hagdowns and shags and sea maws. Then the sky emptied, a blank blue slate week after week, until they drew close to the Banks of Newfoundland, invisible to the eye but recognizable from the dram of whisky given to the seamen, a marker that the North Atlantic was safely at their backs.

That morning, out of the north, she spies a flock of birds heading into the sun, hundreds of them, thousands, the white flashes at their throats lighting the darkened sky like so many stars. Then creatures that might be black pigeons, with startling scarlet legs and a crimson lining in their mouths. And sooty brown birds, no bigger than robin-redbreasts, that scrabble about the masts. The seamen call them Mother Carey's chickens, but they seem to her like butterflies or dusky moths drawn to the sparkling brightness of the sails.

There are saddlebacks and blueys and all manner of other maws, which the seamen call gulls, and others that might have flown ahead from Fife to welcome her, so familiar are they to Margaret – plump sea parrots flitting across the surface of the waves, beating their little wings, their thick, painted beaks straining forward as if their bodies could be lifted by sheer will into the air. And once, off the starboard bow, a veil like snow that separates as the ship approaches into a thousand soaring birds, white as down, with sun-splashed heads, wearing the same blue mask Margaret marvelled at as they screamed their triumphs to the Pittenweem cliffs, their unblinking eyes on a level with hers.

And so the *Deirdre* sails on under skies thickening with wildfowl, past gleaming ice-cliffs, peaks loftier than spires, the sun shattering against the prism of each crest, so that meltwater cascading off the ledges leapt through rainbows to the sea. By day, the waves seethe with fishes. By night, they blaze with phosphorescence, signal fires to the emigrants' dreams.

The ship comes up against the fog before Margaret sees the land that made it.

A real Scotch mist, one of the English ladies remarks, peering into the white marl through her opera-glass.

The deck is damp with it. The sails wilt. The birds roosting on the yardarms fall silent, except for an occasional flapping as one or another readjusts its position. For days the sun is shut out by a gauzy cloud that swathes the ship from stern to bowsprit. Even the top of the centre mast is smothered, snapped off by God, for all she knows. The water licks lackadaisically at the hull as the ship drifts between Newfoundland and the island of Cape Breton, sidling toward the unseen continent, then into the cleft of the St. Lawrence River, the foghorn now and then sounding its plaintive bellow, the ship's bell clanging anxiously like the tap-tap-tapping of a blind man's stick searching to give shape to what lies ahead.

Fog and ice-cliffs and gales born far up the Arctic sea – these are the perils of an early crossing the MacBaynes were fore-warned against, but Margaret's father was determined. They would leave, he said, at the close of the prawn harvest, which was still decent on that coast, and before the herring drave began, when he could sell his boat to someone who still believed that the silver darlings would come back to the shores of Fife.

Through the autumn and early winter, her mother resisted the plan.

You are used to such uprooting, she'd say. Driven from the Highlands, moving up and down the coast alongside the herring 'til you found a place on my father's boat, which now is yours. Why leave just when the time has come to pass it to your sons?

Because they deserve more than a skiff to sail on waters empty of fish, he'd exclaim, slamming up the stairs to the attic, where Margaret would hear him singing through the night his songs of solitude, his *'S mi leam fhein,* he told her when she asked, climbing the stairs with his tea just before first light.

Her mother resisted his laments, his rants, and his cajoling, until the morning she opened the door to waves frozen as far as she could see. All up and down the Shore, those who had lived all their lives in the wake of the sea's endless motion stood mute on their doorsteps, transfixed by a glittering stillness that made it a labour just to breathe.

It happened once a century, that freezing of the sea. Some said it meant good fortune, the herring would return, but most predicted tragedy, for that is what is hoarded in the memory. The sea froze the month the coal-mine opened, drawing villagemen down into the earth, where seven of them died a suffocating death. The sea froze the year witches were found among them and thirteen were left to hang from the bowsprit of a ship. And so, when the sea stiffened again, her mother took it as a presage of calamitous events and agreed at last to leave.

For more than a week, the emigrant ship idles in the fog, its breathing sails moribund. Except for the anxiety, when one thinks of it, of ramming into another ship or running aground, it is not an unpleasant time. Rather, it has the air of an unexpected holiday. The hatches are kept open and the passengers stay on deck. They haul up their bedding, wash what they can, and spread the rest to air on the rails. Some of them drop lines into the water. Others knock Mother Carey's chickens from the rigging with long poles and roast them on spits beside the fish. No one complains of the delay, except for the stout merchants pacing the first-class deck. But the emigrants are grateful for the chance to make themselves presentable, for they know that Grosse Île lies somewhere in the haze ahead.

Margaret awakens one morning to the sight of land, not in the distance but close enough to touch, or so it seems after all those weeks at sea. No rocky cliffs or stony shores, just a furzy bolt of greenery that drapes to the river's edge, here and there a thread of smoke drifting up into the sky.

She tries to picture the cottages concealed within the seamless fabric of trees, tries to conjure the pleasures of a narrow sky, a strip of fancy cutwork overhead. But she has been nourished too long on far-reaching views. She cannot imagine the horizon caged behind a wattle of limbs and leaves, cannot conceive of what it means to be confined to what lies immediately at hand.

When the emigrant station appears at last, a jagged silhouette against the wildly setting sun, a low murmur sets up in the men and women at the rail – *Grosse Île, Grosse Île* – as though a strange, unnatural beast has risen from the river. The ship sidles into the bay and drops anchor before the hasty arrangement of sprawling sheds. Fat geese amble among the hawthorns at the shore, nibbling grass from between hummocks the dimension of graves.

The passengers, ordered onto the deck, are herded behind a rope stretched rail to rail across the bow. Another rope cordons off the empty stern. In between stand the doctors. One by one, the emigrants are called before the medical men to be turned this way and that, their mouths opened, the skin of their arms exposed, their eyelids drawn down, their tongues examined, fingers prodded rudely into the glands at the back of their necks, under their arms, between their outspread legs. Even the boldest among them holds his breath. Will he be waved toward the stern and permitted to carry on? Or will he be escorted down the gangplank onto the skiff that waits to row the sick ashore? For a doctor can see in the linings of their eyes and in the hue of their flesh, the first signs of what they allow themselves to contemplate only in their most desperate hours.

The cabin passengers are examined first, only one amongst them, a young gentleman of dissolute habits or so it is rumoured, ushered off the ship. Next come the men, women, and children of steerage. The emigrants watch in dismay and alarm as wife is parted from husband, father from sons, and in one instance, both parents removed with scarcely time to ask a stranger to care for their three small girls.

And then it is their turn. The boys, then Margaret and her mother, with her father, as head of the household, inspected last. They are all familiar with the signs of cholera – her father's mother was the first to succumb when the Black Death finally found the village of Pittenweem – and so, during the voyage, they practised rigorously the rules for its prevention. Cleanliness, Comfort, and Temperance. They swept out their berths as often as they were able, took exercise in the fresh air whenever they were allowed, pitched spoiled food overboard even when they were hungry, generously sprinkled salt on all they ate, and avoided acid foods, especially pickles and fruit, staving off the threat of scurvy with onions. Even Margaret, who loved the sharp taste of oranges, refused the dripping segment a seaman offered, deterred as much by her fear of loosened bowels as by what he might ask in return. The MacBaynes are thin – five weeks at sea has emptied their kists of the eggs and salt herring, the dried beef and bannocks they brought until all they have left is a few handfuls of meal and tea – but none of them has that blue cast to their skin, none has the blackened tongue, the endless shivering, the red spots on the shoulders that are the dread marks of the disease.

None except Margaret's father. When he lifts the gansey from his back, as he is ordered to do, he peels it up slowly, his eyes on the planks of the ship's deck, knowing the doctors will find what he has kept so well hidden.

Wait for me in Montreal, I'll find you there, he instructs his wife, then to his sons he recites, be steady of heart and stout of hand, with the will to do, the soul to dare. He kisses Margaret on the cheek and then he is gone, leaving her to replay forever the touch of his fingers on her hair, the lost look of love in his eyes.

*Our Father left us at Grosse Île. There was nothing we could do to save him. In the end, He took our Mother, too.*

They hardly notice when the river straightens, when the forest at the shoreline thins and squat, whitewashed cottages appear, not clustered in villages but spread evenly along the banks, as if sown by God's imperturbable hand. Their hearts linger behind on Grosse Île or race ahead through the shambles of their plans, so much so that what actually passes before their eyes appears chimærical. The city, when the *Deirdre* moors at the wharf at Quebec, seems enchanted. Tiers of tin-plate roofs glitter silver in the sun, a brilliant counterpoint to the Citadel glowering over its parapet and the periodic boom of cannon, which strikes terror in Margaret until a seaman assures her it signals nothing but the passing of the hours. The river that takes them from Quebec to Montreal erupts in rapids one minute and the next, solidifies to a platform of wood comprised of thousands of squared logs resting one upon another, and rising from the surface, a dozen masts with sails billowing, little huts with cooking fires, and as many men as might populate a village walking, or so it seems, on the sturdy water, the whole phantasmagoria pulled along by a steamer that booms a greeting to their riverboat as it squeezes slowly past.

The MacBaynes have made no provision for a stay in Montreal. Their intention was to travel to Toronto or to Ottawa and from there, directly into the Back country to procure a parcel of land, but their father's detention forces them to take rooms in the city that they can scarcely afford. The three boys find work unloading steamboats at the docks, which is the best place, they determine, to intercept a message from Grosse Île. Margaret and her mother join in their landlady's enterprise, baking baps and bannocks, Scots crumpets, treacle gundy, and mealie candy to sell aboard the emigrant ships to passengers eager for anything not cooked over an open fire, for something that tastes of home.

Margaret carries the baskets to the ships, moving in a fragrant vapour of browned butter and yeast between the tall buildings, over the squared, rigid streets. How she misses the slope of stone beneath her feet, the twisting wynds, the ceaseless wind! Even at the wharf, the air in this new place is overheated and still, as if coals smoulder under the plank sidewalks, ready at any minute to kindle the city to flame.

Midsummer's Day passes and still no word from Grosse Île. Margaret and the boys lose the gaunt look they took on during the passage, but their mother does not thrive. Her eyes seem bruised and she suffers from a sick stomach and a fatigue so profound that she sinks into a chair for even the smallest task, dusting tantallon cakes with fine sugar or breaking hardened gundy into bits.

It is not the cholera, she murmurs, patting her daughter's hand, but Margaret worries just the same. For all the strangeness of her present circumstance, it is the change in her mother that unsettles her the most. Where is the woman who carried her husband on her back the first day of the herring drave, hoisting him to his boat so the sea would not taste his flesh? Where is the woman who swiftly bound her fingers at the chime of the gutting bell, who sang as she hoisted heaped creels of fish from door to door, who mended nets and baited hooks all day, plaiting seaweed with the winkles Margaret found, then sat through the night by a neighbour's bed, spooning bitter, curing teas between a sick man's lips?

A frail, sighing crone sits in that woman's place. Margaret ties on her apron and takes up the salt in her own hand, lavishing it on her mother's food. Once a week, she rubs her mother's body with a damp cloth, vigorously, and at the end of every day, when she has finished her own work and her mother's too, she walks with her to the hill at the centre of the city where the air is fresher, and where, looking across the rooftops, she can almost believe the decrepit woman at her side will one day disappear and her real mother will return to her.

On an evening in late July, after Margaret clears their meal from the trunk that is their table, William Wallace spreads out the pages of the *Canada Gazette* and directs his mother's attention to a small square of print.

SETTLEMENT LANDS IN THE

MADAWASKA HIGHLANDS


Notice is hereby given, that the lands adjacent to the Opeongo-Ottawa Colonization Road in the County of Renfrew, Upper Canada, are open for settlement.


For lists of lots and conditions, apply to


T.P. French, Crown Agent,

John Brady Hotel,

Mount St. Patrick


The lots are free, a hundred acres to any settler, eighteen years of age or more, who can take possession of the land within a month of application, erect on it a house eighteen by twenty feet, and live there, putting into a state of cultivation no less than twelve acres in the first four years. Fulfill these conditions and title to the land will be theirs.

Margaret has listened to her brothers make their plans as they return from the dockyards at the end of the day. Only a handful of white men are settled in the northern reaches of the Madawaska, they say. At least one is a Scot from Fife, from further up the fringe past Pittenweem. Robert Bruce met him on the wharf as he arranged for provisions to be sent to his trading post in the Bush. The stories he told! Of bottomless lakes and rivers fat with fish. Of boulders the size of mountains and trees that grew to such heights that to climb one was to risk looking into the eye of God himself. Of soil that could be made to grow whatever a man could wish.

No more waiting on the whimsy of the silver darlings, said Robert Bruce. No more serving the fickle pleasures of the sea.

It is a somewhat altered argument they lay before their mother. Other Scots will be lining up for locations, they say. She will have neighbours who speak as she does, who will keep the old Scots ways. Why, the county itself is named Renfrew, after a Scottish shire. If they leave now, they can build a cottage before the winter, prepare a place for their father away from the city's filth, breeding ground for the fevers that bring death.

But the argument that convinces her comes from within. Whether her husband is alive or no, his child will be born on the land he dreamt.

# ALYSON

*Autumn 1990*

Alyson pulled off her mitt when she felt it, a brief, distinct flutter in her lower abdomen. She slid her fingers under her coat, under the waistband of her jeans, cupping the faint roundness just above her pubic bone. She'd known for months that she was pregnant, but she'd held herself back, afraid to hope too much, and now, all of a sudden, it was certain. Her baby was alive, moving about inside her.

Though it didn't feel like a baby. More like a bird stretching one long feathery wing, a fish wriggling upstream. She recalled a story she once heard of a woman whose belly grew big until one day in the bath she felt a squirming between her legs, and believing her child was coming, she looked down and saw a long, white tapeworm swimming out.

But she wasn't going to think like that.

She pushed the image out of her mind and cast about for another, finding it in her garden – a seedling taking root, the first true leaves unfurling against the wall of her womb.

She felt a longing for her baby, then. A sweet anticipation that swept through her, the sort of rush she associated with those days of early spring when the air was sharp but the sun was warm and every seed and bulb and bud was swelling, not with ripeness but with readiness, a taut willingness to become.

She shifted her buttocks on the perforated metal seat and drew her spine up straight, raising her rib cage and drawing her wide shoulders back, conscious of how imperfectly her hips and pelvis knitted together, a restlessly flexing cradle. She tried to keep herself erect, thinking Walker might notice the change in her posture and she'd tell him, the baby's moving, it's going to be fine. But he didn't look up. He stayed bent over his shovel while she sat cross-legged on the tractor, facing backwards, as she had sat for hours, looking out over the streambank, over Walker digging his clay.

The gardener and the potter – that's how she'd come to think of them. Not as partners or lovers, not as city people transplanted to the country or almost thirtysomethings, not even, if the truth were told, as Alyson and Walker, a mother- and father-to-be, though all those terms were accurate, some of them even pleasing. But none made her smile the way she did when she was thinking, the gardener and the potter. Both toilers in the soil, she liked the sound of that, too, though she'd never say it, for he'd correct her, it wasn't soil, it was clay he was piling onto the stone boat, her body set to rocking with every shovelful he pitched.

He was digging close to the water where the earth would be warmest. Even so, he'd had to take up the pickaxe to loosen the clods. His body arched with every upstroke, a tremor running through his limbs as the claw bit into the ground. He'd tossed his jacket onto the tractor, unbuttoned his shirt, and rolled up his sleeves. She could see the muscles of his forearms coil and stretch under the skin, and she felt a rise of desire for him, as if it were summer again, everything sprawling and open, not the last day of October, the dying end of the year, the earth already turning cold and hard, resistant.

Too late to be digging clay, she was thinking. But then, their whole life was in disorder, everything done at odd times, in unaccustomed ways. Her routines so upset she never knew what to expect of a day except that it would be different from how she liked it to be. Her body grown treacherous. The landscape altered, too, riddled with risks and temptations where before there'd been just the hauling and the lifting, the planting and weeding, all the things that were hers to do. Instead, there she was, sitting idle on the sidelines.

It wasn't like her, she was thinking, it wasn't like her at all.

In the ten years since they bought the land, she'd hardly stopped to catch her breath. She'd ripped off the siding, put up drywall, laid a brick hearth in the kitchen while Walker built the studio in the barn. They'd rarely worked side by side, and yet she'd always felt they moved in tandem, both straining toward the future they'd planned. When the weather warmed, she'd started on the gardens, prying up the sod, levering boulders out of the ground, reshaping the soil into terraces, her muscles growing strong, her mind and heart, too, so that even when their plan altered, she never broke stride, always pulling her weight, and more.

It was the baby that had transformed her, reduced her to a casing, a fragile shell. Afraid to lift a shovel or bend too close to the ground, afraid a bloom of blood would appear and she'd end up on the toilet, weeping as another unborn child slipped out.

It's okay, he'd say, wiping her tears with his thumb.

No, it's not. I want a child, don't you?

I like having you all to myself.

And in the beginning, it was enough, just the two of them on the old abandoned farm, the work laid out in steps so clear and definite that nothing seemed more natural than to turn the earth, build the kilns, make the pots, grow the herbs for the container gardens they'd sell.

Their meals were picnics in the grass under the shade of the giant spruce. Walker would tell her about the glazes he'd mixed, the gouge he'd made from a jawbone he found or the whisk he'd tied from the stiff grasses by the stream. She'd bring basil and fennel to lay on the first tomato, the first cucumber. A working lunch, they'd laugh. Sometimes, Walker would take the extra sprigs back to the studio, where later he'd show her the lines in the clay inspired by the swelling curves, the feathery strokes of the leaves. In the evenings, when they were too exhausted for words, he'd pick up his bandoneon, his little red squeezebox, and she'd tune up her violin, and they'd fill the space between them with music, her strings tracing a light, high-pitched harmony around the melancholic tune he returned to again and again, their instruments playing off each other, finding a pleasing balance, just as their natures did, or so she'd thought then.

Some days they would escape to the villages around, playing at being tourists. They'd stop at roadside taverns for cabbage rolls or plate-size perogies, once landing at a church supper where they feasted on sand-baked beans and peach schnitz pie, though after a while the outings stopped. There was always something wrong with the place – someone staring at him too long or whispering as they ate – something would set him off and he'd withdraw into himself, the adventure ruined. It was better with just the two of them, at home, though sometimes she'd set him off, never meaning it, but then she'd forget and do something he'd asked her not to do, like turning off all the lights when she went to bed so that he'd come back from the studio to a pitch-dark house, and then he'd shrink from her, too.

That fall, it might have been the pregnancy or maybe it was something else, she'd given up trying to figure out why, but he had become more irritable than ever. It got so she hated to ask him for anything, but the doctor had warned her to stay off her feet, and there was so much that needed to be done – annuals to lift, perennials to divide, the bay laurel and rosemary to move inside, garlic to sow as well as spinach and lettuce, leaves to rake into piles for mould, compost to turn, soil to mix for next year's seeds, everything manured and mulched, fruit bushes to prune, trees to wrap against winter-starved mice. The list, when she'd set it to paper, seemed endless.

She could have stayed in the house, read, and sipped her tea, but she would have seen him anyway, the hard line of his mouth, his wide, amber eyes, inset into every page. So she'd bundled herself up and settled close to where he worked, saying, I'll just watch, okay?

What's the matter? Don't you trust me?

It's not that.

Yes it is. Admit it, you don't think I can handle it.

You can handle me, she said. Anytime you want.

That made him laugh and she'd relaxed a little, grateful her silliness could still relieve some of the tension between them.

It seemed to her she'd passed the entire season watching and waiting, perched on some rock or hay bale or overturned bushel basket, her eyes never off him, waiting for the first sigh, the faintest gesture of complaint, worried that he would give up, or worse, that he wouldn't do it right. His hands, so skilful at shaping clay, became clumsy in her garden soil, mutilating roots, crushing stems and leaves. It hurt her to see her plants so abused, but she'd rationed her responses, for if she'd said what she felt — that it was like a blow to her own skin — he would have said she was exaggerating, he didn't mean it like that, which she knew was the truth. He was just being careless. A blow of a different sort, she thought.

And when at last she would make a comment, ask him to do things a certain way, he'd erupt. Christ, what does it matter what I do with the fucking cornstalks? he had shouted at her just that morning, and she'd started to tell him how she layered the garden waste, setting the stalks crosswise for aeration, adding leaves, then manure, grass clippings, weeds, each one in order, turning and watering the pile all summer, just for the thrill of thrusting in her trowel on some cold spring day to feel the black humus crumbling warm in her hand, a living thing . . . but he was already slapping the stalks into a grid, exactly the way she liked, though the pleasure she'd taken in that simple arrangement was spoiled.

While he finished the job, the last on her list, she had sat tracing the fault lines in the slab of granite that, years before, he'd wrestled to the head of the garden, taking three days to manoeuvre it down the slope and position it where she could sit to shell beans or just stare out over the hills, his surprise birthday gift to her. And she'd thought again what she'd thought so often when he was in one of his moods – that he was kind to her in many ways, that he didn't mean to speak so sharply. That if only she could convince him of her own good intentions, he wouldn't set himself against her. That in the meantime, if she wasn't careful, he'd trample what she loved.

She readjusted her position on the tractor seat again. She shouldn't be so hard on him, she thought. He'd put off his fall chores until hers were finished, even though the digging was harder now than it would have been earlier in the season. She circled her hand on her belly in sympathetic rhythm as she watched him on the streambank, his compact body built for shovelling, tireless in its devotion.

As though waiting for a certain interval in the slide and pitch of Walker's shovel, the baby moved again, a lithe little dance under her palm.

She started to call to him, to raise her arm, wave him over, but then she paused. She told herself that if he were separating a mound of mother-of-thyme or spreading leaf mould under the currants, she wouldn't hesitate to interrupt him. But he was excavating his own earth now. So she left him to the work, kept the baby's stirring to herself.

A rift, it would feel to her when she thought about it later. Not at all the way she hoped things would be. Though at the time, nothing changed. She still sat on the tractor and he still shovelled the red soil, heaving it onto the stone boat where it steamed under the cool October sun, filling the air with a fragrance that was faintly sour.


It had taken him months to find that clay. All through the trailing end of their first winter in the Madawaska he walked the property, impatient for the snow to be gone, trying to formulate a plan, a system of searching for what he was convinced lay under the snow, the leaves, the thin scrim of topsoil.

Mother-rock was everywhere, uplifts of granite glittering with feldspar. Glaciers would have long since scraped the clay from around the stone, he said, but what he hoped for was some vestige of a glacial pond where the clay had filtered out. A varve lens, it was called – she looked it up. A shallow dish of accumulated earth, the layers of sediment so distinct you could count them like rings on a tree. Soil laid down in strata of black and grey and buff and sometimes in a wide, russet vein like the one Walker had found at the back of their land, where the stream that was the boundary cut across the base of a granite ridge.

The clay was good, he told her so, but still he kept searching, pulling soil samples all through the spring and summer, bringing them home in plastic bags that he emptied onto the kitchen counter, leaving the earth to soften under damp cloths like mounds of rising dough. It was thrilling to watch his hands work the clay, kneading it firmly, then unexpectedly tender as he rolled a small lump into a ribbon that he bent to a ring, his fingers deft, the way they felt on her skin, so that seeing the row of clay loops lined up along the windowsill to dry, she'd feel a sudden craving, even after the red and yellow ochres faded and they all looked the same to her, grey links of a chain that held nothing but promise.

She garnished all the windowsills with what he'd dug up that first spring. He would come into the house with his fists behind

his back and make her guess what he had found, and she'd say anything, a garnet ring, a gold doubloon, just to keep the game going,
until at last she'd give up and he'd present his gift to her — a short
twist of barbed wire, a broken horseshoe, a hand-forged spike,
and once, a small bottle, cobalt-blue, with its cork still intact,
which he begged her not to remove, certain it contained some
ancient poison, though it didn't, she'd sniffed the blackened
stopper to prove how safe it was, how unfounded his fear.

Sometimes while he was searching, she walked the woods,
too. One day she came upon an incline where the soil had been
recently disturbed and then so resolutely tamped down that she
brought a shovel and dug into the broken ground, unearthing a
cache of heads, pale pink dolls' heads, which she brushed off and
laid out in rows, their faces to the sun. The bisque skin of their
cheeks was unmarked, though the skulls were caved in at the back
and the hair was missing, the eyeballs too, so that the lids, those
that still blinked mechanically, lifted blankly up at her. She
thought of taking one home and playing Walker's game but, in
the end, she buried them all, never mentioning what she found,
just as he never spoke of them to her — not a secret or a lie so
much as a kind of mutual protection.

When she'd asked Réal about the heads, he'd said, sure he
remembered them, he'd delivered them himself, fifty years ago
or more, when he was just a kid. He'd always been the mailman,
though now he was old, his skin like putty left too long in the
sun, his manner so uninquisitively friendly that it drew her down

the lane to the mailbox every day at noon. The woman who used to live there, he said, made dolls for a time, dressed them up to look like lumberjacks. *La vieille fille*, they called her, the old maid.

He chattered on, but she stopped listening, even when he tapped her arm and winked, Who knows what else you'll find back there, eh? The truth was she didn't care, then, who else had lived on that land. They'd abandoned it. She had scrubbed away every trace of them, made the house her own, telling herself that the forged nails and barbed wire and battered heads had migrated through the soil from some other farm, one that was cherished, held in a family for generations, just as theirs would be, handed down to their children and their children's children's children, that flutter in her belly, a beginning.


It was dusk by the time Walker hauled the stone boat heaped with clay back to the barn. She followed on foot down the bush road for a while then veered off toward the maple grove, weary of shovels and tractors, ready to wrap the woods around her.

The back of nowhere, her mother called it, never understanding her need for unenclosed space. It was something she hadn't understood herself until Walker had come along with his dream of moving to the country and she'd said, yes, that's what I've always wanted, too. She'd made an effort to explain it to her mother: how suffocated she'd been in that tall, narrow city house with its drapes always drawn, what relief she'd felt the summer

she was twelve, when she was sent away to stay with Aunt
Catherine on her farm.

You won't last a year, her mother had replied.

But Alyson had proved her wrong. Right from the beginning,
she'd felt safe there among the trees, safer than on any city street.
And it was still true, she thought. Her breath came easier when
she was alone in the woods, away from all the constrictions, the
wearying convolutions of human interaction.

The path through the bush was steep. She had to watch her
step. She imagined watching herself from a satellite, a tiny creature inching down the eastern lip of the Canadian Shield, though
it wasn't a shield, Walker told her, so much as an enormous stone
saucer set on the heart of the continent. When the bedrock was
lifted up, it had slumped and warped like badly fired clay, leaving
the surface crazed with fissures that had worn down over thousands of years to a landscape of hills and valleys, ridges and
scarps. All of it was thickly forested, though the granite was never
far below the surface, erupting here and there as a reminder of
ancient, altering forces. Even where the stone was covered, the
soil was thin and tentative, so that the ground seemed uncertain
where she walked, the sound of her footsteps reverberating as if
she were crossing over a cavern, the earth's crust an empty shell.

A wilderness, she'd called it, the day they bought the place.

They'd been looking for months, setting off every weekend
in her father's old blue Dodge Dart, Walker taking charge, direct-
ing her out through the gridiron of city streets, past farmland

surveyed into squares, until she was driving the thin, grey lines that meandered across the map. Then, they both relaxed. The farther north and east they went, the more the roads followed natural contours, going around a lake, a hill, a stand of old pines, not obstacles so much as things to be considered, accommodated, as one person accommodates another, stepping aside, acknowledging in the other certain rights of place. Something she'd never thought of when she drove north with her parents every summer on their holidays, the world appearing to her differently with Walker at her side.

All day they would cruise the back roads, copying telephone numbers from real-estate signs, heading down old logging roads at night to pitch their tent among the trees. They'd zip their sleeping bags together, but they'd be too full of dreams to sleep, and at daybreak, they'd set off again, intrepid explorers, travelling roads that funnelled higher into the hills, deeper into the woods, until late one afternoon, Walker had pointed her up a path not marked on any map, a trail so faint, so pocked with boulders and overhung with limbs that she'd thought it would be crazy to continue, though the moment she'd said so, the lane opened to a clearing and Walker jumped out of the car, shouting, This is it! This is it!, as he strode toward the trees, leaving her squinting through a slant of snow at the derelict house, the tumbledown sheds, the forest closing in.

Lost Nation, the real-estate man had called it when he drove them up the lane again. Walker sat in front, folded into himself in that way he had with strangers. She'd taken the back, leaning her forehead against the glass, seeing the landscape as if for the first time, the forest going on forever, undisturbed, pristine. The house looked charming under the fresh fall of snow, the heart of a quaint settlement of rustic log sheds and barns. A century homestead, the man said. Trees sheltered it all around except for a break to the south where they seemed to part like an invitation to the overlapping hills and valleys layering into the distance.

A wilderness! she'd exclaimed then, and thought again, standing on the granite bluff that marked the boundary between the woods and the lawn. Not a wilderness, really – the land had been logged, the forest was second-growth, maybe third, not a virgin tree among the lanky conifers and scrubby hardwoods, no trunk so thick that she and Walker couldn't circle it with their arms – yet she'd clung to the word, for the wildness in it, she supposed, but also the wilder, as in bewilder, for that was what enthralled her, the way the landscape after all those years still refused to deliver all its mysteries.

Below, in the clearing, the pressed-tin walls of the house caught the day's last light and shone a homing signal up to her, making her think she'd got it right the second time. It *was* a settlement, the buildings bound together now with paths she'd made and walked a thousand times. The place could never be for her what it would be for her child, a birthplace, a birthright, but still, she felt well-positioned there, like an alpine herb transplanted from a meadow to a barren, rocky slope. It wasn't where she'd started out, it was harsher in many ways, but it was where she belonged.

She took the long way from the granite bluff to the house, along the path that skirted the chicken coop and the drive shed where she could see the tractor already parked, past the log barn that was Walker's studio, past her greenhouse and the garden beds mounded with leaves like rows of children tucked safely under their quilts.

She paused by the garden closest to the path, regarding it with the affection one reserves for first mistakes, innocent errors easily corrected. The spring she'd turned that soil, she'd stood lost among its furrows, struggling to remember all her aunt had taught her that summer on the farm. But it wasn't lessons that came back to her, it was Catherine's hands. Wide, blunt fingers with ropy veins that slid under the skin as she smoothed on the glycerine balm she made in a pot on the stove. Capable hands. Too rough for the teacup her mother had set before her, their conversation hushing the moment Alyson came into the room, carrying her small red suitcase, the worried frown on Catherine's face lifting as they drove away from the city. Then, it was just the two of them, collecting eggs from the hens, working in the orchard, in the gardens, Catherine always singing, taking up her work with enthusiasm, nothing like the woman Alyson had imagined when she'd heard her mother say, poor Catherine, all alone out there on the farm, no one to love. And it was the songs she remembered, too, rousing hymns and sweet ballads and the old-fashioned rhyme they sang together as she pushed her first seeds into the ground – *One for the rook, one for the crow, one to die, one to grow.*

Books had taught her the essentials. The rest she'd had to discover for herself, worrying over her first seedlings, creeping out on cold nights to pull blankets over their heads, piercing hoses to lay up and down the rows to feed their roots, weaving rushes from the meadow into mats to shade their leaves from the intermittent, burning sun. At times, she'd despair of ever learning it all, or even enough, and then she'd turn back to her books, not for instruction so much as reassurance that the tender sense of duty she felt was not peculiar or obsessive, although it often seemed so to her, coming as she did from a family that called it gardening when they set a row of red geraniums along the concrete patio behind their narrow brick house, her father measuring and measuring again, her mother leaning over him, insisting, Leave it, will you? Just leave it alone.

She waited by the shade garden under the old Manitoba maple, thinking that when Walker finished unloading the clay, she'd meet him there and they could continue on together. She would tell him that she'd felt the baby move, a quickening, and at the word, she saw her mother again, pouring oil into a glass and handing it to a friend. Heard her saying, it's worth a try, even though it was too late for me, the baby had already quickened. Then her father's voice, she tried to get rid of you, did you know that? She wants to get rid of me too, his face contorted, bent close, as he blocked her way up the stairs. When he gets like that, her mother told her, just ignore him, it's crazy talk, he doesn't mean a word.

She shivered and pulled her coat closer. The sun had dropped behind the trees, abandoning her to shadow. She hurried through the darkness to the house, thinking, it must be the pregnancy, stirring up all those ancient, useless memories. And she banished them again, the way she always had.

She pushed open the kitchen door and stepped into a pool of heat.

Walker? she called.

The fire was freshly stoked, steam rising from the kettle.

She called to him again, but there was no answer. He must have stopped in on his way to the barn, she thought. He was like that — thoughtful in small, unexpected ways, balking at her requests, then surprising her with something she didn't know she wanted, like the sitting-stone at the head of the garden, a warm kitchen on a cool fall night. She threw off her coat and crossed to the stove, trailing her hand along the bundles of herbs suspended from the ceiling, releasing waves of musky scent, lemon balm, chamomile, a dozen different mints.

A witch's hovel, Walker had said the day she hung her first harvest to dry.

Careful, she'd laughed, I'll put a spell on you.

Too late, he'd whispered, burying his lips in her neck.

That evening, after supper, as Walker got up from the table, she reached for his hand and laid it on her belly. Her fingers spread long and thin over his, taking on the contour of the scar that flowed up his arm, obscuring it.

Do you feel it? she asked.

No, he said, then, Feel what?

The baby.

He leaned over her awkwardly, moving his hand under her shirt, over her skin.

It's getting bigger?

No, it's moving, she said.

Although it wasn't, not just then.

And it had troubled her, that disjunction between them. The whole day had been like that, a series of closely missed connections, the kind that happened in dreams, though they were both in the same place, it was their words that were out of sync, as if whatever bound sentences into a smoothly oscillating conversation had worked loose, a cleat fallen out, some part misaligned, so that the whole thing felt wobbly, ready to fall apart.

She waited until the door closed behind him, then she pushed herself up to clear the table. The plates made a hollow sound she could have let herself fall into, but her hands caught her up, kept her moving from sink to cupboard to stove. Glasses polished, pots in a row, tea towel folded and hung by the fire — succinct, reliable pleasures.

But then, as she shifted the everlastings to wipe the crumbs

from the table, something in the motion, or in the feel of the jug
in her hand made her think of the bird of paradise she'd once
brought home on a whim. A flower like that should stand alone,
Walker had said, and so she'd put it in a slender glass, then
another that was taller. She'd laid a woven placemat underneath,
a tatted doily from her aunt, then a cloth she found at a yard sale,
stitched with blue armadillos and rainbow-spotted jaguars. But
nothing had looked right until she set the exotic bloom in the old
earthenware jug with an armful of flowers she'd brought in from
the garden – Adam's-needle, angelica, obedient plant – tucking in
a wisp of adder's-tongue, feeling pleased with herself but uneasy,
as if the arrangement were a betrayal, though Walker had said
nothing about it, hadn't even noticed.

The memory flushed through her, leaving her irritated and
confused. Why would her mind dredge up such an insignificant
incident? It was meaningless, she decided, a random piece of the
past stirred loose by the baby's movement.

She paced around the kitchen, straightening and picking up,
then she laid the table for their breakfast. She chose the yellow
bowls and indigo placemats, feeling cheered just by the look of
them, sunflowers against a dawning sky.

In the doorway, she turned, thinking what a lovely room it
was, really. Cozy, with its thatch of herbs overhead, the scarred
pine table oiled to a gloss, the hearth of salvaged brick, the curtains
a slightly warmer red, which picked up the gold in the table as
she'd hoped it would, fingering the airy weave in the fabric store.

The unequivocal satisfaction of details. She focused on each in turn, waiting for the feeling of contentment to fill her up, annoyed that it was so slow in coming, that it refused her altogether, on that day of all days, when a tiny flutter in her belly had brought an end to her idleness, and she could resume her life again. Yet there she stood in the darkened kitchen, feeling neither happy nor relieved, just disconcerted, disoriented, as if she'd lost her bearings, forgotten what was supposed to come next.

She fought the urge to rush out after Walker, like the nighthawks that swooped across the yard as he went to his work, filling the empty air behind him with their wild, anxious shrieks. She'd come upon one once near the stone pile, a nighthawk squatting on the rocks, not bothering with a nest, and she'd raced back to the house, pulling Walker from their bed to where the mother was flapping about, trailing its wing in the underbrush, trying to distract them from a clutch of pink, speckled eggs. But they were too clever for it. They'd crouched motionless in the forest duff until the bird returned, settling so near they could see each striation in its feathers, all marvellously vermiculated, an illusive pattern in brown and grey that Walker had tried without success to replicate in glaze. He'd become obsessed with the birds, calling out to them as he crossed the yard, using all their secret, sacred names. Wind-swallower. Moon-crier. Ghost bird. And the nicknames the Germans gave them: *Kinder-melker, Hexenführer, Totenwogel.* Child-sucker, witch-leader, death bird.

She heard the door slam behind her before she knew what

she was doing, racing into the night. The frigid air against her
face stopped her halfway to the barn. From there, she could see
Walker's shadow moving in the window of the door. Sometimes
that was all she needed, the sight of him, remote and oblivious,
their love refined by the distance, seeming purer to her somehow,
more enduring than what passed between them face to face.

But the smell of snow was in the air, winter was breathing
down her neck, waiting to smother the landscape. She felt it like
a hand across her mouth, the foreboding that always came with a
change of weather. Her biorhythms were askew, that was it, she
was thinking as she headed toward the light, not intending to
disturb him in the studio as he worked, just wanting to be close,
to lean against the door, rest her fingers in the shallows of his
name carved in the wood.

WALKER FREEMAN, MASTER CERAMIST.

What do you mean, it's a made-up name? she'd asked.

Everyone's is, isn't it? It's just that instead of using the name
my parents thought up for me, I picked one out myself.

But names aren't just made up, she'd insisted, though if he'd
challenged her, she wasn't sure she would have been able to say
what she meant, for at some point, in the beginning, hadn't every
word been invented?

He'd named himself for what he was, he said. A free man
walking away. Part of that was bluster: he couldn't have been
more than sixteen. When he showed her the scar on his arm
where his father had pitched the hot grease, she'd felt a surge of

sympathy for the child he'd been. But more than that, she admired the man he had become as he worked his way back and forth across the country, starting from some place in the east, exactly where he wouldn't say at first, though eventually he told her. New Brunswick. He'd planted trees, baled hay, pumped gas, harvested tomatoes, tobacco, apples, wild rice. He'd run away from home before he'd had a chance to finish school, but he was smart. In the shops and on the streets, she'd heard him speak in half a dozen languages without a discernable accent. And he was enterprising. When they met, he was doing maintenance at the art school in exchange for ceramics courses, and he'd built his own kiln in the backyard of the rooming house where he lived.

He only has to look at something once to know how it works, she'd said, trying to think of something that her mother might approve of.

You don't know anything about him, had been her reply.

But she did. He was independent. Someone with real talent. And he had plans. That he had cut his family from his life, she didn't count against him, even though, from time to time, she would wonder why, what else had they done? But she didn't press him. If he told her everything, she would have to do the same, and she was determined not to do that, drag into the open all the details of what she had left behind. She didn't mind that there were gaps in his story — it was only the fabrication of the name that disturbed her, for it threw into question everything he'd ever said.

But what's your name really? Just tell me the truth.

They were sitting under the ginkgo tree on the university common, their picnic of strawberries and bitter chocolate a jumble of hulls and crumbs at his knees. She'd been pestering him for weeks, and still he wouldn't tell her. He never had, not yet, though that was the day she stopped asking.

He had spread his arms wide and cocked his head, tossed her that lifeline of a grin.

What you see is what you get, he'd said.

She could see him clearly through the barn window, bending over a bin, lifting out a bundle of clay, and she thought how little he'd changed since the summer they met. He'd always seemed age-less to her, though he was a little thicker now, more toned from the physical work of the country. But the sight of him still stirred her. The muscled shoulders and narrow hips. The way his hair swung against his collar, a blond more of the earth than the sun. And it was still true what she'd finally said.

I love you, Walker Freeman, whoever you are.

He raised the clay to his nostrils, and she breathed in, too, for she knew that smell. It had hung like a vapour in the basement room where he lived. The first time he took her there, he'd made her wait outside the blanket that served as a door, then he'd led her through a sea of candle flame to the mattress on the floor. As he undressed her, her eyes had drifted past his naked shoulder to the small relief figures in the shadows, twisted bodies, their heads and limbs missing.

Maquettes for an army, he'd told her later. Clay warriors, like the terra-cotta soldiers that were buried in formation with the first Chinese emperor. Though his would lie scattered, he'd said, sowed lightly under the earth in a remote, forgotten field.

*Gehenna, Hephaestus, Ephialtes, Phoedima, Vesta, Hestia, Memento Mori.*

Seven life-size figures hung on the walls of the loft above the studio, awaiting their burial. The front of a female, neck to navel, wrists crossed over her breasts. The back of a male writhing. Another from a three-quarter view, one arm extended as if to shield his eyes, although the head was gone, severed at the jaw. They all lacked faces and hands. Otherwise, the anatomy was detailed, not carved from a block of clay but built up from the core, bones fashioned to cradle organs, the skin laid on in thin clay sheets, sometimes smoothed to sheathe the body, more often left to curl, the edges lifting like scorched tissue off a partially exposed scapula or hip bone. Once a figure was fired, he would cut the limbs across with wire twisted from copper strands, or he'd embed bits of glass that he'd collected on their strolls through the city, picking shards out of the gutters, not saying what use they would serve but saving them just the same, moved by their shapes and colours, by what they might have seen.

Or that's what she supposed, for although she was welcome in the studio when he was making pots for her gardens, he kept the door locked when a warrior was underway. He'd withdraw for weeks, then, speaking to her curtly, if at all, and never about his work.

In the beginning, she'd try to pry it out of him, the details of the composition, his inspiration, complaining that he kept so much to himself, but he would turn on her: And you don't? What do you tell me about what's going on with you?

And he'd choose an example calculated to hurt, needling her for never saying what it was she had against her mother. And what about your father? he'd snapped at her once.

I'd tell you if you asked, she said, starting to cry.

And he'd flashed back, But I don't, do I?

She had learned to wait until the piece was finished, then he would show her, making a ritual of the unveiling, letting her help him with the firing, stoking the dragon-kiln he'd designed especially for the figures. It was on those days, working beside him in the woods, that she would catch glimpses into what she called his brilliance, the darkness at the heart of him.

The mass of clay was on the floor and he was unlacing his boots, unbuttoning his shirt, folding it neatly on the old, green wingback he called his groaning chair. When he slipped off his jeans, she stepped back, out of his line of sight.

He reached a hand to the beam above his head and, steadying himself, lifted one foot onto the clay and plunged it down hard. He stepped on with the other foot, sinking in his heels, one, then the other. Slowly, he walked in place, a slight rotation to each step, a twist of the hip that made her think he was about to turn toward the window, though he didn't, he just kept ramming one foot down and then the other in a deliberate, relentless piston motion.

She could feel the clay's resistance, how slowly it yielded, submitting with reluctance as he quickened his pace to a plodding tread, a march, a run. He kept his hand raised to the beam that he bore like a standard or struggled to tear down, she couldn't tell which, but what pushed her stumbling back into the night was his face, a man she barely recognized, his features contorting with his efforts, warping like a mask held too near a searing flame.

A spring baby, the doctor said. The middle of April, more or less.

She paused at the door of the clinic, reading the sky as she always did before stepping through a door. It was the same worsted grey it had been for a month, one snowstorm after another, the banks along the sidewalk already up to her knees though December had scarcely begun.

The air outside was still, the light opaque, as if somewhere high above, snow was already falling. Just wait until I get the errands done, she thought, pulling out her lists.

Now that the risk of miscarriage was past, they had resumed their usual routine. She woke early in the mornings, craving the first light, feeling disgruntled for hours if a bank of cloud robbed her of the moment when the sun burst above the trees. Walker was just the opposite. He loved the darkness. For a while he had tried to keep country hours, too, but he'd soon slipped back to his city habits, rising late in the day to work through the night.

How can you stand it? You hardly see each other, her friend Renata once said.

It's fine, it works for us, was all she could think of to say, though later she figured it out. Most days, he was up at three and at work by eight, which gave them five hours together, including the evening meal, which she always took care to prepare, laying a cloth on the table, lighting candles. The truth was, they saw more of each other than a couple who commuted from the suburbs to work.

In the summer, she was up and in the gardens before he came to bed, but in the winter, the dawn was so delayed that she could lie under the quilts, as she had that morning, listening to him shuffle about the kitchen while he made himself something to eat, waiting for his step in the hallway, his hand on the bedroom door. Then it was her in the kitchen, humming, welcoming the day, despite all she had to do, despite their unfairly balanced burdens.

She headed down the street, waving to people she knew, and some she didn't. She imagined them staring after her, the baby invisible between her hips, then the shock on their faces as she turned, the cape she'd bought for a dollar at the Sally Ann flapping open, her belly unmistakably rounded now, a long, full curve that started high under her breasts, dovetailing smoothly between her legs. When she caught sight of herself in a shop window, framed by blinking silver Christmas lights, she smiled. The Virgin of the village hardware, she thought. And the apparition smiled back.

She no longer felt a fragile casing. Her body seemed made especially for this. She had taken to wearing long skirts and dresses of clingy fabrics, velvets and finely knitted wools, liking the way they draped over her swelling form. Sometimes, in the afternoons, when Walker got up, she would pull off her dress and stand naked by the fire while he sketched her in charcoal, in sepia, in oil pastels and coloured gouaches, and once, in clay, a thick-bellied figure he called his Venus of Madawaska.

Like the Venus of Willendorf, he'd said. In the spring, I'll bury it by the stream. A thousand years from now, some anthropologist will dig it up and write a paper on how we worshipped pregnant women.

When he said that she thought, he wants this baby, too.

It's beautiful, she said, then paused. You seem happier. For it was true, his irritation had eased and she took that as a sign.

And he'd agreed: I always feel better when I'm working.

By the time her last errand was done, the snow was falling in loose, fluttering flakes that settled like moths on her cheeks, her sleeves, her mittened hands. She hurried to the van, gunning it a little to make it start, patting the dashboard in encouragement. They'd bought it at the beginning of the second summer, painting EARTHWORKS POTTERY AND GARDENS on the side. Every weekend they would set off for some small-town fair or festival, the back jammed with Walker's pots planted with her herbs. During the week, they'd work like fiends, Walker bent over his clay, her kneeling in her gardens, pricking out seedlings, potting them up, planting more, their fingers twitching through the night in imaginary clay, imaginary soil, dreaming that the next fair would be the one to pay the mortgage or the fuel bill, though it never was. She wanted to keep trying, but Walker sank into a disparaging mood and they had quit the fairs, one by one. He retreated to his studio while she laid out the tea garden, then a sachet garden, and when that wasn't enough, she'd sowed bed after bed of culinary herbs, which she bundled fresh for grocery stores in summer, drying what was left and packaging it in muslin bags tied with labels, which she printed from an old computer Renata passed on to her — *Fines Herbes, Bouquet Garni, Brier Rose Sachet, Sweet Cicely Hyssop Tea.*

The van skidded slightly as she turned onto Hopefield Road. She forced her foot to ease up on the accelerator, but her mind raced ahead, stripping leaves, mixing teas, so much still to do before the Christmas sales, when she would set up her display in church basements and high-school gyms, instead of on fairgrounds and roadblocked streets, filling her small electric kettle from the jugs of water she brought, offering infusions of sweet woodruff and apple mint to cautious country women, a pot or two of parsley and bay laurel arranged around the booth, though the pottery was incidental now.

By the time she carried the groceries into the kitchen, Walker was up. He took the bags and started putting things away, while she brushed off the snow, the flakes still whole and white, like bits of lace in her hair. Botticelli curls on a Degas body, that was what he'd said when he crawled in beside her that morning.

Another sign. She collected them, stored them up, these small portents of love.

She came up behind him, took a package from his hands, and turned him around, wrapping his arms about her waist.

Did you miss me?

I just got up.

She kissed him, and he said, What?, so she told him.

The baby's fine, it's due on May the first, she said, sweeping the doctor's prediction from her mind, for she'd made a calculation of her own. Their baby would be born in May, a month of endless possibility, it was there in the name.

When Alyson moved in with Walker, she switched her courses to the evening, then when she quit the university altogether – the degree in botany was her mother's idea, she could get a Master Gardener's certificate by correspondence – she found jobs that coincided with his schedule. She worked the late shift at a convenience store, cleaned offices, closed up for the owner of a large, independent bookstore, staying long into the night to enter inventory, restock shelves, set up the displays.

She thought she'd be lonely otherwise.

But later, in the country, when Walker went back to working through the nights, leaving her to her daylight hours, she was surprised how agreeable she found the arrangement. It was then that she grew to appreciate the particular pleasures of solitude. From dawn until mid-afternoon she ordered the hours to suit herself. She looked forward to the interlude with Walker, the force of his character – his ambition, his tightly trained focus – acting as a catalyst to strengthen her own, so that by the time he left for the studio, she felt renewed, eager to pass the evening with her books.

Though she spent most of the day on her own, she rarely felt alone, for at any given moment, she knew exactly where Walker was, could imagine what he was doing. He was in his studio reaching for a tool, a paddle carved from a root or a stone so gnarled with pebbles that rolling it across the belly of a clay figure left the impression that swarms of tiny creatures were burrowing under the skin. Or he was at the dragon-kiln, splitting wood for a firing. Or he was in the bed they'd pushed up against the window, a tall, narrow pane that extended to the floor, so that from the outside, when she passed by, she could see him sleeping, always restless, lips moving, legs twitching, kicking the covers loose.

She often paused by that window as she went about her chores. If she was farther from the house, she'd stop and listen, which was what she was doing that afternoon, standing with her snow shovel poised in mid-air. She was clearing the path to the chicken shed, moving carefully, as the doctor advised, keeping the scoops small though the snow was light, indulging in the rhythm of the work, when she thought she heard a voice in the scrape of metal on stone. She paused. In the lull she heard nothing but the soft puff of her breath, snow squeaking under her boots, the clothesline screech of a jay. Not Walker, after all, she thought, but then the cry came again and she turned back toward the house, wading through the snow until she saw him framed in the bedroom window, arms and legs flailing as if he'd slipped and lost his footing, was falling into an abyss.

By the time she got to him, he'd retreated to a corner of the mattress. She yanked the bedding off the floor and bundled it over him, then she was kneeling on the bed, murmuring, shhhhh, go back to sleep, though he'd never been awake.

It was something she'd had to learn, that a man could look at you with horror, fall crying at your feet, or strike out at you, and still be fast asleep.

But I never dream, he would say when she'd tell him about it later.

She slid her hand down across his forehead, his eyes, his lips. Small strokes in slow succession. When she'd calmed him a little, she pulled the quilt up close, smoothing it over his chest, over the tiny scars scattered among the hairs. She'd often wondered if they were the spark for his nightmares. He'd only been five or six when he found the shiny cylinder lying in the woods, not far from where his mother and brothers were hunting mushrooms. He didn't know it was a gunshell until he struck it with a rock and it burst apart, driving shards of metal into his chest and blasting the tips off the fingers of his left hand, the one she kissed now and tucked underneath the blankets.

The nightmare was almost over. She'd missed the worst of it. Still, she felt a residue of apprehension, stirred up from all those other times. A sharp remnant of the dread she always felt, not that she'd be hurt, but that the man she loved was an illusion and the dreaming man was real.

It was a simple, fleeting fear, easily dismissed. The fears that clung to her were his. When he finally told her about them, reciting their names — cleithrophobia, hypsiphobia, dystychiphobia — she thought of insects, multiplying, swarming. He had fears she could hardly imagine: bright lights, long flights of stairs, large panes of glass, the shrieking of a streetcar. That was the sound that had sent him crouching into a doorway the day they met.

Hey, are you okay? she'd asked, and he'd turned on her that look of his, a savage cat at the mouth of its cave. Others would have backed away, she knew that now, but she'd moved in closer, leading him to a bench in a quiet corner under a tree where she'd sat watching while his fists unclenched and he forced himself to breathe, counting along with him, One one-thousand, two one-thousand.

Recalling the moment, she thought again how remarkable it was that fate had brought her to him, for it was something she knew about, calming an anxious man. She'd seen how her father needed to be led out of the dark labyrinths of his moods, watched and learned that the more a person retreated, the more you had to give chase, throwing open every door as it was being slammed shut, though her mother had grown thoughtless and had left him alone, no one there on that afternoon when he slipped away from them both.

She'd never been able to forgive her for that.

She lay down on the bed, cupping her body to Walker's, drawing him to her, the rhythms of their life familiar, a comfort to them both.

At home on their hillside, it had always seemed to Alyson that the world held just the two of them, their place a tiny clear spot on a map of nothing but trees. But roads wound like veins all through those hills and the bones of buildings stood concealed beneath the leaves – square log structures, frame houses, a few grander ones of brick, and the dwellings people made themselves from whatever was at hand, hay bales, cedar posts, rubble stone. In the summer, she never noticed them, set back as they were behind rangy shrubs and trees, as if everyone who lived there conspired to perpetrate the fiction that no one lived there at all.

In the autumn, the camouflage fell away. Driving across the township in the middle of December, she glimpsed clearings as she passed, and she imagined the hill people building their canoes, boiling vats of soap, tending beehives and apple orchards, raising goats for milk and rabbits for meat, shaping dark loaves of bread and bright rounds of cheese. The images appeared to her as miniature dioramas fixed with labels such as Earnest Enterprise and Human Goodness, for she admired those men and women, their frugal habits and liberal politics, their easy, open ways. The locals she met at the feed store or the bank were cordial, but it was the hill people – the back-to-the-landers, draft dodgers, and dropouts who had moved up the Opeongo ten and twenty years before – who had made her feel welcome. One by one they'd come to visit, bringing clumps of their best ruby-heart rhubarb, braids of garlic, sourdough starter for her bread, offering the use of a peavey or a come-along before she knew what the words meant, inviting her and Walker to a midsummer party, a seed swap, the spring sugaring-off, so that now, every month or so, she'd find herself driving to one of those houses in the hills, a pan of burritos or a Thai salad balanced on Walker's lap, just as her father had carried plates of butter tarts and egg-salad sandwiches to the monthly meeting of the couples' club at the church. Though there was a difference, she'd tell herself, for it wasn't Christian obligation, it was the rituals and necessities of the seasons that drew her into the company of others.

Without that, she was thinking, she might never leave her hillside, which was why it was so surprising to watch her mental map expanding, transforming as she drove along, her little clearing in the wilderness slipping off to one corner, the space filling in with roads and long lanes and lush sketches of other farmsteads, the place she thought of as home growing more substantial, more plausible the farther from it she went.

She parked the van and got out. The whine of chainsaws was thick as insects in the air. Walker handed over the tray of maple-baked squash and left to join the men already in the bush. It was the last of the fall wood-gathering parties, when the friends moved house to house, sharing their tractors and splitters, helping each other bring in the winter's supply of fuel.

Not friends, she was thinking as she walked alone up the lane. More like acquaintances, people who knew her name and where she lived, but not her parents' names or what she'd left behind when she chose her life with Walker. She'd never had a lot of friends, there was always her father to consider, he needs his peace and quiet, her mother would say, and after she moved in with Walker, she'd had so little time. There was a woman she'd met at the bookstore, a regular who sometimes stayed late to talk. At her father's funeral, she'd seen her near the back of the church and the woman had written her several letters after she moved to the farm, but she'd never replied, feeling too remote, as though in leaving the city she had emigrated to another country where the customs and even the language were different.

Renata was her only real friend.

Aha! Another fringe-dweller! Renata had exclaimed at that first midsummer party, sitting down beside her on the rocks above the lake. From the beginning, talking to Renata had been almost like talking to herself, they had that much in common, both of them addicted to thick novels, and plants that came back true to seed. At the end of the night Renata had invited her to lunch, then she returned the invitation, and it became a habit with them, sharing a bowl of soup in one kitchen or the other, talking non-stop about their gardens, the children they planned to have, the books they were reading, the aches and intermittent discharges of their bodies, the boys they'd loved, the men they were living with.

Shacked up, my mother calls it.

Mine says Walker's not the marrying kind.

They told each other everything, though on the subject of Walker and her life at home as a girl she maintained a certain reserve, so much so that even when Renata admitted she'd had an abortion in high school, something Abe knew nothing about, Alyson had been unable to bring herself to offer a revelation of her own.

For a time, she thought the four of them would be close. She imagined playing euchre in the evenings or going on weekend trips.

Maybe just to Ottawa for the day? she suggested once to Walker.

But he'd said, You go if you want to, I don't need a friend.

It was the differences she had come to notice between herself and Walker, but with Renata she still marvelled at how much they were alike, not only in their looks, both tall and strongly built, with dark, wildly curling hair, but in the way they walked and carried themselves, always leaning slightly forward, as if in anticipation. They were often mistaken for sisters, especially when they were overheard talking in that way they had, completing each other's sentences, answering questions before they were asked, weaving such a cocoon around themselves that as soon as she opened the door and Renata waved at her from across the crowded room, she felt as though they were in her own kitchen, about to catch up on each other's news.

How are you feeling? Renata said when they'd found a corner for themselves.

Great.

Really?

Truly. If I wasn't, you're the one I'd tell.

If you told anybody, you mean.

Alyson laughed.

You know me too well. Where's Abe? Did you bring the girls?

Renata and Abe had two daughters, born just eleven months apart. They were three and four now, but it was still like having twins, Renata said.

They've all got the flu so I left them at home, bundled up together in bed with a pile of books. Even bringing in wood looked to me like a rest.

When the others went out to work, the two friends stayed inside, organizing the supper and babysitting the children too young to haul brush or stack wood. All through the afternoon, women stopped in the kitchen on their way to the bathroom or to put a child down for a nap, exchanging gossip, just as the men did when they paused to sharpen a chain or give their lower backs a rest. Casual conversations, words passed mindlessly along or forgotten as soon as they were spoken, though later Alyson would try to reconstruct exactly who had said what to whom, for at the time, it all seemed so inconsequential – talk of children and school and Christmas and who was doing what to get them through the winter – that it came as a shock when Walker told her on the way home there was a job if he wanted it, felling trees with a logging crew up north.

Her first thought was a memory: Walker's back growing smaller as he walked away from her through the snow. She was standing with the real estate agent, she'd shut her eyes for just a second, and Walker was gone. His trail stopped abruptly at the wall of trees, which from a distance looked to her like a hoarding cleverly painted with limbs and trunks. She'd stamped her feet, trying to stay warm, but it was too much for her. She'd set off after him, fitting her footsteps to his, thinking of the first night they'd spent together, when he'd wrapped a cord around her waist, then his, all their body parts measured and compared, ankles, wrists, thighs, feet, only one place where she was larger, and he'd kissed the skin all the way round where the cord had lain, whispering, Wide hips make good babies.

It's for the baby, she was thinking as he was saying, It's just the money.

I'd be in the bush for the winter, but I'd be back by spring, he went on. Réal can clear the lane. I talked to Abe, he said he'd help with the chores.

When would you leave?

New Year's Day. A couple of guys from the party are driving up. I can get a ride with them.

He'd done it before, come at her out of the blue with some scheme for improving their economic situation. Raising chickens that laid coloured eggs for Easter. Making rustic bent-twig furniture, though there were no willows on their land. Trapping beaver and muskrat in the stream: that was the winter the bottom fell out of fur prices. Keeping bees. Tapping the maples to boil syrup. In the beginning, she had tried to discuss the details of what he proposed, pointing out the costs of setting up, the work of marketing what he would produce, making sure he understood that she couldn't be involved, she had her hands full with the herbs. But talking only seemed to attach him more firmly to his plan, however impractical it might be, and she'd worry for weeks that the money they had set aside to see them through the winter would be lost on some obsolete ski-trail machine or a portable, collapsible mill he'd seen advertised in the back of a magazine. Left alone, he would go on about the idea for a while, then one day the catalogues and sketchbooks would disappear and she'd never hear a word about it again.

She pulled into the lane and stopped the van beside the house, leaving the motor running to give herself time to think.

The best way to deflect him, she had learned, was simply to agree.

If that's what you want, she said finally. I'd miss you, though.

He reached across to pat her arm, his hand sliding to her belly.

You'll be fine.

I know. She flicked off the lights and pulled the key from the ignition. I always am.

# MARGARET

*Autumn 1859*

It is the good fortune of the MacBayne brothers, as they set out to become men of the Bush, that they carry distributed amongst them all the attributes normally accorded the Scots.

Already at twenty-five William Wallace is a sober man of disciplined habit, abiding by the twin lodestars of order and hard work. Patient of hunger and every sort of hardship, he has a captious manner uncommon in one so young, an asperity to his silence, and a certainty in his own correctness that pronounces itself as an obdurate pride.

Robert Bruce is the canny one. Shrewd, close in making a bargain, he is honest too, and daring. Ambitious. A man of deep feeling and ready impulse who, once he pledges his loyalty, will follow a friend to the ends of the earth. Of the three brothers he, least of all, requires a prod to gaiety.

Harry Douglas, the youngest at eighteen, is far and away the easiest with himself and others. He has a sly sense of humour, a sharp curiosity, and a sensitivity to the created world that might be due to youth or to character, it is too early to tell. As industrious and frugal as his older brothers, he is also given to quiet acts of generosity, and in him, the Scots habit of seeing things through has taken its strongest hold.

It is fitting, given the various strengths of their characters, that William Wallace and Robert Bruce proceed ahead to search out a suitable location, leaving Harry Douglas to bring the women and baggage by steamboat to the city of Ottawa. There, they transfer to a stage that crosses the river to follow the opposite shore, rumbling north and west past a series of rapids to a village where they board a steamer with a throng of others like themselves, drawn by advertisements in the *Canada Gazette* – a dozen Scots, a handful of English, a tangled knot of Irish, although these keep to themselves on the far side of the boat.

Cauld iron! Margaret whispers, reaching her fingers to a metal strut the moment she sees the black coat of a priest among the emigrants, but she is not quick enough. A storm blows down the river just as they pull free of the wharf. For hours the steamer pushes west into the wind, bucking waves that lift the contents of the passengers' stomachs over the rails and into the water that bristles around them. At one point the engines stop, and the heaving grows intolerable, even for Margaret who has good legs for the sea, but then machine noise overtakes the howl of the gale again and, eventually, they reach Farrell's Landing, a tiny settlement cleaved by a road that points farther west like a finger into a wall of trees.

They leave their household goods on the wharf and board a rough waggon that takes them the final miles to the village of Renfrew, where William Wallace and Robert Bruce await them on the steps of the hotel. The brothers are changed. Not so much that Margaret fails to recognize them, but enough that she feels awkward in their company, the way she might if they were uncles or older cousins rarely met. Their physical appearance is altered. Thick auburn curls hide their cheeks and chins, and where the skin still shows, it is stained the colour of earth and marked with welts and scrapes. They have exchanged their serviceable Scottish boots for ones that lace to the knee and they wear their shirts rolled at the sleeves, laying bare the muscles of their arms, so swollen with use that she almost believes the story they told her as a child, that the MacBaynes were descended from a race of giants.

But it is their demeanour that is most transformed. They stride down the street with unaccustomed purpose, even on a Sunday while showing the family the town, indicating with an oddly proprietary air the grocer's, the smithy, the kirk. Their voices are loud and sonorous, as though they intend what they say to be heard by every passerby. And later, in their rooms at the Renfrew Hotel, when they declare they require all that remains of the family's modest funds, they speak with such authority that their mother hands over the purse she has held guardian through all her married life.

Margaret watches from the shadows cast by her brothers, men she no longer dares to tease or make do her childish bidding. It is the Bush that has changed them, she thinks. It bears on them more heavily than the sea, for while a fisherman returns to shore and builds his house beyond the water's reach, in the forest they would find no relief. Soon she will be plunged inside, too, altered in ways beyond imagining.

*William Wallace and Robert Bruce purchased a Holding in the Bush, a place of Trees run through with Rivers where no Man had walked before. They took pride in their selection. They made the Land theirs with Words and Dreams long before they touched it with their Hands.*

The men — for they are no longer boys, even in their mother's eyes — have already determined the number of oxen to buy, what seed grain to carry in with them, which tools. They are not acting on their own. Their father, before he made his way down the gangplank at Grosse Île, pressed a book into William Wallace's hands, *The Emigrant's Guide to North America*. It was on the advice of its author, Rob MacDougall, that the family left the bannock spade, the brander, and the iron girdle hanging from the ramtree in their stone cottage in Pittenweem, although they packed their tin plates, their augers, gimlets, and spades, layering the metal goods between bolts of cotton and canvas and heavy woollen cloth. The forged nails to build their log cottage and the axes to fell the trees, the brothers purchase in Renfrew, abiding by MacDougall's judgment that Scottish smiths would not know how to make any that would be of use.

Robert Bruce leaves first, taking an ox and cart back to Farrell's Landing to retrieve the family's household goods. The next day, William Wallace and Harry Douglas load the purchased supplies onto a second cart with a milch cow tied to the back. The men walk ahead, while Margaret and her mother take their place on either side. For sixteen miles, they journey past farms that Margaret takes at first for settlements, so numerous are the buildings clustered together, clinging to a ridge or filling an indentation in the overlapping hills. The villages themselves are sprawling. They line the road on either side of taverns and postal offices that bear names such as Ferguslea and Burnstown, which, together with the dry stone dykes that enclose every field, make it seem as though their journey has circled the family back to some odd, forgotten glen of the nation they just left.

Shortly after nightfall, they reach Mount St. Patrick on the banks of Constant Creek, taking rooms in a small hotel, adjacent to those of the Crown agent, Mr. French. All through the evening, in the hotel's cramped and overheated parlour, the agent holds forth on the merits of the Opeongo Road. Its advantageous position between two great rivers, the Madawaska and the

Bonnechère. Its future prospects as a major thoroughfare, once it is joined to the Great Lakes by the surveyed road known as Bell's Line, which at the moment is a pencilled arrow passing through the heart of the wilderness.

What the entire effect of these splendid works may be upon the future of Canada, it is impossible for the human mind accurately to comprehend, he sputters, wiping his forehead of the effluvia produced by the exertions of his monologue. But with the railway and ship's canal completed from Ottawa through to Georgian Bay, the best economic minds estimate that the region is capable of sustaining a population of eight million, of which you, my dear friends, he says, beaming at the MacBaynes, are among the privileged first.

Heartened by the Crown agent's words, the family continues north as soon as Robert Bruce catches up to them. Within a few hours of their departure from the hotel, they arrive at the Opeongo Oasis, where they fill their jugs with fresh spring water. By the end of the day they are settled among the sacks in one of the many outbuildings belonging to the Scotsman the brothers met on the wharf at Montreal. The next morning, through a break in the trees, they spy the prodigious hills that face them. The land, which has been rising steadily since they stepped off the steamboat at Farrell's Landing, rears up sharply now. Margaret and her mother fall behind, the way too steep for them to keep pace with the carts. When the women reach a height of land, Margaret pauses for her mother to catch her breath. Below them lays a swath of green as far as they can see, cloud-shadows rippling across the surface in shifting patterns of darkest jade.

So like the sea, her mother says as soon as she can speak. A boundless sea of trees.

When the brothers notice their mother and sister missing, they stop the carts and Robert walks back along the road to find them, catching the last of the older woman's words.

This sea we can conquer, he declares, laying a hand on her thin shoulder.


It isn't until they penetrate the untouched forest that Margaret feels the hinges of her bones loosen, feels her breath rise from the deepest recesses of her lungs.

Dense foliage hems the road on either side, limiting her gaze to what lies directly ahead and behind. At first it seems as stout a barrier as the high stone walls of the wynds, but gradually the greenery yields and she can make out leaves of varying shapes and colours, clusters of red and blue-black berries, dangling nuts, trunks smooth, gnarled, corrugated, a latticework of vaulting branches and creeping vines that do not so much keep her sternly to the path as embrace her in her progress.

Nothing about this landscape is familiar. Not the bald, grey rock, not the endless towering trees. Not the stillness of the wind nor the awful heat of the sun. Certainly not the peculiar fragrance, though she will learn to put names to it — pine and hemlock, granite damp with dew. She has never in her life encountered anything like it, yet from the first moment, it strikes her as home.

*The land drew me to itself. I cannot explain it, the way it gripp'd my heart, like love.*

For forty miles, the colonization road is a broad channel opened through the forest. Waist-high stumps stand where trees once grew. Tangled heaps of brush bank each side, restrained by trunks as wide as Margaret is tall. On swampy borders, flowers flourish, sprays of purple, white, and pink, tall spires of yellow. Most of the blooms are unfamiliar, although the asters Margaret recognizes, the sticktights and lady's bedstraw that grow in the grassy meadows that open here and there among the trees.

All day the family walks, leading the oxen through the maze of stumps, stopping to lay evergreen boughs over rain-soaked mud holes so the carts can pass. Margaret holds her breath as the wheels roll over the uncertain roadbed, watching the load tilt dangerously, then right itself again. The terrain is rugged and wild, with steep ridges of bare rock that give way to deep ravines spanned by makeshift log bridges. Now and then the varied timber yields to a forest of Colossus pines that block out the sun and the daylight too, so that it seems to Margaret even at midday that night must surely have fallen. Their passage through these

pineries is swift, for there is little underfoot to impede their way
and the heavy sighs of wind-tossed limbs far above their heads
speeds them on.

It is early October and once the sun is set, the air takes on a
chill. The moon, as it climbs, draws pale mists out of the earth,
but the travellers easily find their way, for the moon is gibbous
and the freshly cut stumps shine like torches in its light.

When their mother grows too weak to walk, William Wallace
makes a place for her on one of the carts, loading yet another
creel onto his back. Margaret walks alongside, her hand on her
mother's skirts, a reminder to enquire after her well-being, for
without the touch of homespun cloth, she thinks, she might
submit entirely to the flickering light, the tantalizing scent, the
beckoning leaves.

Her brothers seem immune to the forest's wiles. They stoke
their steady pace with talk, describing to each other the land as
they intend to shape it: smooth fields of wheat and oats, livestock
grazing in a meadow, neatly fenced, a frame house on a rise set
back from the river, a cellar dug into the slope, bursting with
barrels of tatties and neeps. They calculate how long it will take
to clear an acre, to clear the twelve that will make the land theirs,
seeing already the heavy heads of winter wheat they will harvest
before another summer passes. Harry Douglas, having scoured
*The Emigrant's Guide* as they waited for William Wallace and Robert
Bruce to purchase stores, joins his brothers in discussing the
advantage of peas over barley-corn, the number of piglets they

should pen in the spring, although occasionally, William Wallace and Robert Bruce silence their youngest brother with recollections of the wolves they've encountered or the three bears' heads they once came upon in the Bush, severed and impaled on the boughs of a pine, or they compare strategies for felling trees and for bartering with the Indians, subjects that affirm their superior knowledge of where they find themselves.

Their conversation comes to Margaret in snatches, carried on the breeze over the grind of the cart's wooden wheels and the noises of the forest. Only once does she pay them any attention, when they call out to a woman in a clearing some distance from the road. There is a stream, and on the edge of it, a cottage with three walls made of logs stacked one upon the other, the fourth a blanket suspended across the opening. A faint echo of an axe can be heard, but only a solitary woman is in evidence. She is dressed in a fine pale gown, and strolls back and forth along the water's edge, comforting a child squalling in her arms. Margaret has seen the discarded wheels and broken shafts of those who travelled before them into the wildwood, but the woman is the first bush-settler she has laid her eyes upon and the open ground she walks, her first settler's clearing. The woman pauses for a moment to acknowledge the passing caravan, then returns to pacing calmly within her chamber of spired evergreens.

The vision of this woman alone, at home in the forest, sufficient unto herself, sustains Margaret through the rest of the journey. It is there in the front of her mind when she awakens with the rising sun, and it is a portal to her dreams when at last she wraps herself in her plaid and lies down beside her mother on the boughs her brothers spread for them under the canopy of stars.

It is late in the afternoon of the fourth day when they reach the end of the travelled portion of the colonization road. From this point on, a line has been cut, the undergrowth hacked low, and trees toppled in the forest to tear a ragged path, but the road itself has not been cleared. Their progress slows as the oxen pick their way through the debris, occasionally stopping altogether as the brothers move thick limbs aside.

At the sign of a red head scarf dangling from a branch, the carts turn west, following a line of blazes cut into the bark that mark where the side-line will be opened. The oxen, until then placid in their plodding, balk at the contortions required of them to draw the carts between the trees. More than once, Margaret and Harry Douglas take hold of the yoke and coax the animals back while William Wallace and Robert Bruce pick up their axes to clear the way. Flakes fly long and golden as rizzled fish until a moan far above drops their arms to their sides and they let out a great whoop as a tree hurls to earth with a tearing crash.

Whalers of the woods, Margaret notes to herself, observing the grins of satisfaction lurking within her brothers' grimaces. On the sea, they were lowly prawners and herring dravers, scraping fish off the ocean floor like scullery maids, while whalers held the place of honour, wrestling giants a thousand times their size, as her brothers do now, playing David to the Goliath pines. And the thought brings to mind her father, something he always said, that pride goeth before a fall, and she wishes he were there, watching over her brothers, his hand on her hair.

The sky is beginning to lighten, the birds warming to their chorus, when the weary group passes the post that marks one corner of the MacBayne land. In choosing this location, the brothers put their faith in the counsel of *The Emigrant's Guide*, for while they could tell a sea ripe with herring from the swell of the wind and a certain stipple on the waves, they had no means by which to judge the quality of soil that lay beneath a growth of trees. Where they saw clumps of cedar and yellow birch and swamp elm, they moved on, as Robert MacDougall advised, lingering where the sugar-tree, the beech-tree, the white ash, and red elm grew. They eyed each specimen, trying to determine whether the branches might be called *juicy* and *tender*, if the leaves before their eyes were indeed *soft* and *robust*. The more crustaceous the bark of the sugar-tree the better, although the bark of the beech-tree should be green. The trunks should be tall and untangled, bare of branches for the first fifty feet; the forest floor, sparse. The heaviest forest, MacDougall wrote, grows most often on the poorest land.

All this William Wallace and Robert Bruce kept firmly in mind, assuring each other that the piece of land they chose exhibited none of the disadvantages and all of the merits detailed in the guide. Its author could have found no better, they declared. They saw past the gnarl of trees and the infernal biting flies to the time when the colonization road would be a thoroughfare, not a line cut roughly through the Bush. That vision bright in their eyes, they stomped through the underbrush until they found a narrow river that coursed toward the Madawaska, and there they scrawled the MacBayne name across three lots on the Crown agent's survey map. Two hours' walk to the colonization road, an easy paddle to the waterway that flowed to the colony's city markets, and all other criteria met, as close as they could manage to the forty-fifth parallel of latitude, in deference to their father who had grown attached to the notion of living in perfect balance between the top of the earth and its precise midway line.

By the time the family arrives at their own clearing, the sun is resting on the treetops, as if pausing to admire the river view before continuing its daily climb. A lean-to of evergreens greets them near the riverbank, a fire pit at the opening, a tea-pail hanging from the crosspiece in a welcoming way.

Margaret walks past the rough home her brothers have pre-pared and pulls off her boots to hop barefoot along the crossing stones to a wide, flat boulder that lifts its back out of the river. She scoops a palm of earth-coloured water to her mouth. It tastes sharp, faintly seasoned. The tang of water sprung from roots and stone.

*Our Clearing was by a River that my brothers named the Tea for its well-steeped colour. I called it the River Stone.*

Margaret never trusted the sea, with its teasing tides that offered revelations one minute, concealing them the next. But she feels at ease with the little river that flows so steadfastly by the clearing, its pace steady, its relation to the land constant.

Only the shadows change, lengthening from one shore in the morning, from the other by afternoon. The colour of the shadows alters, too, as the leaves on the trees ripen red as berries, or wax to a yellow so intense that long after the sun has set the forest glows as if a bonfire burns somewhere deep within. But a tree is still a tree, the river keeps its width, and the earth slopes reliably to the water's firm shore.

Each day, from the rising of the last star to the first, the family works in the woods, pushing the forest back from the riverbank in an ever-widening arc. While Robert Bruce and William Wallace and Harry Douglas chop the trees, Margaret and her mother clear the brush, heaping branches and foliage in great piles according to the brothers' instructions.

Margaret does most of the hauling, for by now their mother's condition is in plain view. They do not speak of this new presence, just as they do not speak of their father's absence. So long as no voice is given to their worries, they can maintain the faith that they labour toward the same purpose they devised by the hearth in Pittenweem.

By the time the first snow falls, a cottage made of logs is standing in the clearing by the river, a thin thread of smoke rising from its roof. Its dimensions are not unlike their stone cottage in Pittenweem, although instead of an attic for the fishing gear and her mother's herbs, the room is open to the rafters, so that the smoke from the fire ascends straight to the roof where it noses along the slabs of bark shingles until it finds a gap for its escape. The brothers cut straight, young trees to make pole beds and a table – their kists serve well enough as benches and cupboards – while Margaret and her mother mix clay from the riverbank with wood chips and moss and poke it into the cracks between the logs. By the time the bed frames are ready, Margaret has to shake thick tufts of snow off the evergreen boughs she collects to lay on the criss-crossed ropes as a mattress.

The brothers never stop their work of laying low the forest, although the hours of the day shorten and the cold grows so intense the linings of their nostrils fuse each time they draw a breath. Margaret stays with her mother inside the cabin, mending clothes torn by clawing branches, preparing porridge and brose and stews from their meagre supplies. When the days are at their shortest, the hens are killed, one by one, and roasted over the fire, since it is clear there is not sufficient grain to keep them through the winter. In the lean-to the family abandoned for the cabin, the oxen and cow huddle together, turning their backs to the wind and shivering through the storms. Twice, when the temperature sinks so low the trees explode like cannonfire, they are brought inside the cabin, animals and humans each benefitting from the other's warmth. The ground turns to stone and the river stiffens too, so that hatchets must be pressed into use for water as well as wood.

Margaret marks off the days on the calendar that she hung beside her bed. All Hallows' Eve passes and Christmas too. They see no one but each other, hear no other human voice, only the rustle of small animals and the desperate shriek of birds. On Hogmanay Eve, they put their work aside and gather around the fire to sit the old year out, searching their hearts, as they have always done on the final day of the year for the sins they have committed in the past twelvemonth and counting the blessings they hope are to come. As midnight draws on, a silence falls upon the family. They think of the one who should be there, the one who set them on their journey. When the hand of the clock moves to five minutes of twelve, Robert Bruce begins to sing, and after the final chorus of Auld Lang Syne is through, William Wallace offers up the prayer that their father would have said. It is a simple invocation but it reaches deep into each of them, Margaret especially, who feels most keenly the absence of her father, for, being the youngest, she had him least of all. Her meditations stir remorse for each unkind thought, each selfish act, every shirking of what she knew to be

her duty, and added to these self-recriminations is the certainty
that her father will not return, so that what rises from the cauldron of miseries in her heart is a longing to be at one with the
others who sit around that fire, to succeed as William Wallace
prays they will, prospering among the lakes and trees as her
father promised.

The next morning, Harry Douglas sneaks outside while
the others sleep and bangs loudly on the door, calling out the
Hogmanay blessing,

*Gum beannaicheadh Dia an t-ardrach,*
*Eadar chlach, is chuaille, is chrann,*
*Eadar bhithe, bhliochd, is aodach,*
*Slainte dhaoin bhi daonnan ann.*

The sight of this wilderness first-footer, a pile of clinkers
from old fires in one hand, a dry bun and a mound of salt in the
other, his hair and moustaches blackened with ash to cover the
tint of red that would surely bring bad luck into their house for
all the year, makes them lighthearted. Even William Wallace does
not insist they keep to their work. He joins Robert Bruce in one
song after the other, and late in the day, after they have sampled
their hoard of whisky sufficiently, they dance to the tune of the
whistle that Margaret plays.

Their mother keeps to her bed, her hands never straying far
from the bedcover's fringe. Although her eyes for the most part

are closed, her lips curve in a faint smile to hear her children so happy, playing together again.


The berries hang shrivelled from the branch, more black than red and crusted with snow, but the tree is young and the cluster within easy reach, so Margaret stands on her toes to pluck it, deciding that it will do.

In the cabin, she ties the sprig to a knot protruding from the log above her mother's head. There, she says, smoothing the hair from her mother's cheek, no harm will come to you now.

But when she lifts the blanket to remove the cloths soaked with her mother's waters, she recoils from the body she sees. The skin is pale, the flesh shrunken, the tight roundness of her belly like a bolus on a wasted stalk.

All through the day her mother lies in bed, taking sips of the warm water Margaret offers, never complaining of her pains. The brothers stay outside in the woods as long as they can, and when the birthing continues into the night and they have nowhere else to go, they sit by the fire, avoiding one another's glance, not speaking of what is transpiring in the bed at their backs.

Harry Douglas stands at last, declaring, One of us must go for help.

But William Wallace stares him down. And where will you go? There aren't half a dozen families settled in these highlands.

Robert Bruce's tone is kinder but still matter-of-fact. You

couldn't make it to the nearest clearing and back in time to do any good.

The baby, like her sisters Isobel and Bride, is born without uttering a cry. The effort of pushing the dead child into the world exhausts their mother and the uselessness of it siphons whatever last strength she has. She lives four days more, never speaking a word, her breath coming in spasms. On the morning of the fifth day, she seems to rally, sitting up in bed and moving her lips as if to speak. Margaret leans close, anxious to make out the words, and in the doing, she breathes in her mother's last breath.

Harry Douglas pulls off his gansey and covers the clock, first dampening the chime. Robert Bruce douses the fire. William Wallace picks up his axe and goes outside, leaving the door open so that his mother's spirit can find its way out. Margaret places small flat pebbles on her mother's eyelids, knowing without asking that they do not have the coins. Then she pours salt into a plate and sets it on her mother's breast, gathering nails to drive into the butter to keep it from going rank.

All of these precautions made, Margaret washes her mother's body and dresses her in the dead-clothes she had brought from Pittenweem in the knowledge she would be buried in this foreign place. The men lay her out on the table, and Margaret cradles the baby in the crook of one arm. Then she gathers every candle she can find and hands them to Harry Douglas who arranges a tracing of light around their mother's still form.

Put them back, William Wallace says, when he sees what they have done. There will be no wake.

Margaret protests, She should lie three days!

But William will not be moved. In the absence of kirk and preacher, father and mother, he declares, the rules they follow will be his own. With the child so long departed and only one small room to shelter the living and the dead, surely God would forgive their haste, he said.

Margaret takes the sheet from her bed and sews her mother and sister inside, then she stands apart as the brothers carry their burden to the hollow they have chiselled into the frozen bank of the river. Snow begins to fall as they lay the bodies in the shallow grave, arranging pine boughs over top, then stiff clods of earth. Not knowing how else to keep the wild beasts from their mother's flesh, they heap boulders on the mound.

That done, the brothers stand empty-handed, uncertain what more to do, for they always relied on their father to give them guidance in difficult times. A heavy snow is falling, gathering shawls across their shoulders, blanketing the stones. At last Harry Douglas starts to sing and the others join in,

The Lord's my Shepherd, I'll not want.
He makes me down to lie
In pastures green. He leadeth me
The quiet waters by . . .

Margaret stays inside by the hearth. She knows as well as they that a woman brings bad luck to a grave, and it will come soon enough, she thinks, the moment when the snow will dissolve and she will have to look upon her mother's marker, a mound of stones at the water's edge.

*When I thought the days could get no Colder, my Mother left this Life bringing forth a Sister who never drew a breath. But I had seen Birth before and I had seen Death. I was already Fourteen years of age.*

# A L Y S O N

*Winter 1991*

It started to snow the minute Walker climbed into the truck. Alyson stood at the window waving, the snow falling so thick and fast she could hardly see, big flakes crocheted together, the landscape obscured no matter where she looked, as if a luminous shroud had been pulled over the house.

Walker hadn't let go of the idea of a logging job, as she'd thought he would. He'd gone on about it through the rest of December, making a special trip into Renfrew to price out felling gear, insulated steel-toed boots with ballistic nylon in the tongues, hard hats fitted with visors and ear protectors, felling pants and gloves and jackets, all with special inserts to save vital body parts from the tearing teeth of the saw chain. He'd found books on felling techniques and selective harvesting that he pored over, reading aloud passages on the three types of notches, the proper use of wedges, winches, and fairleads, how to fell

against the natural lean of a tree. By the time she'd stopped pretending she would be fine no matter what, it was too late. She'd
tried to talk to him, then, tried to persuade him to stay, but none
of her arguments made any difference.

What about the baby? she finally said.

What about it? I'll be back the end of March, at the latest.
You said the baby's not due till May.

So you're really going to leave me here alone for three
months?

He didn't answer, he never did when that wheedling tone
crept into her voice, but a few days later he told her he'd been
talking to the man he was driving with to the camp.

He's planning to come home the last weekend of every
month. Four weeks and I'll be back. That's not so bad. You'll be
fine, you said so yourself.

But she didn't feel fine, she felt shaky. Not on the verge of
collapse, just unsteady. The way she'd felt the time she broke her
finger stacking wood, her hand uncertain in its movements until
the muscles learned to compensate. The adjustment had been
just as hard when the splint came off, feeling odd to have the use
of all her fingers again. Only the transition was a problem, she
thought. She would adapt. It was unfamiliar territory, that was
all, which didn't seem fair, since she was the one still at home.

She made herself some tea and settled by the woodstove
with the novel she'd chosen to get her through her first few days
alone. When the snow stops, she was thinking, I'll take a walk.

Then I'll make myself something to eat. One of her favourites, a leek frittata with tarragon and sharp cheese. If Walker were there, she'd have to grill a sausage, too, fry some potatoes, make a salad, get out the canned plums and something sweet if she had it, and if not, she'd probably start baking right about then. Instead, she opened the oven door and propped her feet on the edge. In one way, she thought, Walker's absence, like the storm, would be a holiday.

All afternoon she read by the fire. The snow changed hour to hour like a sweater unevenly knitted, sometimes the air uniformly thick with it, sometimes flakes falling loose, gaps opening up between. The next morning, the snowfall was fixed in its pattern, dense and steady, so that by the time she came back from feeding the chickens, the footprints she'd made going out to the shed were already filled in, as though she'd suffered a loss of memory and spent hours instead of minutes with the hens.

Perhaps it was the mesmerizing effect of the snow, but she hardly felt that Walker was gone. She'd find herself thinking he was in his studio or asleep in their bed, and she'd be so comforted by the thought that she allowed herself to indulge in the pretence that their routines were going on the same as always.

The snow continued all through the second day and the third, the air so still that white caps accumulated on the fence posts and a feathery piping lined every branch. It made her think of the gingerbread landscape her father made her one Christmas, bending over each little pine tree to daub the tips with icing, swirling whiteness over the hills and down the roof of the house he made, an exact replica of theirs, tracing the plans onto the rolled-out dough with tender concentration, fitting slivers of coloured gumdrops into the window openings, rigging up a light inside that she could turn on herself and she would, tiptoeing down the stairs every morning while it was still dark so she could peer through the stained-glass at the gingerbread family he'd set inside. Every year she would ask if he could make one for her again, and her mother would say no, he isn't up to that now, yet there it was outside her window, his whimsy and devotion finding her in her future, and she felt happy and sad both at once.

On the fourth day, a wind rose out of the east, rattling the pressed-tin siding and shifting the snow into sharp-edged sweeps, raising a drift against the kitchen wall. She sat by the woodstove, her feet propped on the oven door, the edge softened with a towel. She only pampered herself like that when she was sick, and she thought how lovely it was to be so warm and lazy and yet so completely well. She watched the snow piling up against the window, climbing the glass inch by inch as she daydreamed of her baby, just a hand's-breadth long, no heavier than the hummingbird she once trapped in the cage of her fingers, its heart pulsing against her palm as she carried it out of the house. When she opened her hands the bird just sat there, then suddenly, it took flight.

She must have been dozing, for when she looked up, the living room was brightening. The storm had passed, though the kitchen was still dark, the window swallowed in a drift. She pressed her nose against the pane, squinting to make out the contours of trees or a shed through the covering of snow, thinking, my baby's world must be lit like this.

The drift filled the entranceway, too. When she pulled open the door to go to the hens, she faced a white ghost-door, its panels embossed in reverse, a hollow where the knob should have been. She gasped, more in wonder than in alarm. She had the feeling that if she could just find the handle, the door would open to a preternatural landscape, a crystal garden of flowers that only bloomed inside a blizzard, each a different shade of white.

She trailed her fingers over the ghost-door, wanting to leave it be, but there were the hens to consider. So she got a broom and with the handle broke a hole in the snow, reaming out the drift until she could see the sky, half-expecting a different vista – ivory birds soaring over an alabaster sea – only partly relieved to see the familiar spires of black spruce, the distant, changeless hills.

Frigid air was seeping in through the tear in the snow. The temperature had dropped. She pushed the snow out of the doorway, dug the shovel out of the drift, and cleared the path to the hens, working quickly in the dimming light. Inside the coop, the birds were huddled together on the roost, their heads tucked under their wings, their bodies such a mass of feathers that she had to count several times before she knew for certain one was missing.

She'd spared eight of the best layers from the fall slaughter in the hopes they'd go broody in the spring. Her days were filled

with such small economies. That's what makes all the difference, she'd told Walker, still hoping to convince him not to leave.
She'd helped him stack bales along the walls and heap straw on
the floor, thinking the body heat of the chickens and their com-
posting dung would keep the coop warm. But he'd been right,
the flock was too small.

She followed a thin, high-pitched whine to the nesting box,
and there she found the missing hen, its beak gaping as it
wheezed. She smoothed the feathers on its back and slid her hand
under the breast, feeling for an egg. The wool of her mitten
caught on the broken shell, stuck to the albumen that glistened
icily between the cracks.

They'll all die, she thought, hurrying back to the house with
the frozen water-bucket, stopping at the barn to gather an armful
of bricks leftover from Walker's kiln. She heated the bricks in the
oven while she cooked a warm mash for the hens, spooning it
into their trough, laying the bricks on the straw under the roost.
She crouched close, worried that the heat in the clay would burst
the straw into flame. The only thing worse than the cold, she
thought, would be a fire. When the bricks cooled, she lugged
them back to the kitchen and brought another steaming tray,
crouching to the straw again, trying to think what else to do,
tugging at the bales, pulling them nearer to make a smaller space,
but still she couldn't get it warm, couldn't get the hens to eat.

When at last she fell into bed, she dreamt wandering, fruitless
dreams of doors that wouldn't open, of buildings that collapsed as

she passed, of a baby, a tiny thing someone thrust in her arms, telling her to care for it, although the moment she looked up, the baby vanished, and she ran searching through the house, a stranger's house, full of people who couldn't see her, couldn't hear her, not even her mother, who kept straightening a picture she was hanging on the wall, as if her daughter weren't beside her, pleading for help.

Silliness, she thought when she woke. But the dream unsettled her nonetheless. Not the story so much as the setting. She'd never been in the house she dreamt, had never seen it before, and yet there it was in her mind, in minute, exact detail. She remembered the precise shade of rose and cream and willow-green on the walls, the swirling pattern of the carpet on the stairs, the curving banister and brass-handled doors that opened to rooms furnished beautifully, if somewhat too formally for her taste. Her mother was wearing a dress she'd never owned although it was just the sort of thing she'd buy, a white shirtwaist with a narrow red belt, her lipstick the same shade of red, the colour she always wore because, she said, it went with her dark, chestnut hair, which she always kept short, swept like a mane from her face. Her mother was hanging a picture of their farmstead as it might have looked when it was built, the image worked in slivers of wood, Walker's name spelled out in red cedar in a bottom corner, although he had never, would never, make such a thing.

It was all so authentic, so convincing — as if she'd caught herself living another life. The one threw the other into doubt, and as she moved through the snow-cave of her kitchen, brewing her tea of flowers and leaves, it was the dream that seemed to have more substance.

The haze of unreality was still clinging to her as she went about her chores. When she saw the hen dead in the nesting box, the water a white ingot of ice, she reached for the axe Walker had left leaning by the door as if this was what he'd intended all along. Lifting a bird from the roost, she knelt with it on the straw and stretched out the neck, bringing the axe down hard. Blood sprayed across her cape. The neck was not cut through. She struck again, breathing fast, her glasses steaming in the cold. Struck again, blind to where the axe blade fell. Birds flapped squawking to the ground. A wing scraped her cheek. She hung on to the flailing hen as its head slapped the straw, the wound gaping like a mouth, splattering blood across her hand, the way it had the first time they'd killed a hen, the bird so quiet on the stump, its neck slipped between the nails, jerking out of her hands as Walker slammed the axe down, the hen darting into the bush, blood raining on the leaves, like a doomsday prophecy, Walker had said while she stood dumbfounded, staring at the bird as it zigzagged headless through the woods, finding its way among the trees, muscles still alert to nerves though all connection to the brain had been severed.

She raised herself on one knee, pushed up her glasses with her wrist, missed and knocked them to the ground. She reached for them, swearing, determined not to let go of the hen, losing her balance instead. As she toppled over, the heel of her hand landed on something hard that she heard give way with a sickening crack. She shook the broken lens free and shoved the bent frame back on, but the hen was already limp under her hand.

The clothes next to her body were drenched, an unanticipated side effect of pregnancy, she'd discovered, that profuse sweating. The baby was kicking madly. The whole scene struck her as preposterous, another dream she would waken from soon. She threw the slaughtered bird into the nesting box with the other dead hen and scattered fresh straw over the floor to dampen the sharp, metallic smell of blood. Then she picked up the axe and turned back to the house, steadying herself by focusing on what she'd have to do next. Find a file. Sharpen the blade, Walker's job. Kill the rest of the hens. Quickly. Cleanly. Properly.

The cloying warmth of the kitchen made her nauseated. The baby refused to be still. She dropped the axe and slumped into her chair by the stove, massaging her belly in slow circles, murmuring to her child, trying to calm it, calm herself. Under her hand she could still feel the bird's struggle, feel herself pinning it down, that awful squirming under her palm, then something else, water lapping at her wrists, the writhing of the bodies, thirteen of them at least, though she could hardly see under the piece of old tin roofing where the dog had crawled to give birth. She'd appealed to Walker, How could the poor animal look after them all?, But it was her dog, he'd said, hardly more than a puppy itself, nosing its mewling offspring out of the way as yet another one slid out, and without thinking, she'd grabbed a stocking from the clothesline and reached frantically under the tin, not counting how many she took, half, maybe more, averting her eyes as she lowered the writhing mass into the rain barrel, sobbing as she held them down, her arms aching as she leaned over the water, waiting for the life force to wear itself out.

It undid her, the way those memories swept in, so real her palms felt wet, her cheeks, too. But she wasn't going to spend her time weeping. When Abe called the next day, she asked him to take the rest of the hens and he did, gathering the birds in a gunny sack, which he stowed in the back of his old Fargo. She stayed inside, watching from the window as the red truck disappeared between the snowdrifts, hoping he intended to add the birds to his own flock, wondering if he'd taken the nesting boxes and what was left of the feed, her mind fixed now on practicalities, her heart aching for Walker, the dreaminess of those first days by the stove brought abruptly to an end.

Renata telephoned every afternoon. Alyson looked forward to the call. It gave her something to structure her day around. January was the month she did her accounts, balancing her books for the year just past, setting up the new ledgers. It was a job she liked, the certainty of numbers a respite from the intricate contingencies of growing things. But that year, though she tried, she couldn't settle to the work.

Everything feels wrong, she said to Renata. I don't know how else to describe it.

She didn't say she felt abandoned, although that would have been the truth. But he hadn't left her, she told herself. He'd just gone away to work.

When's he coming back?

In a few weeks, she said, or at least that's what he promised. She heard in her voice that tone of complaint her mother used on the phone to her friends.

And I'm sure he will be, she added quickly. That's one thing about Walker, he's reliable.

From then on, she steered their conversations in other directions, rarely mentioning Walker except to say he'd called. It didn't help to talk about how lonely she felt. Dwelling on it only makes it worse, she said to herself, her mother's phrase, and she thought, in that one thing, at least, her mother had been right.

You look good, said Renata, picking her up in the Fargo at the end of the second week.

I'm not sure I want to do this, she said, climbing in.

It's my Christmas present, remember? *Your future foretold.* How can you refuse?

And she had to admit, it felt good being out. Since Walker left, she hadn't ventured far from the house, as if she worried that he'd come back unexpectedly and find it empty, though she knew that was ridiculous. With the freezer full and a stack of library books to read, she'd had no reason to leave. But now, driving along the country roads, she felt her spirits lifting. The radio, her friend's chatter, the places they passed — it was all mundane and familiar yet somehow invigorating, so that by the time Renata slowed, watching for the turn, Alyson felt excited.

She leaned back and turned her head toward Renata. Thanks for this, she said.

The fortune-teller's mailbox, when they finally got to it, looked promising. It was painted a deep twilight blue, stuck all over with stars and moons, *Nadine of the North* scrawled on one side in a loopy silver script.

It'll be a lark, Renata said as they pulled into the lane, but Alyson wasn't listening. She was watching a boy, maybe eleven or twelve, running in a crouch alongside the truck, dodging tree to tree. When the Fargo stopped, he threw himself into a snowbank, rolling over and out of sight.

Did you see that?

See what? asked Renata, slamming the door to the truck and coming around to her side.

At the sound of gunfire, they both jumped. The boy was propped up on his elbows, firing an air rifle into the trees.

Kids! Renata said under her breath.

Alyson felt her mood shift. She wondered how much damage a gun like that could do, if she should duck behind her friend, a cowardly thought, though she allowed herself to lag behind as they walked toward the battered trailer set among the trees. Mobile homes, her mother called them. Tin breadboxes, her father scoffed when her mother suggested they buy one to set up near a beach, their own summer place, instead of renting a different cottage on a different lake every year, no two holidays ever the same.

Nameless shanks of rusting metal poked up through the dirty snow, as if whoever tried to bury them had lost heart and given up. Farther back in the bush, Alyson could see the hulks of several cars and trucks, parts broken or rusted off or cannibalized to keep some other vehicle on the road. She could imagine the clearing almost pleasant in the summer, the junk hidden under sprays of goldenrod and jewelweed, but it looked desolate in the snow, the trees wasted and scabbed, leaves still hanging from the limbs like rotting bandages.

A pack of liver-coloured dogs were pitching themselves against the wire walls of a cage, howling in a frenzy, then abruptly they stopped.

A woman was standing in the doorway. A-lyson, she breathed, in a way that sounded like, at last! She laid a hand on Alyson's arm and drew her inside, calling back to Renata that she should wait in the truck.

The trailer had been gutted, opened up to one long, narrow room that was empty save for two chairs arranged to face each other across a white circle painted on the floor. As her eyes adjusted to the gloom, what appeared at first to be a shimmery coating on the walls differentiated into hundreds of icons and charms – pentacles and scarabs, horseshoes and crosses, a devil's mask, the Horus eye, a plaster-of-Paris ascending dove. There were dolls twisted from corn husks, dream catchers bent from bittersweet, necklaces of cowrie shells, and a rosary of sharp blue stones. She saw the skulls of several small animals, one large enough to be a cat. Plastic figurines hung from push-pins, coloured threads knotted around their necks. Snow White, Saint George and his dragon, a herd of My Pretty Pony unicorns, more Virgin Marys than she could count, some with the Christ child in their arms, others with the hands upturned, empty and forlorn. A curtain of crystals hung across the one, small window, flickering rainbows over the landscape of Nadine's wide forehead as she lowered herself into the red plush La-Z-Boy at the centre of the room. The ceiling above her was painted the same blue as the mailbox and glittered with a galaxy of miniature, flashing lights.

All the constellations and astrological signs, Nadine said, pointing out two of them, the Twins and the Virgin.

What a coincidence, she thought wryly. Walker's sign and hers.

Is that what you do, she asked. Read astrological charts?

The woman didn't answer. Instead, she indicated the plain wooden kitchen chair. Have a seat, dear, she said.

The hand she extended was so small, so delicately formed, the nails so perfectly painted that Alyson thought for a moment it must be fake. Everything else about the woman was uncommonly large. Fat billowed from her jawbone, accumulating in soft rolls at her midriff and thighs, flowing out from under the cuffs of her cushiony pink sweatpants to swell over the banks of the narrow, black slippers she wore. Her skin was very white, which made her seem unbaked, the dough of her flesh overspilling its form, still rising.

Her voice belonged to the hands, thin and delicate. You're worried, aren't you, dear?

Nadine lifted her hand. No, don't answer. Don't even nod your head.

There's a man, she continued. He's mysterious. Not a wanderer, that's not the problem, not the problem at all.

She said something about his hands, how they were healing hands, a doctor's or a minister's, but then she shook her head, saying, no, she had it wrong, he made things with his hands.

Not beautiful things, oh dear me no, she said. She was staring at a spot on the wall behind Alyson's head, as if she could see something there. She frowned. No, not lovely things at all. But he'll be known for them. People will come knocking at his door.

Quite a performance, thought Alyson. Renata must have put her up to it, though the woman was droning on now about her father, how he worked with numbers, a quiet man alone in a room, a man who liked to fly, things she'd never told Renata. Then the woman was folding her hands in the vast plain of her lap.

Is there something you'd like to ask me, dear?

She looked down at her own hands, nicked and scarred from ten years of digging in the earth, swollen with the fluids of pregnancy. So unlike the smooth, clever hands she'd looked down on

at cash registers, computer terminals, all the work she'd taken
on so Walker could devote himself to his clay. And so unlike the
slender girl's hands that had carried her books and quilts and
plants up the stairs to the apartment her father had made for her
in the attic, understanding her need to be alone, although he'd
never said as much, never said much of anything at all, silent for
weeks at a time all through her growing up until, one day out of
the blue, he would pull her onto his lap and tell her stories about
the haystack he'd once lived in or the plane he flew over the ocean
— The only time I was truly happy, he said, was when I was in the
air. Or he would make up stories about people known only to
them, winking at her over dinner, saying, Cornelia grew those
peas, you'd better eat them up, and she would, her mother scowl-
ing that his foolishness should succeed where the logic of good
nutrition failed. Jealous, too, or so she'd thought then, for she
was the apple of his eye, the light of his life, he'd told her so, his
sandy-coloured head the one she searched for in vain in the sea
of parents as she was called again and again to the stage to pick
up the blue ribbon for penmanship, for English composition,
for the best perfume-bottle collection at the fair. But that was
all such a long time ago, before the summer she was sent away, the
summer she grew breasts, the two things somehow linked in her
mind, for when she came back he no longer seemed to recognize
her, wanted nothing to do with her, and it was her mother who
took her aside and said, He's sick, you're old enough to understand that now, and she'd felt then the way she felt sitting in front

of Nadine. It was petulant and childish, but she couldn't help herself, she blurted, What about me?

What is it you want to know?

Nothing, she thought. Not from you.

She stood up abruptly. It's getting late, she said.

This won't take long. I can tell you what I see. An aura that is pale, smudged with all the unresolved sorrows of the past.

She'd had enough. She pulled her cape off the back of the chair, and threw it briskly around her shoulders.

Nadine raised her hand.

One more thing. I see flashes of sulphur. There is a lot of anger in you. Be careful, my dear.

How she laughed with Renata as they drove the winding roads back home. Laughed at Nadine's yard-sale attempt at psychic ambience, at the mistakes the fortune teller had made, telling Renata she was better off without the husband who had left, consoling her for her barrenness.

Man, did she get that wrong! exclaimed Renata.

Alyson laughed, though she'd felt Nadine's eyes still on her as she paced up and down the lane, waiting while Renata had her turn. She'd felt the woman staring through the wall of the trailer to a spot behind *her* head, so that beneath her laughter flowed a thought as slippery as truth – what the fortune teller told Renata was meant for her.

The first month of Walker's absence passed slowly as she adapted to the rhythms of her absolute solitude. During the day, she'd go about her work, imagining Walker at the camp instead of in the studio or at his kiln in the woods. But in the late afternoon and evening, through the hours she was accustomed to spending with him, she would sit disconsolate by the stove or wander through the rooms of the house, scanning the bookshelves for a story, some pioneer reminiscence, some native legend she could lose herself in.

That was where she found it, the embossed leather notebook her aunt sent her the Christmas after she stayed on the farm. *For your heart's desires,* Catherine had written on the inside leaf. It had seemed such an adult gift, too fine to contain her jumbled, adolescent thoughts, and so she'd tucked it away, forgetting all about it until the night she pulled it out and laid it on the table at Walker's place.

She left it there, coming to it several times a day, whenever a thought struck her or she found something in the magazines or newspapers Renata dropped off that Walker might enjoy, jotting down notes or sometimes pasting in a clipping. At four o'clock each afternoon, she would make her daily entry, noting the weather and the mail. Then she'd prepare herself some dinner, and as she ate, she'd write down all she would have told him if they had been sharing the meal – a new species of basil she'd read about, hardy in the north; the pillow stuffed with fragrant herbs she was thinking of making to sell; who among their friends was pregnant or breaking up, selling out and moving south, back to the city, all the gossip she gathered eagerly now from Réal, Renata, and Dorothy, her nearest neighbour on the farm a mile down the road.

She would have preferred to write him letters. A correspondence seemed more like a conversation than hoarding words in a book. She missed him desperately, especially in the mornings, missed the reliable warmth of his body as he slipped into bed, the weight of his leg slung over hers, and it would have helped to ease his absence to write, or occasionally, to prepare him a parcel of the things he was missing — muslin twists of her tea, a pair of the booties she'd knit, the latest ceramics magazine — but mail into the camp was erratic, he had told her. By the time a letter arrived, he would practically be home.

But I'll phone every Sunday, he'd said.

They'd never made a point of weekends, their schedules unchanged from one day to the next. But now Sundays took on the feeling they'd had when she was young, when even the commonplace became special, a bath in the morning instead of at night, their big meal at noon after church instead of at five o'clock, the unhinging of the pattern making it seem as though anything was possible, everything could change.

On the morning of the third Sunday, she lay in the steaming water of her bath, lingering until the sunlight through the window was full on her face and the warmth of water and light joined around her, buoying her up. It was the first of the stepping stones she'd set in place to lead her through the hours to Walker's call at three o'clock.

After she towelled herself dry, she looped the measuring tape around her belly, taking note of the new circumference. Then she stood naked in front of the mirror and snapped a Polaroid picture that she tacked up in the hall, the third in the row. She stood back and squinted at the sequence, a time-lapse of a swelling bud or a waxing moon, and she tried to complete it, her belly growing, the curve changing, dropping, flattening on top. That was as much as she could imagine, though she knew it wouldn't stop there, with the birth, any more than a moon remained full or a flower held itself open forever.

By noon, she was at the table, thumbing through her books, making notes on how the baby had grown. *Now its bones are beginning to harden*, she'd written at the end of the first week. Then, *it can tell which way is up. It can distinguish sweet from sour. It can taste what is bitter.* And the one that stopped her breath now. *Its heart beats faster when I speak.*

For an hour she sat with her notebook, filling page after page. The front of the book had grown splayed with her additions, while the layer of crisp, white pages at the back diminished week by week, a visual measure of the passage of time that she clung to, like the sound of his voice on Sundays, for otherwise, she thought, she'd sink into the sameness of the days where his absence had no beginning and no end.

*Nothing seems quite real,* she wrote on that third Sunday of the month, the same words her father had sent her mother in his fine, upright hand, writing every day from flight school, from the mess an hour before he suited up, from the locker room when he returned, writing all that ran ragged through his head as his plane dodged back through the searchlights over the Zuider Zee, writing even after he was shot down, living in a haystack hollowed out and furnished with a table and a bed, the entrance hidden inside a doghouse where the soldiers who came to find him never thought to look. Her mother had kept all his letters, the ones he mailed and the ones he brought back, stacks of flimsy airmail paper tied with thin, silk ribbons, a different colour for every year. I married him because of those letters, her mother would say, something softening in her voice. If you could read them, you'd understand.

And after the summer of his breakdown she had, stealing one page at a time from her mother's bottom drawer, watching as her father's passion condensed, growing small and distant, like his handwriting, which by the end was hardly legible, a series of tight, secret circles attached to sharpened sticks. The same change she'd begun to notice on the pages she was writing, the lush open vowels, the confidently rising stems, all of it compressing, and she made a point of broadening her stroke, consciously drawing her letters larger so they would seem more assured.

In the last minutes before Walker's call, she read through her notebook, going over what she would say, arranging the conversation the way she liked to do, edging in slowly, not asking too much, letting her desire for him take him unawares. Cautioning herself, as well, not to expect too much, since by now, she knew the pattern – all week longing for his voice, just a phrase, a single sentence, and then when she'd finally hear him speak, it would never seem enough, for it wasn't just any words she wanted, it was something in particular, though she never knew exactly what.

And then it was three o'clock, the telephone was ringing, and she came to it as if he were walking through the door, so happy to hear him that she forgot all the things she wanted to say, she just closed her eyes and tried to see him, standing there at the pay phone in the corner of the barracks, just as he'd described it the first time he called.

She could hear him breathing at the other end of the line. She pressed the phone tight against her cheek as she talked, twining the cord between her fingers, thinking how amazing it was that they could be joined like that, the thin black wire trailing from her hand along highways, through forests, across streams and swamps, climbing the slope to the logging camp, miles from the nearest town, hundreds of miles from her, the wire in her hand attached directly to the one he held.

I can't wait to see you, she said.

Then, Are you still coming next week?

As far as I know.

He let go the details, one by one. They'd leave Friday after work. Arrive sometime after midnight.

I can't say when I'll get there. You'd better not wait up.

How long will you be able to stay?

We'll have to be back on the road by noon Sunday. Unless the weather's bad. In that case, we'll go sooner.

But that's not much more than a day!

The exclamation was out of her before she had time to moderate the thought.

It's the best I can do, he said, his voice sharp.

The line buzzed empty between them.

Look I should go, he said at last, there's a line of guys wanting the phone.

She said goodbye, though she stayed where she was, sitting cross-legged on the floor, the cord stretched to its limit, the receiver cradled in her lap, her hand still on the mouthpiece, reluctant to let it go.


And then he was home.

The stilted phone calls, the empty evenings, all of it would be dispelled, she thought, by the fact of him in the room, across the table, under the quilt, leaving his imprint in the air, renewing her sense of him, something to carry her through the month to come, and the next, and then he would be home for good, a thought she found so convincing that when he walked through the door what flashed through her mind was, thank god! he's here to stay.

They hardly said a word, just stumbled to the bed.

She woke early, conscious of his body beside her, twitching with his dreams. She curled into his arm, and thought how strange it felt, though he'd only been gone a month, and then she realized that it was her, the contour of her belly fitting differently now to his.

She noticed changes in him, too, his muscles firmer, his hair grown long. Let me cut it for you, she said, later, after breakfast, wanting to keep her hands hovering close. Thinking that the intimacy of barbering, something she'd always done for him, might help to ease the awkwardness that had sprung up between them once the meal was over and the day stretched empty before them, waiting to be filled, though by whom and with what they both seemed unwilling or unable to say.

For days she'd been imagining how the visit would go. She'd stocked up on all their favourite food and, on a whim, had sewn a mound of oversize cushions in soft, luxurious fabrics, thinking they'd lounge through the day, making love or playing music, the way they used to do. She'd restrung her violin and set out his bandoneon, just in case. But most of all, she thought, they would talk, the weeks apart bringing them back to the way they had been at the beginning, when they'd lie in bed for hours, telling each other everything that happened during the moments they weren't together. He would tell her about the camp, the men he'd met, the ideas he was gathering for the new figures he would make. And she'd show him the photographs, give him the notebook, leaning back on the cushions while he took it all in.

I can't read this, he said, after she brought it to him at the table, watching as he paged through it, remembering all she had written.

What do you mean?

It's too hard, he said, handing the book back. It makes me feel awful, thinking of you here alone.

But I wrote it for you.

Maybe later. If I read it now, I won't be able to go back.

If she didn't say it then, she thought, she never would.

So, she said, softly. Why not just stay?

He pushed himself away from the table. Don't start, he said, pulling on his coat. We've been through all that.

He went outside to the studio, then, leaving her sitting there. It was the one thing she hadn't thought of – the time he'd want to spend with his sketchbooks, his clay.

The more she tried to put it out of her mind, the feeling that he wanted to leave, that he couldn't wait to be gone, the more it seemed like the truth. She no longer felt abandoned – that implied a certain carelessness. She felt set aside, like the notebook. Not worth the effort.

He stayed up late into the night and woke late in the morning, as if all he'd come home for was a taste of his old routines. Once she'd had that thought, nothing he did could please her. The interest he took in the Polaroids, in the kicking of the baby, seemed calculated and forced, a feeble attempt to make her happy so he wouldn't feel guilty when he left. The whole visit such a letdown that by the time he climbed into the truck shortly after noon, she was almost glad to see him go.

Alyson fell into silence the way she fell into sleep, never thinking how strange it was not to open her eyes for hours, not to make a sound for days, until one morning she whispered some sweet thing to the baby inside her and the roughness of her voice startled her, a rusty key in an iron lock.

She cleared her throat and spoke again, surprised at the way the sound filled the room. She talked to the baby, then, describing the day, all the things she planned to do, lunch with Renata, a trip into town for milk, butter, eggs, nothing out of the ordinary, though hearing the words out loud gave them substance, and she carried out the tasks with a sense of purpose she hadn't felt since Walker left.

From that day on, she was rarely silent. She thought of her baby as a kind of shut-in, like the elderly men and women her mother sent her to visit, carrying roast-beef dinners or plates of brownies and Christmas shortbread, bringing books from the library or tapes of the morning sermon, stopping by old Mr. Ferguson's house because although Parkinson's gave his fingers a drunken man's quaver, still he loved to play duets with her on the piano. She would dawdle on the sidewalk, resentful, knowing the errands had been invented to get her out of the way, though what she remembered now was how welcoming the old people had been, how happy they were to sit and listen to her stories.

In the same way, she brought the world to her womb, thinking of her baby's heart beating faster, just to hear her speak. She talked about what she heard on the radio, what Renata told her when she called. She read aloud from the books she left squared on every surface — books on gardens and herbs, on soil, natural history, and history, books on child development and birth. She explained everything she did, techniques for separating seeds from their hulls, tricks for lifting stains, and when there was something she didn't know, she discussed that, too, matters of information as well as those of habit and belief.

From early in the morning until she murmured her last goodnight, she kept up her running commentary, saying whatever she pleased, no one else to consider, no misinterpretations to forestall, no need to hold anything back or put anything forward, every thought that came into her brain flowing unimpeded through her mouth, the words pure and unadulterated, unequivocally hers.


On the first day of February, she woke up thinking of her father, of a game they'd played when she was eight or nine.

A pinch and a punch for the first of the month, she'd yell, diving out of her bedroom the minute she heard his footsteps, pinching his arm and jabbing him with her fist. A pinch and a kick for being so quick, he'd shout back, making a grab for her, chasing her down the hall until she fell squealing onto the carpet. Now you're mine, all mine, he'd say, tickling her so hard her sides would ache for hours just from laughing.

But how often had it happened like that? she thought, for she could remember with equal clarity, waiting in her bedroom and peeking down the hall, willing his door to open, growing chilled in her nightie until finally she'd get dressed and go downstairs alone, knowing even then that if he wasn't up before she went to school, she wasn't likely to see him for days.

And if it happened to be February when he descended into one of his moods, then her mother would be crabbier than usual, for that was the start of their busy time of year, when the telephone would never stop ringing and people would show up at the door at all hours carrying shoeboxes and file folders and fat manila envelopes stuffed with receipts that her parents would stay up half the night putting in order. Her father was an accountant, he'd once held important jobs with insurance companies and large corporations, even the income tax department, though for as long as she could remember he'd worked at home in the little office by the kitchen. It's the only job he can handle now, she had overheard her mother say to Catherine. And he can't manage that without me.

That's where my apprehension comes from, she thought, for February was the start of her gardening year, too. Inevitably, as she prepared to draw up her plans, the potential failure of what she was about to begin would weigh so heavily against her hopes for its success that she would see-saw through the days, alternately believing it would all work out, she'd earn enough to see them through another year, and being certain that she wouldn't, they'd go bankrupt, lose the land, starve to death.

But she could see now that Walker's earnings from the winter might well keep them through the summer, and with what she'd make in the gardens, they might even get ahead a little. Perhaps Walker was right, she thought. The separation would be worth it in the end.

She spent the day with her preparations, pulling books off the shelf and stacking them in neat rows across the table according to subject, squaring a sheaf of drawing paper in front, laying out charcoal sticks and coloured pencils to the right, each one sharpened to a perfect point. On the left she stacked the sketches of Walker's clay pots she'd drawn in the studio the day before.

By the time the sun rose the next morning, she was already in her chair, thumbing through the catalogues, sticking coloured flags between the pages, green for herbs, yellow for edible flowers. It didn't take her long to fill out the seed order for what she'd sell through the grocery stores and at the Christmas sales. Except for an occasional new variety, she grew the same thing every year. Basil, dill, parsley, and cilantro to sell fresh. Oregano, savory, sage, and thyme to dry. Cornflowers, clove pinks, hyssop, and marigolds to mix with her perennials in sachets and teas.

It was the designing of the potted gardens that she lingered over. Walker had built the containers by hand from thick coils of clay or from slabs he rolled out like dough, working texture into the surface with his gouges, paddles, and whisks. Because of the injury to his hand, he'd never used a throwing wheel, and she was glad of it. The pots had the unconscious, inevitable look of stone. The raku firing produced an iridescent finish she'd seen only in nature, on the neck of a raven or in a fragment of mica. Occasionally, she thought she saw the influence of a certain plant in the way Walker designed or glazed the clay, but for her, the pot was everything – the standard of form and colour against which she selected and arranged each species in her miniature herbaries. Digging in the soil of the terraced gardens by the house, she sometimes lost sight of her ambition, but sitting with her drawings, she knew exactly what she was striving for: the perfect marriage of Walker's art and hers.

She lined up the sketches in front of her and started to page through her books, mentally transposing plants to one pot or another until something felt just right, then she took up her charcoal and roughed in the leaves, shading them with coloured pencils to test the effect – a tumble of yellow cinquefoil against a stand of blue flags in the tall pot with the carmine glaze, maybe a fragrant mignonette, some comfrey and rue. She checked the list of seeds she'd collected, made note of what she would need to buy, then she pulled out fresh sheets to sketch the seedlings in their garden beds, shade plants in the lee of the house, those that loved the sun on the slope below the granite bluff. Papers spilling to the floor, her pace quickening as she gave herself up to the work. By the end of the second day, the drawings were spread like leaves through the rooms, the herb beds along the seat of the couch, the salad garden on the steamer trunk, the tea garden and sachet garden taking over an armchair each, the nursery bed on the floor between.

For a week, she lived in her gardens at their loveliest, stepping carefully between the pages on her way to bed, wandering the paths in the morning, teacup in hand, imagining swaths of German chamomile shining chartreuse in the sun or mounds of chocolate and cinnamon basil nestled under a hedge of dwarf grey sugar snaps. Seeing a flaw in her plan, she'd pull her chair to the table and pick up her pencils again, once rising in the night to add a plant she'd dreamt, bluish-green with lacy yellow blooms, thumbing through her books until she found it, *Ruta graveolens*, the one her aunt called the herb of grace.

Sometimes, exhausted by her imaginings, she'd bundle herself up and plow across the yard to Walker's studio. She'd given up the daily routine of making entries in her notebook. In fact, she'd made a pact with herself to ask nothing of him at all, and because of it, she thought, their calls since he returned to the camp had gone better. She'd told him about the gardens she was designing and he'd told her about a dream he'd had, the first he remembered, though it was nothing but an image — his own body inside a kiln, encased in flames.

She climbed the ladder to the loft and moved around the walls, reaching to touch Walker's figures like a pilgrim marking the stations of the Cross. Through all the hours of her conjuring she was silent, her mind too filled with sprouting seeds, unfurling leaves and blossoms, to marshall thoughts into words. But in the old log barn, she leaned back into language. She told the baby stories about her life with Walker, adding a detail here, losing a bit there, until even to her they sounded like fables she might have read in a book. Their enchanted, fateful meeting. Their journey into the wilderness. Their quest for a home. She told stories about the games she played with her father, about the summer she spent on the farm. Stories that she'd pried out of Walker about his mother, a Frenchwoman who taught him to play the bandoneon and took him mushroom-hunting in the woods, the stern Norwegian father who gave him his pale good looks. Some stories she kept to herself, stories it did no good to remember. These she barred from her mind, shaping the baby's past and its future with the same firm hand she'd used to shape her own.

And so the second month slipped by. Once the seed order was sent, she busied herself stripping seeds from her mother-plants, sterilizing the planting trays, preparing tubs of her special propagating mix, getting the greenhouse ready. Late in the afternoons, if the day still held some light, she would strap on her snowshoes and wander up into the trees. In every season, there was something to draw her into the woods – spring leeks for a pie, fall mushrooms for a stew, wintergreen for tea, the dark juniper berries she sold as a pungent flavouring for hearty soups — so much to gather from the wild that she'd come to think of it as a large and unruly extension of her garden, a ramshackle outdoor pantry that never needed to be restocked.

It was the baby that took her into the woods just to see what might be there. She saw the way the snow, after a wind, clung to one face of the trees, as if it felt safest there. The way fire scarred a pine trunk, flat and smooth as a door. She saw squirrels flying from branches like birds, birds burrowing under the snow like mice, mice making tracks across the snow like stitches on a quilt. And once, she saw a wolf passing so close to where she stood that she could hear the snow crust collapsing under each paw, though the animal kept its gaze fixed on the ground, as if by refusing to look, it could believe it was alone.

She snowshoed the bush trails and the logging roads, stopping often to rest, telling the baby how to distinguish a red pine from a white by the number of needles in a cluster, explaining that the finches would soon turn blotchy with gold and the spruce grouse silently browsing in the crown of a wild apple would erupt like a diesel motor in the spring. She'd heard it first the day she started ripping up the sod for her gardens. She called to Walker, who was raising a wall in the barn, and they had listened together, trying to place the loud, erratic thumping that seemed to come from everywhere, out of the trees, off the hills. It was something they'd already learned, how the stillness swallowed sound and spewed it back, amplified and distorted, so that the woods seemed full of women with wildly scraping shovels and gangs of hammering men.

It was Réal who told them it was the pump from Sauvage's gravel pit – Goes all spring during the melt, he said – though it wasn't, it was a mating grouse, but they didn't know that then. They'd hurried back to the stream, crossing on the stones laid down like a footbridge, pushing through the prickly ash and spreading juniper until they found the pit, a canker eaten into the landscape.

She'd felt it like a wound at her back. A disfigurement she should have noticed before handing over the inheritance from her father as a down payment on the land. But there was nothing to be done about it. She put it out of her mind and kept it there until the crusher started up and the wind blew from the northeast, then she would flee into the house, slamming the doors and windows shut no matter how oppressive the heat, revving up the vacuum or pulling out pots and pans, obliterating the hideous grinding with noises of her own, railing against the fools they had been, against the pit and the man who owned it, Henri Sauvage. He'd come to their door late that first year, wanting to buy a right-of-way for his trucks. Walker had stayed silent and withdrawn, leaving it up to her to say, No, they would never sell, though Sauvage had turned to him for confirmation, which made her angry, even in remembering it, her word never enough, though this was one of the stories she kept to herself, saying nothing but, It's late, we'd better get home.

Then, it was the end of February and there was no time for excursions into the woods or up to the loft. Every hour was absorbed with planting and monitoring the flats, making sure each had the proper moisture and temperature and light for germination. Walker called to say his friend's truck had broken down, he wouldn't be coming for the weekend after all, news she heard with relief, she was so busy with the plants.

As soon as the first true leaves appeared, she moved the seedlings into the greenhouse, the sunlight already visibly stronger, spring coming on fast now, the willow tips reddening, the breasts of finches flashing gold, the inner flanks of the snowbanks she shovelled showing a clear, auspicious blue. By the time the last seeds had germinated, the snow was shrinking from the granite bluff, abandoning the bright sides of the trees.

More than once, tending the seedlings, her gaze would drift out through the glass and she'd think she saw Walker, the baby in his arms, walking toward her out of the woods, and the ache that she had managed to stave off with her work would shaft through her, a longing for everything to be in its place — Walker in his studio, her with the baby in her gardens, their life going forward exactly as they had planned.


It was the third week of March when her nightmares began.

Trees pitching down. Branches bristling, piercing like horns. Walker trapped, alone, or crawling out from underneath the

carnage with a mass of other men, men who huddled like butch-
ers over slain beasts, slicing off their crowns, dragging their limbs
free, frantic to bleed them, gut them before the flesh spoiled.
Skidders with muscled arms yanked trees out of the earth. Saws
cut with chains of thorns. Felled trunks seeped resin the colour
of blood.

Sometimes the dream would shift and the men and machines
would remain what they were. She would hardly mind it, then,
watching Walker cut through pines that never fell, with a chain
that wouldn't stay sharp, until one night, with a single pass of his
saw, he cut through a mountain ash and through the man who
leaned, dreaming, against the other side.

She woke up wet with sweat, her hand shaking as she groped
for the lamp, her mother's voice in her ear, Don't be a baby, it's
just the darkness that makes it seem so bad. She dragged Walker's
pillow from his side of the bed and propped herself up. Then she
forced herself to reconstruct the scene, replaying the monstrous
machines, Walker's terror, her own, until she'd reduced it to a
cartoon, and she could laugh at herself, at her tendency toward
the grotesque. She plumped the pillows and opened her book,
prepared to dispel the dream, though when she turned the page,
her hand was still trembling.

Perhaps it was the new moon on the spring equinox that
made her feel so unsettled. But after March the twenty-first, she
rarely slept a night through. No matter how full she tried to keep
her days, still she would lie awake in the dark, the baby restless

in her womb, her mind a maze of questions: What kind of person would her child be? Would it escape her father's illness? Would she? What else lay hidden in her genes? In Walker's?

Every time he called, he said again that he'd be home by the end of the month. She was certain she could hear the longing in his tone. She imagined him as he worked, watching the snow melt, urging it on like a prisoner counting the hours till his release. And she imagined him on Sunday mornings, taking his sketchbook into the woods, to an isolated shoulder of granite or a fragrant cedar stump, laying down quick pencil strokes, a shape within a shape, one emerging from another, sketches for a new figure, though they all looked like her, for he carried her with him wherever he went, his inspiration, a charm against all that haunted him, her image grown so real in her absence that her voice, when he finally telephoned, would sound unfamiliar and false, and he'd find himself tongue-tied before the woman he loved, unable to respond except in guarded syllables, afraid that if he spoke his heart he'd have to run from the camp, carve his way through the woods home to her.

She soothed herself to sleep that way, although her dreams remained restless, Walker scrabbling through the timber slash, gleaning daggers of slivered wood, digging in the ruts for odd metal shearings and severed lengths of chain, prying bits of resin from the wounds of fallen trees, scavenging like a crow, concealing all he found in the folds of his clothes, crouching alone in the bush, head cocked, listening for the voice that told him to take this, not that, quelling his fears, she decided, the only way he could.

# MARGARET

*1 8 6 0 - 1 8 6 4*

How quickly a situation, impossible to conceive, in the doing becomes common as breath.

*I was Alone in the Bush.*

One afternoon in the middle of that first winter, a man appeared at the door of the MacBayne cabin in the woods, and the next morning, Margaret's brothers were gone, conscripted to the further clearing of the colonization road. They would return in time for the spring planting, they said.

William Wallace took the new axe intended for their father and leaned his own against the woodpile. Margaret eyes it as she carries the water bucket to the river each morning, wondering if it might break through the fresh scar of ice more readily than her own small hatchet. On the third morning, she sets her bucket in the snow and lifts the axe, testing its heft. She raises it over her head and swings it down into the ground. It falls with such force that she fears it might crack the ice beneath her feet and so she leaves it where it is. But on the fourth day, a day so brilliant that the shadows on the snow reflect a blue as intense as the sky, she lingers by the axe again.

She is an orphan in the wilderness, deserted by her brothers, left to tend the oxen and the fire. These facts, when she recites them, sound so like a fable that she wonders, why not fell the giant trees, too?

She picks up the axe and carries it to a slender evergreen at the verge of the clearing. She spreads her feet apart, recalling her brothers' stance, one fist near the axe head, the other near the butt end. Her first strike bounces, leaving the bark unmarked. The second misses the tree altogether and pulls her headlong into the snow. Then her body adjusts to the axe's curve and its weight, and with her third swing, she buries the tip of the blade in the wood. She shimmies it free and fingers the wound. For an instant she regrets what she has begun, but then she feels the draw of the axe on her muscles and she swings, one blow after another, until she hears the tree crack. Startled, she jumps back, though not far enough, for the winnowing branches catch her by the shoulder and knock her off her feet, rolling her screaming through the snow until the tree comes to rest and she picks herself up, breathless, but unharmed and laughing.

The next day she pulls on a pair of Harry Douglas's trowsers that he left for her to mend. They are not nearly so warm as her layered skirts, but she can see her boots to plant them firmly and when she moves, there is no sway of homespun to snag in the underbrush. She secures the trowsers around her waist with a length of rope and, lacking a proper coat, crosses her shawl over her chest as the women of Pittenweem have always done, tucking the ends inside her makeshift belt.

Each morning she spoons her porridge as she stands in the open doorway, choosing the tree she will fell that day. At first she selects only young, thin growth, but as her swing improves and the muscles of her arms strengthen, she plants herself before more formidable specimens, never one of the soaring pines, but others whose leaves have fallen, thick-waisted, gnarled trees or staunch, straight-backed trunks that tremble as she deepens the cut and waver in their death throes, moaning, sometimes shrieking as they lay their heads at her feet.

This is what Margaret waits for: that split second of terror, swooped up and carried off by an exultation the likes of which she has never known.

She gives her days over to the achievement of that moment. The hours spent hacking off limbs and branches, heaping them into brush piles, yoking the reluctant oxen to drag the stripped logs into a stook — through it all she is sustained by the memory, driven by the anticipation of the next tree quivering, submitting to the steady stroke of her axe. On the days when snow falls in clouds so thick she fears she will be smothered, when the wind sends limbs crashing to the forest floor and bends the pines so low she can hear their muttered curses, when she sits wide-eyed through the night, wrapped in her plaid by the fire, her ears tuned to the eerie cries of creatures too hideous to show themselves, her dreams of the trees she will chop and the land she will free calm her heart by giving purpose to her circumstance.

When the brothers return in the spring, they find the cabin empty, the fire banked, the oxen gone.

They think the worst. They think of bears, stumbling from their dens. They think of wolves, the wolves that howled every night at the edge of the road camp, a sound so unnerving two grown men had fled through the night to the nearest settlement. They think of Indians, for the rumour is that the tribes in this territory are pagans still and practise unholy, bloody rituals. At best they think she has wandered off, looking for her brothers. Not once do they pass the thought that she is chopping a tree, clearing an acre, making the land hers just as they have done.

She sees her brothers from a distance, from between the trees, time enough to prop the axe against the far side of the wood-pile, though there is nothing to be done about the trowsers, the makeshift belt. Her skirts are soaking in the river, she explains as she enters the clearing, the lie springing to her lips before it is bidden.

Everything shifts when the brothers return, a subtle realignment, as when a boat, after sailing alone to lift its nets, joins the herring fleet heading home, each Fifie fitting neatly within the wakes of the others. A natural enough adjustment. The extra axe languishes against the woodpile. If the brothers notice the results of her labours in the woods, they say nothing. Margaret no longer goes into the forest except at midday to deliver the dinner she prepares and sometimes in the afternoons, when she brings the men a pail of fresh water, setting it on the shaded side of a tree and covering it over with a green bough to keep it cool.

The brothers are tireless, their ambition fired by what they have learned in their time away. Swifter ways to chop a tree, the knack of dropping it exactly where they please. Names for the trees they fell, for the perils they face: dead stand, withes, chicots and snags, rampikes and stubs, spring-poles, blow-downs, widow-makers, windshakes. From those who have already cleared a farm in the Front, sold out, and moved north to the Back country to lay low the virgin woods again, they have learned how to make the soil prosper, how to plant, how to burn.

Within a week of their return, the brothers put torches to the piles of brush and logs on the land they have cleared. Branding, they call it. Leaving their indelible mark on the land. Day after night after day flames leap into the sky. It is wild work, for the massive logs must be rolled in close as the centres burn away, gaps in the flame fed with stray branches and limbs. Ash falls like a blizzard of grey snow. When the wind rises, lifting embers from the burning logs and casting them down on the cabin, Margaret hauls buckets of water from the river to douse the roof and walls. She soaks headkerchiefs for her brothers to tie around their mouths and nostrils to keep them from fainting with the fumes. They look to her like bandits roving round Beltain fires, guisers on All Hallows' Eve. The heat is unbearable. Her brothers' faces are blistered and scorched, yet none of them dares walk a distance that might bring relief, for one stray spark might reduce their cabin to cinders, set the forest aflame, start a blaze that would sear the face of the earth, for they have told her that the Bush is one great, green veil that stretches north to Hudson's Bay, west to the Prairie and east to the sea.

When the ash cools, the task is given to Margaret to spread it over the soil, plant a garden. She takes up the work willingly, slipping into her mother's place, which helps relieve the loss she feels once the brothers return, the assembling of the family remnants making visible the gaps where her mother and father once stood.

While the brothers go back to the business of felling trees, she pokes at the earth between the stumps, opening it enough to take the seeds for neeps and barley-corn, squash and beans, the eyes of tatties she saved through the winter. Robert Bruce paddles to an Indian village at the junction of two lakes to buy seed corn from the pagans. He takes the waggon to Renfrew and brings back three piglets and a crate of pullets along with baking supplies for Margaret and news of another dozen settlers. There is a letter at the post office from their mother's twin sister, Jean, in Pittenweem, but given the choice of paying to collect it or buying another hen, he purchases the hen, recounting his decision without apology. Margaret passes the summer tending the animals, weeding the wild plants from amongst her seedlings, harvesting the fruits of her garden and of the forest, too, though she is cautious, picking only those berries and nuts that she sees have been sampled by the birds and the small striped squirrels that Harry Douglas calls chatterers.

She makes no complaint. It is fine to work in the garden while her brothers work in the Bush, each at their given task. But when the men leave again in the autumn, engaged as choppers at a logging camp, how she welcomes the return of her solitude. How familiar the heft of the axe, how thrilling to hear once more the moan of a tree felled by her own hand.

*I became a Chopper like my Brothers. The Forest fell before me, the Sky opened up Above.*

Within two years, the MacBayne brothers fulfill the Crown agent's conditions, earning title to their land. They lay the deeds on the table alongside a fair copy of the survey map, their names penned corner to corner inside three adjacent lots — William

MacBayne, Robert MacBayne, Harry MacBayne. They have let go the heroic doubled Christian names their father gave them. Let go, too, the hope that their father has survived, taking this as their inheritance.

For the MacBaynes, the earth proves a kinder master than the sea. While it does not always yield its fruits as the brothers would like, neither does it rise up to swallow them. And although the trees stand as endless obstacles to their ambition, they are a means of survival too, for the lumbermen who own vast tracts of northern timber hire settlers at a rate of ninety cents a day to chop the pines and transport them across the snow to frozen streams, piling them on rollways to await the spring thaw that buoys the sawlogs along the rivers to Quebec, where they are loaded onto ships and sailed back to the very harbours the settlers so recently left.

Every summer the brothers work to clear and fence another field. With the straightest logs they build a piggery and a barn with a loft for the beaver-meadow hay they scythe and a room for pumpkins and grain as well as the livestock it feeds. They also make small improvements to the cabin, more for Margaret's comfort than their own. They raise a chimney of mud and river stone, cementing in place the crane they brought from Pittenweem. They lay a floor of rough planks and cut a window that Margaret seals with greased paper when the weather turns cold. They build a shelf for the Bible, the hymnal, and the stories of Sir Walter Scott that their father favoured so. By the first snowfall, there is a full barrel each of flour and salt pork in the pantry corner, braids of onions and vines of squash and beans drying on the rafters, and a flank of venison aging in the chimney's smoke.

Margaret grows accustomed to her winter solitude. Sounds that once frightened her, the cannonshot of frost-gripped trees, the hammering of the cock-of-the-woods, become her familiars. She takes pleasure in the company of the forest birds, more brightly coloured and more hospitable than those of the sea – black-headed balls of fluff that never stop their chattering, blue crested birds that strut like lords, shy grouse pecking among the evergreens, occasionally a black bird with a crimson breast and the sweetest whistle, and one of scarlet with a beak of burnished gold. She is kindly disposed to the animals she sees, especially the rabbits and foxes whose faces she knows from home. Lacking a gun or much of an appetite for flesh, she thinks of them as neighbours more than as prey, although once, when she is weakened from her monthly bleeding, she clubs a thick-witted, prickly hedgehog with a stick of firewood and boils it for her dinner.

She learns to read the seasons. When green mists dance across the night sky, winter will come on soon. The arrival of the white birds that Harry calls snow fools heralds winter's end. Then the forest begins its slow costume change from the wispy greens of spring and summer's lush linens to autumn's crewel tones, a bright embroidery that drops at last, welcoming her deep among the trees again.

This is the season when Margaret blooms. In the days after her brothers depart, she washes the clothes they leave behind and folds them into the kists with sticks of cedar to keep them fresh. She puts away their papers and bowls, the tart preserves she makes just for them. She scrubs the plank floor and washes down the walls and the hearth, then she rearranges the sparse furnishings to suit herself. One chair before the fire instead of three. A small chest pulled close for the story she will read through the snowbound days and nights, rationing the chapters like sweet biscuits. And on the floor, a basket of wool to knit into socks that Harry will trade at the Renfrew store for seeds, all the necessary vegetables and herbs but also love-in-a-mist and prince's feather, flowers that serve no purpose but to gladden her heart. On the nails by the door reserved for her brothers' coats, she hangs her trowsers, her shawl, and the heavy gansey she knit for herself. Below them she leans her axe, sharp and ready.

When the river ice begins to melt, Margaret withdraws into herself. She puts away her axe and her book, prepares the house for her brothers' return. She cooks for them and listens as they speak of neighbours they have never met but with whom they feel a kinship, for the Bush to them is peopled now with the families they've heard about as they sit around the campfire, the sweet Sheilas, Janes, and Madeleines, the strapping young Thomases and Jacks, the pretty little Euphemias and Laura Mays. Phantoms of the woods, these people seem to Margaret, for with the exception of her three brothers and the stout road-crew boss who conscripted them, she has not seen another human soul since she walked into the wildwood four years before.

That is not the strict truth. In the night, in the winter, her cottage door sometimes opens and figures enter, dark soundless shapes that settle on the floor by the fire, rising before first light to steal silently out. Days later she might find a brace of grouse hanging from the door latch or a sack of meal corn on the table. They are savages, hunters caught far from their huts, she supposes, but she sees a woman, too, more than once, never in the cottage, always at a distance. The way the woman hides herself among the pines, slipping out of sight when Margaret turns her way, makes her think of the crone who haunted her in Pittenweem, although this woman's skin is dark and her hair hangs loose and black to her waist. Margaret puts her out of mind, as she did the other one, for she has work to do, and she has long since outgrown such childish games and imaginings.

Late in the fifth spring, a stranger appears on the path.

Margaret watches him approach, a small man with a shock of red hair that flames through the greening woods. His step is light and he whistles as he walks, a tune so bright that more than once he breaks into a jig, his feet kicking high, scattering the debris of last year's leaves.

He stops a respectful distance from where she stands, hoe in hand, in her dooryard garden.

Ewan Calder at your service, he says, bowing from the waist.

It is months since she has spoken to a person, though she has not been entirely mute. She sometimes makes soothing sounds to the oxen, the pullets, the cow, and sometimes her thoughts take shape in the air around her, but she has lost the knack for discerning whether she is speaking aloud or not, and so, although she thinks a welcome of sorts and poses a question or two, what reaches across the dooryard to the handsome young man is silence, pure and simple.

But it doesn't matter. Ewan Calder holds his smile wide open and Margaret MacBayne tumbles in.


William and Robert follow at a distance, appearing among the trees as Margaret stands listening to the young man. Ewan Calder is not tall and broadly built like her brothers. He is sinewy as a squirrel and just as smart, which is why the lumber company hired him not as a chopper but as a land looker, a timber spotter. Since the age of thirteen, he has been travelling through the wildwood, he says, with a lumber merchant, a map-maker, and an Indian guide. They send him shimmying up the tallest tree, where he hangs from the topmost branch like a sailor in the rigging of a ship and scans the rippling greenery for an island of conifers that rises above the rest or a skein of darker green that runs like a cool current through the weald. When he spots the treasured pines, he breaks off a limb and pitches it down to point the way. Then he calls out whatever landmarks he sees – a flash of waterfall, a shield of stone, a copse of birch or trembling aspen, a blaze of tamarack in a distant swamp – for he's come to know the Bush as well as the freckles on his hand.

The brothers brought Ewan in Harry's place. One of the loggers, they tell Margaret, sliced his leg nearly through with an axe, and it was Harry who took him home, staying on with the family to clear new fields, for otherwise the man would have lost his land.

Ewan has come to help with the branding, but spying the eye-locked pair at the river or on the path, the brothers can see almost at once that the young man might serve another purpose altogether. They notice the care Margaret takes with her appearance, never, after that first encounter, wearing the old trowsers or the frayed rope at her waist. And they notice how Ewan flushes when she bends to place the bowls of food on the table, and how he offers every morning to draw water from the river, bringing her fistfuls of the blue flags that grow wild along the bank. The brothers tease the two of them, calling it calf-love what passes between them, but the men mean no harm, for they've always taken it as given that Margaret will bring another man into the family, and Ewan possesses as cheerful a willingness to work as any brother could want.

This is how Ewan woos Margaret – he names the wildwood for her. In the mornings, they walk the forest, stealing out of the cabin while the brothers are still asleep. When she fingers the cinnamon bark of a lofty, jade-black tree, he tells her it's a hemlock, its feet always in the water or wrapped around a rock. And when she asks, What's this beside it? he answers, A beech, slow to green in the spring and slow to fade in the fall, the only companion the hemlock abides.

He shows her how the underside of every hemlock needle is etched with two fine white lines, and he tells her how the Indians use the bark to soothe a burn and dye their baskets the colour of their skin, how the Yankees boil the sprigs to make a bitter tea, and how the lumbermen call them peelers, using their slippery, naked trunks to roll the reluctant pines to water.

As they walk along the river, he points to a black spruce growing near a fir with flattened needles, a he-balsam and a she-balsam, he says, the two of them always together, just as we are, he winks, and he lifts the bark of the she-balsam to where the resin swells like milk, and he pries a drop loose, offering it to Margaret who takes it in her mouth, tears springing to her eyes, for in the taste she can hear her father singing through the mad tossing of the ship, hears him too in the alphabet of trees Ewan teaches her, dashing from trunk to trunk, reciting, *Ailm, Beith, Calltuinn, Darach.* Elm, birch, hazelwood, oak.

In the evenings, he brings her gifts he finds in the woods, wild leeks for a stew or sweet ginger for her tea, and once, a pillow of balsam boughs wound with strips of basswood, one for each of them, he says, so that when we lay down our heads, we'll dream of our walks in the wildwood.

In June, he drives a row of thin stakes around her dooryard garden and weaves them with an elm-braid rope, a wattle fence to keep the rabbits out. He steeps the bark of the silver maple, the one with the deeply notched leaves – not the rock maple the Indians tap for sugar to make a soft brown ink. And he shows her how to recognize the hop-hornbeam, the most modest of trees, yet so enduring the choppers call it ironwood. On Midsummer's Eve, he presents her with an axe, its handle carved from iron-wood, To fit the grip of your strong woman's hands, he says, laying a kiss in each palm.

In July, when the musquitos hold them hostage in the cabin, he strips bark from a paper birch and rolls it into a taper that he lights and tucks under his hat, and they continue their walks inside a pale cocoon of smoke, a smudge he calls it. When it rains and the roof of the cabin weeps, he lays great sheets of the same white bark under the scoops to guide the water away from their heads. The bit that is left he shapes to a funnel, which he blows like a horn, dancing about the yard in a demented reel that makes Margaret laugh until her stomach hurts, he sounds so like the pig that caught its tail in the split-rail fence.

When the crimson cones of sumac ripen, he soaks them to make a tea that his Indian friend has told him keeps away the ague. One morning he wakes her gently, his finger to his lips as he points to the rafters where sumac cones dangle from elm ropes like red Christmas tassels, and he whispers, So you stay well through the winter 'til I return.

*From the lumber shanties, my Brothers brought a Man named Ewan Calder. He knew no Home save Canada. With him, I learned to make it Mine.*

Ewan and Margaret search for weeks for a rock that is suitable, one worn through in the centre, but the boulders in that virgin country seem immune to the perforating effects of water and wind. At last, late one afternoon when the brothers are hunting in another part of the forest, the young couple finds a blasted oak on the western edge of Harry's land. The trunk, once split by lightning, has joined again above the wound, leaving a cleft. Though not as round and true as the hole in the swearing-stone at Pittenweem where her mother and father pledged their troth, they agree that it will do.

They perform their secret ceremony early one morning while the sun is lifting into a cloudless sky.

Give me your hand, Margaret says, standing on the far side of the oak. Ewan thrusts his arm through the cleft and she takes his hand in hers. Then she reaches through the trunk.

Now grasp my hand in yours.

She leans her forehead against the bark, blind to him, feeling nothing but the stroke of his finger on her wrist, the pulse of hers on his. Neither knows the proper words, so they make a simple promise: to always hold to each other as they do right then.

In the evening, Ewan lays their plan before the brothers. He tells them of a clearing he knows to be abandoned close by to the south, of the cabin he and Margaret will build there in the spring, of the marriage that will take place the next time a preacher rides through. William and Robert welcome the news, for they are expecting it and have prepared an offer of their own.

*When my Brothers learned we would be Wed, they gave us the land that was Harry's, for he had moved to Golden Lake where he married a Polish girl and worked her father's fields.*

The brothers seal the bargain with a handshake and drink whisky to the family's fortunes, their spirits high, for the betrothal of their sister has stirred the same dream in each of them, of quitting the log cabin and building a house of milled lumber, installing a wife of his own on the hearth.

Margaret waits in the barn with the chickens and the pigs and the carcass of a freshly killed deer, the smell of stale blood and fresh manure becoming for her, ever after, the rank odour of anticipation. By the time they call her inside, they are feeling the effects of the liquor. They raise the small horn beakers they brought from Pittenweem, relics of their father's forebears, and William recites the *shoinneadh* as their father would have done, naming their kin as far back as he knows, though as much has been forgotten as was originally known, it has been so long since a MacBayne spoke these words within sight of a glen.

The brothers sing their sister's praises, calling her Queen, her childhood name, recalling all the Margarets, Queens of Scotland, as they raise their cups to her — Margaret the Saint, Margaret the Maid, Margaret the Beloved, the Invincible. Perhaps it is the drink, or the honours being heaped upon his sister's shoulders, but William's eye turns suddenly mischievous and cold.

Our Margaret boasts a skill no queen has ever known, he says, throwing her a look aslant. She chops a tree as well as any man.

Once, she would have thrilled to hear such a thing from William's lips. In the spring she would linger close by, hoping to catch a comment on the freshly felled logs he would find in a heap, logs he burned with all the others as if he'd hurled them down with his own hand. Yet she feels no satisfaction at the mention of her prowess, only surprise that he should bring it up now and a chill that makes her reach for Ewan's hand, because she knows her eldest brother, his ruthless practicality, a man for whom the effect of every word is calculated closely and always intended. And although she cannot imagine what benefit might accrue to him by taunting her, she knows better than to reply, since the right to disallow the marriage is his.

In the woods she wears men's trowsers, says Robert, taking up William's mocking tone.

Aye, Ewan, and who will wear them on your hearth? Will the lass leave you to stir the porridge while she takes the axe to clear the fields?

A chopping contest! declares Robert.

No! exclaims Margaret.

But William brings his fist down on the table. We will settle this once and for all. We'll prove who is the better chopper, lass or lad.

Margaret grows still, and the notion is swept aside for the moment in the banter of the men. When at last they go to bed, the brothers clap Ewan warmly on the shoulder, saying nothing when he leaves his mound of blankets by the fire to slip under Margaret's quilts, drawing her so close she feels the heat of him along the length of her limbs. They lie whispering together until the snores of her brothers deepen, then they let the words be and find other ways to name all that is in their hearts.


The brothers find two trees side by side on Harry's land. Rowan trees, they say to Margaret, for luck.

Witchwood! her mother exclaimed when she first saw the golden fronds, the berries hanging in red clusters. Like faerie lights, she said. She broke off a twig to tie above the lean-to, and when the log house was raised, she made certain the lintel was cut from a rowanwood tree. Against the glamour, she said.

When Robert scoffed, We've long left the faeries behind, Ma, she answered so softly only Margaret could hear, But can ye be so sure?

William flips a coin in the air, insisting that Margaret call the side.

Ladies first, he says, the mockery still ripe in his voice.

She chooses the leafy garland over the English Queen, winning the larger tree. Ewan protests, but she hushes him. The sooner we begin, she says, the sooner it will be done.

They stand before their trees, hands resting on their axes. Too late, Margaret realizes she has not put on her chopping clothes. She pulls the hem of her skirts up between her legs and tucks it into her waistband, fashioning makeshift pantaloons.

When Robert calls, On your mark!, Ewan and Margaret turn and wish each other well, then William shouts, Begin!, and Ewan takes up his axe. She does the same, feeling awkward at first, for the ironwood is unfamiliar in her hands and the witnesses seem a strange thing, too, for the chopping of a tree has always been a private act, and she feels a certain modesty, as if she were about to uncover herself before her brothers.

But Ewan has already placed his first blow. She spreads her legs and swings, sinking her blade deep into the wood. She jerks it out and strikes again, falling into the rhythm, forgetting her brothers, the contest, forgetting Ewan, their blows so perfectly matched that the two axes seem almost to strike as one. Then Ewan's pace quickens, while Margaret holds hers steady, hitting the mark every time. She has paid close attention to her brothers, tested all their tricks. When the cut is halfway through, she moves behind the tree and strikes her blows again, the axe kept to a single plane so that each cut follows the other in a tight, true line that slashes through the wood just above the notch. She hears nothing but her breath, sees nothing but the widening gouge, thinks of nothing but the shifting hue of the wood chips at her feet, pale yellow sapwood, heartwood red.

*My Brothers set a contest to determine who was the better Chopper, the lass or her swain. Once begun, I could not stop until the Rowan tree was down, and by then, the Harm was done.*

When she hears the tree's first moans, Margaret stills her axe. She stands aside and waits for the rending, the riving, the exultation she always feels at the final letting-go. But she has miscalculated the hinge. The crown is circling, wobbling like a top near the end of its spin. Branches sweep across a hemlock, a green cloud of beech, a spruce, a balsam fir, then the tree seems to pause, as if considering how to proceed, and deciding, it falls faint into the arms of an old jack pine, which collapses under the weight of its unexpected burden, both trees pitching to the ground, in a direction she never intended nor ever would have suspected, and there is Ewan, trapped under a limb, his head wrenched to one side, the skull broken open, blood mingling with the berries of the fallen mountain ash.

# A L Y S O N

*S p r i n g   1 9 9 1*

The cramps began late in the morning, at the same time as the rain.

Alyson dismissed both as insignificant, though she wondered how her body knew to go into training like that, working the muscles with false contractions for weeks, a month, until one day they'd start clenching for real. Was it the baby that set these things in motion? Or were they both blindly following a schedule encrypted in her womb? Either way, it explained the feeling of compulsion that had roused her from her bed long before the sky began to pale.

Now it was almost noon. She switched on the overhead light in the kitchen. She could tell by the curdled look of the clouds that the rain would go on for hours. On the table lay the heap of cloth squares she'd cut out in the night. She'd stitched five of them with figures copied from old children's books she'd found among her aunt's things, some of them inscribed to Kenneth, her father, the others to Catherine, all with love from relatives she'd only heard of, never met. A family that died young. Her father gone and Catherine, too, of a heart attack not long after the summer she'd spent on the farm. That branch of the Thomson line reduced to her and the baby. If it's a boy, she was thinking, maybe they could call him Thom.

She laid out the squares, alternating the embroidered pieces with pale green broadcloth, then pinned and sewed the seams, working quickly, still driven by a strange, untimely energy.

It must be the visit from Renata and Abe that had her so stirred up, she thought. And not just the visit. They'd dropped by unannounced, herding the girls into the kitchen, all curly-haired and boisterous, Abe coming in last with the cradle in his arms. He'd made it himself, he said, from a pine he'd cut near where Walker dug his clay. A tree off their own land to make their baby's bed. Why hadn't she and Walker thought of that?

They'd helped her rearrange the bedroom, the kids bouncing on the mattress as Abe pushed the bed against the wall so she could fit the cradle in front of the window.

I can't wait for Walker to see this, she said, turning to Abe. When does he get back?

In a week or so. He's calling tomorrow to let me know exactly what day he'll be home. It's been so cold up there, the cutting season was extended. But it's supposed to turn mild this week.

Just in case the weather report's wrong, should I fill the woodbox before we go?

No, that's okay, the exercise is good for me. But thanks, she said, putting an arm around each of them. What would I do without you two?

After they left, she'd lain on the bed, the fingers of one hand hooked over the edge of the cradle, rocking it gently. The blanket she'd tucked inside shifted with the movement, as if a baby were breathing there, stirring awake, crying for comfort. Her nipples tingled at the thought, the child suddenly real now that it had its own place in the house.

She spread the finished quilt-top on the table, rolled out a length of batting, then the broadcloth, pinning the three layers together along the edges and through the middle. She glanced at the clock, gauging her progress, intent on finishing by the time Walker called. It was pointless, she knew, these arbitrary goals she set herself, but they worked to occupy her mind. As the day of his return approached, she could feel her senses heighten, becoming alert to faint sounds and unexpected movements, to shifts in the light at windows, under doors, waiting for a knock or the turn of the knob – Walker home early, a surprise! – the sharp swells of anticipation never amounting to anything and never dissipating entirely, a ragged ebb and flow that wore at her heart.

By mid-afternoon on that Saturday, the second to last day of March, the sky was so dark she had to bring another lamp to illuminate the stitching lines drawn on the cloth. She'd copied the pattern from a quilt that hung on her bedroom wall, a log-cabin design her father's mother had made. The edges were frayed, the fabric worn through in places, but she'd salvaged it anyway from the Goodwill boxes heaped with Catherine's things that she'd found in her parents' basement.

How could you even think of giving this up? she'd chided her mother, not waiting for the reply that had trailed after her up the stairs, across the years, until it caught up with her at last, there, in her own kitchen.

It never occurred to me you'd want it, you take so little interest.

Her mother's tone was accusing. She felt her ears half-close against the memory of that voice, the way a person's eyes half-shut against a suffocating sun. And she was back in the old school-house that had been converted to a museum, two small rooms crammed with spinning wheels and hay forks, stuffed birds and fishing creels. It's our summer pilgrimage, her mother would say, taking her hand and leading her to the car, leaving her father to sit alone on the dock by the cottage while they visited the country graveyard, the collapsing barn at the edge of the woods, the little museum where her mother's family had deposited so many of their things. Year after year, always the same dusty exhibits, the photographs the only thing she cared about at the time — faded sepia portraits of women in white dresses reclining in canoes paddled by young men with straw hats tipped back from their faces, men standing splay-legged on stumps as big as gardens. Staring into the pictures, she'd feel the pull of the forest, the placid river. But she was never allowed to linger there. Her mother would hurry her along to the silver tea service or the book of postcards commemorating the visit of the Queen, always that improving tone as she instructed her in the meaning of each object, making her stand quietly and pay attention while she told the newest volunteer how important the Wisharts had been, which streets in nearby towns were named for them, which items in the displays had been theirs, the conversation turning eventually, inevitably, to her, and her mother would pat her head in a show of affection, saying, Yes, I bring her every year, it's a shame she takes so little interest.

And she would drop her eyes and hood her ears, keeping her distance from her mother's past as stubbornly as she reached toward her father's, though when she'd stopped at the museum, years later, during one of her country drives with Walker, she'd been surprised by the affection she felt for the place, not for the family heirlooms, but for the rough-hewn tools, the worn and dented utensils, the sense she had of lives lived in a more intelligible way. Since then, she'd made the excursion on her own, driving across the province every summer by herself, for Walker had no patience with the past. She didn't know how to explain to him that it had nothing to do with her mother, there was nothing she was trying to prove, it was just a feeling she liked, moving down the path between the tombstones, pushing open the museum door. It was the same feeling she got pulling on a jacket she'd had since she was a girl, relaxing in the familiar smells, in the way the cloth settled comfortably around her form. She'd shove her hands in the pockets and find crumbs of the oatmeal cookies she used to sneak from her mother's kitchen, the same recipe she made for Walker, storing them in her grandmother's glass jar, the one she would hand on to her son or daughter, explaining, only if she were asked, that she went on those private pilgrimages precisely because they weren't required.

Bending to the cloth, she followed the chalk lines with small stitches, struggling to make them even. It was close work, and every now and then she had to lift her eyes to the window to rest. The ladybird beetles that had swarmed over the glass earlier in the day were burrowing into the corners, piling up on each other in garnet clusters. The temperature must be dropping for them to crowd together like that, she thought. They arrived every spring on the first day the weather warmed. She'd see one and then, suddenly, there would be thousands, surging up the windows and across the ceilings, dropping onto the bed at night, landing on her knees in the bath, nestling in her hair, attaching to her clothes like sprays of rubies or spotted sequins. The day she and Walker moved into the house, one appeared on his sleeve, and she'd counted the spots on its wings, saying, the more there are, the better the luck. She'd been so thrilled to see even one ladybug. And then there were hundreds, millions, so many that, with any other insect, she would have called it an infestation, though she never thought of the little red beetles as anything but a sign of their good fortune.

When she looked up a little later, she noticed the trees, the dried spikes of mullein, the slope of thin snow, all of it shiny, as if dipped in clear gel. By the time she went to the stove to make another pot of tea, a shell of ice had thickened on the roof of the barn. Icicles were growing from the eaves, ribbing the walls, snaking down the window glass. The patter of rain on the tin roof, a sound she usually found companionable, was becoming insistent, the clickety-click of sharpened nails. The sound of rat's claws, she thought, shivering a little.

She was pushing herself up out of the chair to put another log on the fire when the lights flickered and went out. She looked at the clock — the hands were stopped at ten to four. If the power came on soon, she could still get the quilt finished, she was thinking as she got out the candles, the matches, the kerosene lamps.

Don't worry, this happens all the time, she said. A little freezing rain is nothing to worry about, we're prepared, you can relax.

But the baby did not relax. As Alyson climbed the basement stairs with a tin of kerosene, a cramp forced her against the railing. It was a different sort of contraction, a fist rising from her pubis to push deep into her belly, though as soon as it was over, she put it out of her mind, along with the darkened sky and the rain — temptations to be resisted. She took a candle to the couch and snuggled up under her afghan, something she loved to do, reading on a rainy day, though the book was scarcely open before it fell against her breasts, and hugging the blanket close, she slept.

She woke with a gasp. Her abdomen was a drum, a steel balloon overfilling with some dense, pressurized gas. Her limbs, shrivelled and useless. Nothing seemed to work. Then slowly, the muscles softened, and she could breathe again. She sat on the couch panting, refusing to think.

When she could walk again, she groped her way into the kitchen, where she lit all the candles and filled all the lamps, setting them on tables, on top of bookshelves, in the corners on the floor, so that no matter where she looked, she saw a lively, flickering flame. Then she closed the curtains against the windows' blank stares and returned to the kitchen to stoke the stove, jostling the poker longer than she needed just to hear the clatter of the wood, the spit and crackle of the fire.

Renata, she thought. Renata would know how it felt when the pains were for real.

Alyson lifted the receiver to make the call, but someone was already on the line. She recognized the low, wheezy voice of her neighbour Dorothy.

I won't be a minute, Dorothy said, interrupting herself. Who is this?

Just Alyson.

The woman Dorothy was talking to broke in, and Dorothy explained that Alyson was the girl that grew the parsley for the Foodtown.

Is everything all right up there, dear?

Dorothy always used that motherly tone with her. The day she and Walker moved in to the old abandoned farmhouse, Dorothy had appeared at the door, handing a plate of biscuits across the threshold and following it inside. Dorothy Holmes, she'd announced, taking a good look around. I'm your neighbour from the dairy farm down the road. Edgar, the man that plowed your lane?, he's my husband. And Réal Chabot?, that's your mailman. Anything else you want to know, just ask, I know everybody, I've lived here all my life. From the beginning, she'd embraced Alyson like a stray and Alyson had let her, needing some relief, now and then, from the burden of her independence. Dorothy was older and not at all reticent, but being with her made Alyson feel sometimes that Catherine was in the room. She had the same kindness around the eyes and a way of listening that made Alyson want to confide everything, though she never had.

If it hadn't been for the other woman, Alyson might have told her the truth — that she was worried and she didn't want to be alone. But all she said was, Do you know why the power is off?

No, but if I find out, I'll give you a shout. I'll do that anyway, later on. I have a couple of other people to check on, then I'll call and we'll have a good long talk. I want to hear how the baby's doing and when that husband of yours is coming home.

Don't worry about me, I'm fine, she said quickly. I've got everything I need. Besides, I think I'll make an early night of it.

She should have asked the time, she thought after she'd hung up. She had a windup watch somewhere, her father's, the one she'd unstrapped from his wrist as he lay in the coffin, horrified to see it there, loudly ticking off the seconds for a man who had made certain he'd no longer have a use for them. She'd worn the watch on a leather thong around her neck, but she'd felt weighed down by it, by the memories it kept fresh in her mind, and so, as soon as she moved to the country, she'd tossed it to the back of her underwear drawer, and that was where she found it. She carried it back to the phone, winding it, checking that it still worked, raising it to her ear as she picked up the receiver again.

All she heard was the ticking of the watch.

She'd always thought she would be good in a crisis, and she noted with some satisfaction that she wasn't panicking now, though, clearly, the line was dead. She would set the watch in the morning, she decided. At that time of year, the sun rose at about a quarter to six. She was always awake by then.

She crawled into bed, feeling disoriented by its new position against the wall. Lying on her pillow, she had a long view of the narrow window, pebbled with ice. She should have hung curtains in that room, too, she thought, something that would have muffled the clicking of freezing rain against the glass. Her blood was dancing so fast to the spun-out hustle that she was sure sleep would never come, but she must have dozed, for a crash against the window startled her awake.

The Manitoba maple. She peered through the skim of ice on the window. The tree was cleaved down the middle, its branches scattered across the grass like a barren hedge gone wild.

It was already light. She hurried through the house, window to window, ripping open the curtains to a landscape that wavered, no matter where she looked, under a pebbled veneer of ice. The snow at the back door was slick as porcelain, littered with twigs embedded like ancient relics in clear amber. The pressed-tin siding on the house, the barrel under the eavestrough, the bench by the garden – everything seemed brushed with a viscous preservative that fixed objects permanently in the landscape, a frigid Pompeii. The limbs of every bush and tree slumped to the ground, burdened with ice, and still the sleet poured down, thickening the crystal glaze.

Above the incessant, erratic dripping of the rain, she heard a crack. A tearing crash. Then another. She stood on the doorstep, shivering in her nightgown, counting. Then she stopped, the wreckage too complete to quantify with numbers. Against the horizon, the forest was a jagged paling of snapped-off trunks. Limbs skittered across the enamel snow or hung precariously in mid-air. The row of spruce along the lane had been decapitated, the tips uniformly broken, as if by a single blow. The rain was already letting up, but still, she'd never seen the ice that thick. The damage was shocking, so much so that it was some time before she noticed what had been eliminated altogether – the power lines that tethered her house to the rest of the world. The poles were gone, all except for one that stood alone beside the barn, its black wires dangling helplessly.

A sudden hardening in her belly pulled her back inside, pushed her, hunched, over the kitchen table. When the spasm subsided, she set the hands of the watch, choosing a time for herself. Seven o'clock. At eight-fifteen, there was another. And again at nine-forty-five. She checked her birthing book. Even contractions that regular could be false. She paced back and forth as the book suggested, kitchen to bedroom, living room to kitchen, to see if the contractions continued, if the intervals between them shortened. They did.

My god, she thought, this is real.

A rush of fear swept through her, and she was on the verge of letting go, giving herself up to it, when she saw the need open up in front of her and she slipped in, the way you'd slip into a burning building at the sound of a cry for help. Her baby was being born. She had no choice.

In the intervals between contractions, she put fresh sheets on the bed and a stack of clean towels on the floor. In the cedar chest, she found the mattress pad she'd made, flannel for the cradle, the baby things she'd knitted. She laid them out, though it felt surreal to her, as if she were setting the stage for a play she didn't expect to perform.

Craving company, she found photographs of Walker, of Abe and Renata, to put beside the bed. She looked for a picture of her father, too, scanning through the albums she'd made as a child, the small squares produced by her father's old Brownie camera giving way to larger, coloured photos, but in every one her parents were together, her mother sitting beside, or in front, or leaning over him from behind, her hand always on his shoulder, his knee, his arm. She remembered that hand, those slender fingers so much like her own, resting on her hair as her mother tucked her in, pulling the quilt up under her chin, then reading her to sleep, letting her drift off into one story or another, never leaving before she was asleep, and she felt a sudden yearning for her mother, a sharp desire to have her there, and she picked out an early likeness, from a time when her father's eyes weren't yet so haunted and her mother's were still soft, setting it on the bedside table with the others.

In the kitchen she lined up all eight mugs on the counter, spooning a little honey and a heaping teaspoon of raspberry leaves into each. She filled the kettle and stoked the fire again. Forcing herself to consider the worst, she found a pair of scissors and a spool of stout linen thread and set them on to boil, then she brought in more wood, one piece at a time, shuffling between the stove and the woodshed, stopping only when she had enough to last for several days. She worked slowly, moving carefully, her body a foreign creature, delicate but wilful, liable to turn on her at any moment.

Through it all, she told herself that Walker would telephone at three, and when he couldn't get through, he'd call Abe or the police. He'd hear about the freezing rain, he'd know she was marooned. One way or another, he'd get help to her. She only had to manage until then.

When everything was ready, she sat at the kitchen table, sipping tea and playing solitaire, the version her father taught her, where each game cost fifty dollars and each card on an ace earned back five, a win paying two hundred and fifty dollars, which happened rarely, but often enough to keep her playing.

Between contractions, she could almost convince herself that nothing was happening. Now and then she rose to feed the fire or to make more tea, but it all seemed so commonplace, the minutes weighed down with the boredom of a rainy day at the cottage.

And then another wave would build, inflating her belly, pushing it out, out, out until she thought she'd split in two, give birth like a cell dividing. Colours intensified. The flowers on the wallpaper bloomed. The tin house wavered, disintegrated, its pieces hung suspended. Time stood still, opened up, and she fell through, riding a wave that swelled and surged until it rendered ridiculous a word as paltry as pain.

The contraction subsided, and the world dulled, becoming itself again. She ran her fingertips lightly down over her belly, massaging the skin in the calming effleurage Renata had taught her. As the hours wore on, she settled into the rhythm of her body's work. The baby was early, but only by a week or two, by the doctor's calculation. Not enough to cause her to worry. She felt calm and peaceful between spasms, exhilarated as another swept her up, though she refused the word contraction, disturbed by what it conjured, a narrowing to confine her baby, block its entry into the world, a tightening that would crush its limbs, compress its still-soft bones. Instead, she held to images of expansion – petals unfolding, pods spreading open, releasing their seeds.

Sometime in the evening, the rain stopped, but she pulled the curtains to anyway, and this time, kept them closed. She turned the watch face down on the table. She didn't need it to tell her that the interludes were growing shorter, the spasms more intense. And she didn't need it to remind her that three o'clock was long since past.

The spasms continued, their progress slow and relentless.

Then, quite suddenly, they stopped.

Thank god! she said.

The exclamation was still damp in her mouth when her body reasserted itself, though in an entirely new way, all her muscles pushing in unison. Hot liquid gushed down her thighs. She put a hand between her legs, as if to hold the baby in, and scrabbled to the bed, lifting herself onto the mattress, rising up on her knees as she fingered the rim of her vagina, slick and round, the mouth of a cave, and inside, a great wet mound. Then her body took charge and she was pushing again, one hand firm against the baby's head, yes, baby, yes, yes, yes, the need subsiding, the head slipping back, the urge on her again, and again, as she strained into oblivion, pulled back by a gurgling cry, and there she was, all of her, pink and glistening on the bloodied sheet, such a tiny, perfect thing, and she gathered her in her arms and drew her to her breast, mouth latching onto nipple in a softly writhing circle, the cord that trailed from her baby's belly still buried deep inside her womb, the child sucking, drawing tight the bright thread that ran right down through her, until in a rush of warm fluid, the placenta slipped out.

She would never be able to recall exactly how she cut the umbilical cord, tying it in two places with the boiled linen thread. And she'd have no recollection of where she set the baby, although the tug of her nightgown over her head, that split second of disconnection, would forever fill her with regret. Somehow, she pulled the soiled sheets from the bed and dragged them into the empty bathtub. She would be able to reconstruct that. And the rest — laying down fresh flannelette, crawling back between the covers, wrapping her little girl in her arms, cradling her daughter to her side, skin to warm skin, the quilts shaped to a nest.

That's how Abe found them in the morning.

Later, much later, he would tell her that, looking down at them sleeping, he'd wished he were an artist so he could capture such bliss. He'd thought: Walker should be the one to witness this.

And she would remember blinking awake, the room ablaze with light, such relief to see Abe standing there, her ordeal over at last, smiling up at him as she drew the quilt aside, her hand brushing that small cheek, feeling the chill.

It's not your fault, the doctor was saying. He was standing at the end of the hospital bed, and though she turned her face away, pressed it against the pillow, she could still hear him, the words coming to her as if through a wad of cotton batting, but she didn't want them at all, didn't want to listen to him saying, it doesn't matter where the baby was born, she would have died anyway, no test could have detected it, a malfunction of the heart, his words growing fainter as she closed her eyes and drifted, drifted until the sentences barely registered, like the mouthings of animals or a language she'd never learned, phrases blurring in their own cadences, but what she'd heard had stayed with her, it stalked her inside her head, his low voice circling, not your fault, not your fault, but it was, she knew better than anybody whose fault it was, it was hers.

Then Walker was there, taking her home, helping her into her own bed, covering her with her quilts, sometimes leaving her alone, sometimes sitting there beside her, only once in that first week insisting she get up, pulling her by the arm, walking her into the kitchen.

We have to do this together. You know the answers, I don't.

Papers were strewn on the table. Official forms for the birth or the death, the burial, she didn't know which, she didn't care. He sat her down and moved a chair close beside her, pulling one of the pages forward.

This won't take long.

His voice sounded tight, the words shaved off in slivers.

When was she born?

She put her hand to her chest, certain she was bleeding, her body pricked in a thousand places. Her hand came away damp, with milk, not blood, her body resolute in its mothering.

I don't know, she finally managed, not to the question, but to everything, all her knowing gone, flushed out of her, she was empty, nothing left. I don't know, she said again, so softly that Walker bent close to hear, though when he did, she leaned away, unable to bear the warmth of his skin, the living smell of him.

This hurts me too, he said.

But he kept on, going over the details, as if she could forget. Abe coming in the morning as soon as the sand trucks were out, then the ambulance, the doctor, the storm not so bad after all, and only local, Walker there by nightfall, hunched by the hospital bed, the wetness on his face that she had reached up to touch, thinking it must be rain, she'd never known him to cry.

Abe got here around seven, Walker said. According to the autopsy, she died a few hours before that, between three and four. But they can't tell when she was born. You're the only one who knows. Was it in the afternoon? Was it dark?

A high-pitched tone inside her head was shredding his words to bits, scattering them around her, such a job to pick them up, piece the meaning back together.

The curtains were closed, she tried to say, but she had trouble shaping the sentence, her lips sluggish, as if from a stroke. When the rhyme finally came to her, the one her mother used to sing —

*A child that's born on the Sabbath day is fair and wise and good and gay* – she was too tired to make the effort to get it out.

She watched as he gave up on her, shaking his head and writing *Monday* on the form, adding the date and a time of his own choosing in small, cramped figures in the appropriate box, then he turned back to her.

We have to name her, he went on, it's the law. She was born alive.

And a flare of bitterness burned through her. How would he know? He wasn't there, he hadn't seen her.

Call her what you want, she said, thinking, what difference would it make?


Renata brought her food on a tray and sat with her, stroking her hair, saying nothing, waiting for her to speak.

But she craved only silence, wanted stillness. Even the stroke of a hand felt an abrasion, though she bore it, for to object would require words and it took everything she had to preserve the all-pervasive whiteness that quelled the keening in her head.

She was aware of Walker getting up from the couch in the mornings, putting away his blankets, bringing her tea, sitting folded into himself on the end of their bed. And she knew Renata came in the afternoons, bringing bowls of food, helping in the house, speaking quietly to Walker and the friends who came to visit. Vases of flowers appeared, the leaves became parched and faded, the petals turned brown, and they were taken away. The surfaces around her were stippled with cards and then they weren't. Through it all, nothing was expected of her but to eat, drink, sleep, weep, yet all she could do was lie on the bed or sit in a chair, her eyes dry and open, or sometimes, closed.

When Renata said to her at last, you can't go on like this forever, you have to find a way to live with it, she just stared at the stove.

I know it's hard, it's devastating. Renata pressed on, crouching in front of her chair, But it's already the beginning of May. Walker's back in the studio. Look — she cupped Alyson's chin, and turned her face toward the window — look at your gardens. Are you just going to let them die?

Renata's hands flew to her mouth. Oh Alyson, I'm so sorry.

But she was already out the door, striking off across the lawn. Halfway to the woods, she broke into a run, sucking in her breath until her feet hit the granite edge, then she gulped at the air and plunged on, thrusting branches and saplings aside, scrabbling over fallen timbers, pitching deeper into the bush, the rhythm of her breathing coming right as she found a pace and kept it, moving forward over roots and under ice-arched trees, through gullies and stinking swamps, nothing slowing her, not the thorns that caught at her nightgown, not the twigs that tugged at her hair, scraping at her arms, her face, her feet, the assault welcome, something to strain against at last, the wounds a relief, a reason to scream.

She left in the mornings before Walker was awake and returned when the sky grew dark. Sometimes, he would creep out after her, but she'd hear his footsteps among the trees and she'd stop, not moving again until he gave up and turned toward the house. Often, especially in those first few days, he'd be sitting at the table, staring out the window, waiting for her when she came back through the door.

Alyson, he'd say, his hands on her arms. Where have you been? What do you do all day? Talk to me.

She kept moving, that was all. Kept pushing into the underbrush. Kept the branches scratching at her shins, her arms, the nape of her neck. Sometimes she'd get lost, and then she'd have to wait until the clouds parted for the sun, or the moon rose before she'd be able to find her way. And she always did. She never panicked.

If she could have found the words, she would have said that she preferred the woods. Not because that was where she'd walked before, naming the trees, the flowers, the birds. She scarcely remembered that place, so different from the ice-ravaged labyrinth she found herself stumbling through. But she felt safe amid the chaos. She would have stayed there into the nights, if not for Walker sitting at the table, waiting. She'd make her way back, her muscles tensing, her senses masking over as she entered the house so that she'd hardly see the burrs and pods he'd pick from her clothes, never feel the welts and stings he'd paint pink with calamine or daub with iodine and bandage.

Look at you, he'd say, at least cover your arms and legs, can't you? These will get infected, if you aren't careful. You'll be sick. Is that what you want?

Through the early weeks of May she wandered restless through the bush, avoiding the slopes of meadows and granite uplifts with their long perspectives, keeping to the hollows, the dense stands of conifers, the swamp, never stopping until she'd reach a road or a fence, and then she'd swerve back among the trees. When she came to the stream, she'd pick her way across the stepping stones to the flat boulder in the middle and she'd sit there, gazing into the dividing waters, tracing the bubbles that skittered past her on one side or the other, following them until they burst. Or she'd stare at the roots that lay undisturbed beneath the surface, so transfixed that sometimes she'd settle on the boulder before the sun was high in the sky, and by the time she'd think to leave, it would be so dark she could barely make her way home.

Looking back, she would say she wore her grief out.

One day as she kicked through the forest duff, she gazed down and saw not a vague tangle of underbrush but wintergreen sparked with starflower. Red trillium. Wild leek. There was a trill and she thought, white-throated sparrow, heard the churr of a squirrel in a jack pine.

The silence broke and words spilled from her lips – how could you? how could you? how could you? – uttered first to herself, then to Walker, to God, to the baby, to everything, all of it, to the spring that surged forward, mocking the winter of her heart.

A white trillium about to open, a certain pale shade of green: the smallest thing brought her weeping to her knees. She wept until her eyes swelled shut, until there was no more moisture in her cells to wring to tears, and still she wept, a parched wailing.

So much weeping thinned her skin, so that after weeks of feeling nothing, she was all response, slick and rank. The wound in the bank where Walker dug his clay raised a fury that sent her clambering for stones to seal the earth leaking red into the stream. The sight of the sun high in a bleached-blue sky filled her with inexpressible joy, though when it rained, she cowered in her room, buried under her quilts. When Walker reached for her, she recoiled, unable to bear his touch, until one night, she fell into his arms, overcome with gratitude for his persevering patience, welcoming him back into their bed, yet once he was there, she pushed him away, disconsolate, wondering if forgiveness would ever be possible. For him. For herself.

Her emotions were seismic in their eruptions, rocking her hardest inside the house, though even in the bush she was at their mercy. One afternoon, late in May, when she was roaming near the

stream, she heard the trucks grinding their way out of the gravel
pit and was overwhelmed with a sudden loathing for Sauvage, for
the hollow he'd gouged in the earth, for her own deceiving inno-
cence that had lulled her into agreeing to buy that land. Turning
away in disgust, she stumbled, cursing at what had risen up to
trip her. Then her irritation collapsed, and excitement swept into
its place as she saw what it was her toe had struck.

A square-cut timber, hidden in the undergrowth.

She bent to it, brushing aside the ferns and leaves, moving
along the wood. Its hand-formed edge was such an aberration
among the rounded stalks and worn stones that it drew thoughts
into her mind that had nothing to do with her, and she felt a
shifting, a stirring. She followed the log to its end, which proved
to be a corner, and then with both hands she was tearing at the
forest growth, yanking out the sumac, the maple saplings, the
twining blackberry vines, ripping up the cleavers, the bloodroot
and snakeroot, the false Solomon's-seal, and there it was – the
base of a structure, the bottom logs of a cabin, one side obscured
under a tumble of chimney stone.

She didn't even think to hoard it. She rushed back through
the woods toward the house, and as she ran, she felt the shadow
of her old self with her, running to tell Walker about the nighthawk, about the motor-sound of the grouse. She couldn't wait to
share this with him, too, though she'd hardly spoken to him for
weeks, and she saw how unkind she'd been, when he'd been so
good to her, he'd let her be, so that by the time she burst into the

kitchen, she was eager to speak, but then he turned, and the way he looked at her, wanting not news but explanations for all that had gone before, withered the words in her mouth.

Before she could tell him about the ruins of the cabin, so much else would have to be shared — the rat's-claw rain, the wolf slinking across the snow, the paper gardens she'd wandered through with a teacup in her hand, the months alone — that the prospect overwhelmed her and she pushed the door closed behind her, saying nothing but, I'm home.

It was early June by the time she uncovered all that was left of the collapsed building. Two rows of logs were still intact, and where the spill of stone protected the wood, she found part of a third and a fourth. Shielded from the weather and the creeping vegetation, the timbers there might have been laid yesterday, the edges were that crisp, the chinking still firmly in place.

Standing in a gap in the logs where a door might have been, she imagined the view cleared to the water. She envisioned chickens in the yard, a cow browsing among the trees, a chopping block by a stack of cordwood. A neat garden with a wattle fence against the rabbits and the deer. A footpath to the stepping stones and her flat boulder in the stream, the perfect place for dipping buckets. She could almost see the water sloshing to the ground, splashing a woman's skirt.

I'll restore what I can, she thought.

The work was invigorating. She no longer woke in the mornings to that crushing dread or what had come after — an undifferentiated pain that made her think she must be ill until she remembered and then she'd bury her face in the pillow, willing herself back to sleep. Now, she got up with an eagerness that surprised her. Some days she almost felt good. She still spent most of her hours away from the house, but her excursions seemed less an escape now than a journey she looked forward to. Before she left, she rubbed citronella on her skin, tucked her long sleeves into gloves, pulled a bug net over her head. Sometimes she even thought to pack a lunch. And when she returned in the evenings, if she felt up to it, occasionally she prepared a meal.

The rest, she left to Walker. She had grown used to letting things slip, knowing that he would see to them. The cradle, the quilt, the row of Polaroids — all the baby things had disappeared. The bed had been returned to its place in front of the window. The standing half of the Manitoba maple had been cut down, the limbs sawn into lengths and stacked in the woodshed. The twigs and small branches that littered the lawn had been raked into a pile and burned. For days he'd worked to clear the fallen trees and smooth the ragged wounds of the limbs ripped off by the weight of ice.

He'd done the work without complaint, though in the nights, when she was restless, he would leave their bed, too, sitting with her on the couch, his arm a clamp on her shoulders, his questions heavy in the air.

Why won't you talk to me? he'd say.

And, What do you want from me? What more can I do?

Then, Fine, I'll leave you alone, if that's the way you want it. Let me know when you decide to snap out of it.

Through it all, she said nothing, paying attention to the faint whisper that told her to keep herself apart, raise a shield around herself, though if you asked her, why?, against what?, she wouldn't have known what to say, since it wasn't a thought or even a feeling so much as an urge, the same sort of thing that had told her to push the baby out, cradle it to her breast.

After a while, he had given up. He started sleeping through the day and working through the night again, so that, by the time she found the remnants of the cabin, they were back to their old routines. When she left in the early morning and when she returned as darkness fell, she could see his shadow in the barn-door window, always in the same position, as if he'd grown rooted to the spot, forever reaching up to something just outside her field of vision.

But even that was something she noticed only in passing. Her brain, idle for so long, was given over to her project, devising strategies, identifying tools, imagining the cabin, the height of its walls, the placement of its openings, until it seemed to her as substantial a piece of architecture as the house in which she lived. She cleared a path from the cabin threshold to the stepping stones across the stream, cut back the underbrush from around the low rim of logs, and raked the earth bare within. She piled the stones at one end and brought an old wooden chair from the shed, so that when each phase of her work was finished, she could sit in front of the makeshift hearth and stare into the non-existent fire, trying to think what else to do.

She was prying out a piece of chinking — she had the inspiration that if she could figure out how it was made, she could reseal what remained of the walls — when she spotted the edge of something soft. She pulled on it and a rag slipped out. Behind it was another, cleaner than the first. She picked out more of the loose chinking, more scraps of rough, grey cloth, then reaching deeper between the logs, she touched something smooth, thin but rigid. A thing with weight to it that she pinched out of the narrow gap. A fold of clean white cloth wrapped around a leather bag. Inside that, a book.

She lifted the cover. The pages were brittle, the colour of strong tea. When she touched them with her fingers, small bits broke off the edges. She slid the thin blade of her pocket knife between the leaves, lifting them up just far enough to read.

It was a cookbook, the rules for rising steamed puddings, instructions for roasting caribou, the seven types of stains and how to remove them. The sort of old-fashioned manual of household management she'd often picked out of the boxes of books that Renata's parents sent twice a year, eccentric, worthless volumes culled from the overburdened shelves of their used bookstore in the city.

The pages in the middle were too parched to separate, even with the knife, so she turned the book over and opened it from the back. Bits of dried leaf and stem spilled onto her lap. She picked them up, peering at the veiny texture, trying to identify what they'd been.

The sky was darkening, a wind gathering in the upper leaves. She was picking up the fragments of plant material, thinking she'd tuck them back in the book and take it to the house where she could study them in better light. That was when she noticed the handwriting — six or eight pages of it — the space reserved for cookery notes completely filled with long lists in cramped penmanship so small she couldn't make out the words, and then, right at the end, a few sheets closely written in cursive script, the paper written over twice, side to side, then top to bottom, so that the sentences seemed woven together, and she knelt there by the logs, the wind worrying at the pages as she tried to tease the phrases apart, until at last she found an opening and tracing her finger along the lines, she came at last to the beginning,

*I am a woman Alone in all the wide World.*

*Until today I had three Brothers, William Wallace, Robert Bruce, Harry Douglas, named for good Scots heroes, every one. Margaret the Queen, they called me. Now the Queen has taken her Revenge.*

# MARGARET

*Spring 1865*

*My brothers buried Ewan beside our Mother, laid him in the earth by the River Stone. I set stakes around the mounds and wove elm bark between, marking our Graveyard in the Wilderness.*

The earth holds its breath, as it always does before a storm. William and Robert, smelling snow in the air, leave for the logging camp without delay.

Margaret sits in the doorway of the cabin, staring into the trees, the leaves sulphurous against bruised and swollen clouds. She thinks once of the fire that must have extinguished on the hearth, but she lets the notion pass. She does not weep. The oxen and the cow, their nostrils flared to the advancing tempest, make their own way to their shelter. The hens fly up to their roost. If she hears the lowing and the squawking, she makes no response.

By noon the sky is dark as night, the stillness a suffocation. Then the wind sweeps in, bending the pines before it like a hurricane. With the wind comes lashing rain. Thunder rolls the clouds together, lightning splits them apart. Limbs torn from their trunks crash to the ground, spinning leaves into the whirlwind.

Only when the gale reaches its peak does Margaret rise, letting fall the plaid that Robert laid across her shoulders. She moves into the storm, inviting the wind to tear at her hair, begging the rain, flecked now with hail, to batter against her skin.

The dark-haired woman Margaret glimpsed between the trees crouches by the fire. She brings a bowl of broth, spooning it between Margaret's lips. When the bowl is empty, the woman speaks. Zahgahseega, she says, pointing to herself and then to Margaret, who whispers her name as she sinks back into sleep.

Each time Margaret wakens, the woman feeds her or leads her outside to relieve herself, gives her moss to put between her legs when she bleeds. She allows the woman to do these things, grateful to be cared for like a child. Sometimes the woman is gone for hours. When she returns, she spears meat over the fire, tearing off singed bits for the two of them to eat.

Margaret takes in her surroundings slowly, as if awakening from a dream. A lashing of poles slanting overhead. The softness of fur under her cheek. The warming fire. A section of the wall that blinks open and closed as the woman comes and goes. The woman herself. Hair like a blackbird's wing. Skin not red or brown or copper but the colour, Margaret decides, of new cloth dyed with lichen and rinsed with woad. Her throat is long and stretched thin as a wading bird's, or perhaps it only seems so against the silver disk she wears at her collarbone.

As the curved room comes into focus, Margaret remembers the cabin, its square wooden walls, the animals. With a burnt stick she draws on a flat hearthstone the outline of a cow, a house, and the next day, the woman leads her through the forest to her brothers' clearing.

The path they follow through the snow ends at the barn door. Inside, the oxen huff funnels of steam, an impatient welcome, though their mows hold remnants of hay and their troughs are damp. The woman moves shyly to the barrel of grain and scoops handfuls to the hens that flop down from their roost to mill about her ankles. Margaret smooths the soft hide of the cow, dropping her hand to the swollen udder, then, gathering the bucket and the stool, she positions herself, her body leading the way, steadying itself against the furred flank, her fingers palpating the fevered teats, massaging gently until the milk bursts forth in a thick stream, the animal lowing in sweet relief.

By the time she is finished the milking, Zahgahseega has brought water to the oxen and the hens. The two women leave the barn together, Margaret pausing to slide the bolt on the door. She looks uncertainly at the cabin, snow drifting at the door. The window is dark, the chimney cold. No sign of human habitation at all, except for the tips of the stakes that mark the graves by the river.

She takes a step toward them, but her foot has scarcely creased the snow when she pulls it back. She stands, unable to move in one direction or the other, until the woman takes her hand and leads her into the trees, the way they came.

*woman of the Forest took me into her Weegawum. I stayed
through the Winter. She lived a solitary existence, which in time
gave me to believe that I could make my way Alone, too.*

One late-winter morning when the ruddy tips of willows
promise spring, a man pushes open the flap of the *weegawum*
and Zahgahseega gives a shout of pleasure, pulling him toward
Margaret, pronouncing syllables that come to her ears more as
music than words. He bows as any white man would, and stretches
out his hand.

My English name is Peter, he says. Peter Constant. The
cousin of Zahgahseega.

The sound of her own language releases a torrent of words
inside her head. She has passed the winter in silence, having
nothing to say that could not be expressed with a gesture or a
glance. In the absence of expression, her mind has emptied of
thought except for what lodged around her most basic needs, but
now it is filling up again. Words arrange themselves into sentences, lamentations, bitter reproaches, demands and appeals, all
eddying together, though for the most part the barriers she has
set in place hold, and all that surfaces is a question:

Did you know a Scotsman, red-haired, a tree-spotter for the
lumbermen?

Peter nods. He was my friend. We called him Shingua, the
pine.

Zahgahseega speaks to her cousin.

My sister says you must have a name, too. Omiskabugo, the red leaf.

Shingua. Omiskabugo. Man of the pines, woman of the red leaf. She repeats the words to herself as the cousins talk together in phrases that heave and sigh so like the Gaelic that Margaret hears in their voices her father singing among the rafters, Ewan whispering through the night. When Zahgahseega rises to prepare a meal, Peter turns to Margaret with stories of Shingua, his bravery, his wisdom, his kindness, his strength, a eulogy that draws out of her all the tears she never wept, so that when the women are alone again, she finds it easier to speak. She points to parts of herself, to the baskets of dried roots and plants, the furs, the stone and copper tools in the hut, to the features of the land around them, the events of their lives, naming them all by turns, her in Scots' English, Zahgahseega in her tongue.

They convey meaning in the lilt of their voices, the swoop of their hands, and the contortions of their bodies, shaping a world between them made of equal parts gesture and sound.

Spring that year comes suddenly, a burst of heat that unfurls leaves and pushes shoots up through the soil overnight. Zahgahseega, who in the winter left the hut only to help with the animals or to fell a deer, now spends every daylight hour among the trees, poking in the leaf litter, gathering dark, shiny leaves that smell of mint, a root that bleeds when broken in two, a starry bloom that spreads like late snow over the forest floor.

She shows the plants to Margaret, miming their uses. As a signal that she understands, Margaret imitates the symptoms too, and together they take the simulated cure. Someone watching in the woods would think them demented, one old woman and one young, both of them bending low, making flatulent noises with their lips, squatting in mock childbirth, pretending to break their legs and slash open their arms, becoming a snake poised to bite, sipping non-existent elixirs from invisible cups, laying imaginary poultices on make-believe wounds.

Now and then Margaret thinks she sees, in the shapes of the leaves and the arrangements of petals, plants she knew from the braes. As she watches the Indian woman press the bruised leaves of buttercups against her skin, raising a blister to drain an inflammation, Margaret has a vision of her mother relieving a sea-boil on her brother's back in exactly the same way. When Zahgahseega chews a sweet-smelling purple flower and mimics its laxative effect, what she sees is her mother pausing to pick the same bloom, heart's-ease she called it. To lessen the pain of being far from one you love, she'd said when Margaret asked about the name.

It comes back to her then, like a story she heard long ago or a truth she knew but let slip. How as a young girl she wandered the meadows and the shores collecting simples with her mother and later, when she learned to tell one leaf from another, harvesting them on her own. How she wrapped the stems with twine and hung them from the attic rafters to dry, their bittersweet fragrance an antidote to the briny odour of the fishing gear. And Margaret hears her mother's voice as she sat by the hearth crushing leaves between her fingers, separating flowers from their stems, tying a pinch of each into small muslin squares, saying, shepherd's-knot boiled in milk is a cure for the flux, remember that, and the leaves of witches' thimbles applied warm, plaister-wise, soothes the pain that follows fever, staunch a wound with a leaf of healing-blade, listen to me, Margaret, you'll find a use for this one day.

Terms long since forgotten find their way to her tongue. Emetic. Cathartic. Cataplasm. Though it is years since she thought such things, she knows instantly that an infusion is a tea, an ounce of herb to a pint of water, while a decoction is boiled to a stronger dose, and a fomentation is applied externally, though the other two are drunk. She remembers that bark must be collected when the tree is in full leaf, then dried in the shade and that an extract is best made from roots dug when the sap is rising in the spring.

The store of her own knowledge astonishes her. As she plunges into the past to retrieve what she once knew, her mind casts ahead to her brothers' return, to the stories from the shanty-fire they will bring, sad tales of settlers' wives dying as they give birth, children drained by dysentery, grown men felled by Bush fever, friends bleeding to death from the slip of an axe or wasting away with the ague or a persistent, bloody cough. And amidst the bramble of these thoughts, a plan opens before her like a path.

*I determined to gather Simples — the Leaves and Flowers*
*I knew from Fife and the Cures my Indian friend taught me.*
*I would raise a Cottage on Harry's land and plant a Garden in*
*the Meadow. As the Bush fell before the Settlers, I would keep my*
*Forest whole and make my living from the Herbes I found there*
*and from what I could Cultivate.*

When William and Robert return, they find Margaret working the soil in the dooryard garden. They are surprised, and pleased, to see her looking so well. They do not remark on how robust she seems, for such a comment might require an admission of what they feared they would find, which in turn might lead to a recollection of the events of the day they left. That, the two men have agreed, is ground best left undisturbed.

Margaret appears intent on her digging, but her mind is wandering the garden she will make in the small, secluded meadow on the far edge of Harry's land. Earlier in the spring, the Indian woman helped her raise a *weegawum* there, teaching her to pray to the trees before she felled them for poles, showing her how to sew strips of birchbark into fabric to wrap around the frame, giving her hides to carpet the floor. When the weather warms, she will turn the soil, plant the seeds her brother Robert will buy for her in Renfrew, following her list, as he always does, without question.

So absorbed is she in her plans that when she looks up and sees the men coming into the clearing, she almost blurts out all that has transpired through that miraculous winter. But the sight of them, William's calculating features, Robert's ready taunting grin, recalls the memory of that autumn hurling-down and it stills her tongue, so that as they pass, she acknowledges their greeting with a barely perceptible nod.

And so it becomes fixed.

The three of them go on as is their custom. The brothers pick the stones that sprout like mushrooms in the fields, they plant the barley-corn and wheat, and when that is done, they set to felling trees again, fencing more land. Margaret cooks for them. She boils the sap and makes the sugar for their porridge. She plants the gardens and harvests the turnips and potatoes, the onions and the beans. She feeds the livestock, which each year grows in number, pigs and sheep now as well as the oxen and the milch cow, the broody hens. She sets eggs in waterglass for the winter and kills the young cockerels for meat. She renders the fat from the pigs and mixes it with the lye she strains from wood ash and lime to make soap to clean their clothes. She cuts the wool from the sheep and washes it in the river, cards and spins and dyes it with lichen she prises from the river stones, spreading it on the bushes to dry, then rolling it into balls ready to knit into the ganseys, socks, and mittens that keep her brothers warm through their winters in the camp. All of this she does, and more.

But she says little to her brothers. They never ask for her forgiveness, and so she never gives it.

The Indian woman moves her *weegawum* with the seasons, leaving the riverbank when William and Robert return from the logging camp, coming back to her winter grounds shortly after they are gone.

But even during the warm months, when Zahgahseega makes her encampment on the shores of a lake to the north, Margaret sometimes hears a soft voice singing a greeting through the trees, and she echoes, Hallo! Friend!

They walk, then, in the damp thick Bush on the land that once was Harry's, far from the level ground where William and Robert clear their fields. Margaret never speaks of the wild place they wander as the woods, preferring words such as forest or Bush that make of it a single entity, like the sea, so she can move through the growth of trees as she would through molecules of water, oblivious to individual parts, for to see them would be to name them and to name them would be to hear Ewan's voice, and she cannot bear that yet. She keeps her eyes fastened on the ground, on the pale waxy pipes that bring relief to sore eyes and the peculiar spotted plantain that eases an ache in the teeth, on the spindle-shaped root that cures the bloody flux and the blue-flowered meadow grass that soothes a cough, on the deadly white mushroom that clears a hut of vermin overnight.

She records it all. From each apronful of plants she collects, she saves one wholesome specimen to press between the pages of her mother's only book, a collection of recipes she bought in Ottawa from a clerk who declared that its advice on how to broil pigeons and make a leech for soap, as well as the directions for Indian pudding and spruce beer, would be indispensable in the Bush. The blank pages at the back, intended for cookery notes, are closely written now with the details of each leaf and root and flower that her friend points out to her — where it grows, its identifying marks, when it should be gathered, the part to be used, how it is prepared, the ailments it relieves, how much should be given, how often, and with what effect.

It has become a compulsion, this recording of everything she learns. Not because she is afraid she will forget, but because it seems to steady her to make these notes in her pale maple-bark ink. It fills up with living things the empty spaces that memory might invade. She writes in solitude, keeping the book in a rabbitskin bag the Indian woman sewed for her and hiding it beside her bed in a crack between the logs where the mortar has come loose.

On the day of the autumn equinox, Margaret is beckoned from the root cellar she is digging. She follows the Indian woman as she lays bits of food and bundles of herbs at the mouths of caves, by the wildest rapids in the stream, in the crooks of contorted trees and the crevices of stones, finding spirits to appease in every orifice that opens in the wilderness.

Margaret finds a certain comfort in the ritual, for in Fife, too, the natural world was never just itself, an arrangement of water, stone, earth, and growing things. Break Boats, Burnt Craig, Sandy Craig, Blind Capul, Meggyhead, Pane's Goat, Ladies' Seat, Boiling Cauldron, Witches Craig – every cliff and every rock had a story to tell. The wildwood, when she journeyed through it, seemed empty by comparison. The rivers and lakes and bays had been named to record a shape or as a geographic marker or some-times, as a reminder of those who had passed through or the home they'd left behind, the new world made serviceable, no room for enchantment. Where the Indian names were kept, it seems to her to be because it made men like her brothers feel brave to penetrate a place so alien, not because they believed it has a story to tell.

Once the snow is on the ground and William and Robert are gone to the logging camp, the women spend long hours by Zahgahseega's fire. She makes a pipe for Margaret, moulding a fistful of reddish clay around some strands of twisted grass, baking it hard under a mound of coals. She stuffs the bowl with dried, wild herbs and presses it into Margaret's hands, then she lights a pipe of her own. It becomes their habit, smoking together in the evenings. Margaret puffs on her clay pipe, just as she had seen her Scottish grandmother do, while Zahgahseega sucks on a bowl of black stone carved in the shape of a woman, both of them smoking the herbs down to ash, making peace with the spirits.

Then the stories begin. The Indian woman tells Margaret of the man-gods who control the winds, of *Gitche Monedo*, the Great Spirit in the sky, and *Matche Monedo*, the Evil One who lives on *Aukee*, the Earth. She tells her about the mermen in the water and the *Pukwudj Ininees*, the little people who live in the forest, and about the *Nimmahkie*, the thunder monsters who set lightning at the trees, and the cannibal giants, the *Windigoes*.

She tells her how the porcupine got its quills and the oriole, its colourful feathers. How the star-maiden became the white water lily and how Lone Bird became the woman in the moon. She tells her the story of *Nanabozko*, who shaped the landscape where they live, marking each day of his journey with a pile of rocks, which became the hills, leaving footprints, which became the valleys, and once, dropping a kettle in pursuit of a stone giant, creating a cave in which Indians leave an offering to ensure their safe passage. And she tells her of the spirit she dreamt, a perfect burning sun, which she took as a husband, forsaking other men to live in the forest alone.

*We passed the Winters with our stories, waiting for the simples to bloom and for the ground to soften sufficiently to work the secret Garden I made in the meadow beyond the Cedars, at the farthest edge of Harry's land.*

Margaret tells stories, too. About boggarts who are full of mischief, hiding cups and breaking plates, and brownies, little men without noses who are hard-working and helpful but quick to take offense. She tells her about the wrisks who are half man, half goat, and about the selkies, gentle seals who become human when they venture onto land, and the kelpies, treacherous water horses that lure travellers to their death. And she tells her what her mother said, that faeries in the mind manufacture all a person's fancies, their dreams and imaginings, their memories, too.

She tells her about the old hag Cailleach, who spat out the lakes and farted the hills that lie across the Firth from Pittenweem. And she tells her about the *fianna*, an ancient race of giants who lived in her father's highlands. One day, the men went out to hunt, leaving Garaidh to protect the women and the children. He was a vain young man and his hair was his greatest pride. To tease him, the women pegged his braids to the ground while he slept, then they locked themselves in the fort and screamed as if in fear. Hearing their cries, Garaidh leapt up, tearing the hair from his head. When he heard the women laughing, he fell into a rage and set fire to the fort, burning every woman and child alive. The men hunted Garaidh and killed him in revenge, but without their women, the race of giants vanished from the hills.

Margaret and Zahgahseega match story for story all through the winter nights, always waiting for the evening star, the woman's star, to come into view before they begin. Margaret often asks to hear the tale of the father who, as he lay dying, begged his children to care for each other in the home he made for them, far from the cruelties of the world. His wife died soon after, leaving the children to fend for themselves. For a time, the three were happy in the woods,.then the middle child grew restless and set off to find others of his kind. The eldest became selfish, too, and left in search of companions, abandoning the youngest son to survive on berries and roots and the leavings of wolves, who abided the child in their midst for many years.

One day, as the ice was breaking up, the wolves moved toward a lake. A man paddling close to shore thought he heard a young voice singing, and he leapt from his canoe, certain he recognized his brother. He reached to embrace him, but the child slipped from his grasp, his singing mixed now with guttural sounds. The nearer the brother came, the more rapidly the child changed until, no longer able to sing, he raised his voice in an eerie howl, saying, I am a wolf! I am a wolf! as he bounded into the forest, disappearing among the trees.

The Indian woman lifts her head to howl, and Margaret joins in, their voices circling the hut, spiralling out through the fire-hole, twining through the trees like an errant wisp of smoke until sometimes, on the coldest nights, a wolf raises an answering call.

# A L Y S O N

*Summer 1991*

The smell of burning roused Alyson from her reading. She looked up from the book, reluctant to let go of the words, though she knew them almost by heart. For a week she'd been coming to the ruins of the cabin to read what Margaret MacBayne had written, transcribing the three pages of her story to memory, carrying them with her in her mind like a missal.

But a fire in the woods was not something to be ignored. She slipped the book between the logs and stuffed the crevice with rags, slouching moss across the place where the chinking had been disturbed. Then she hurried to the stream, veering west along the water, walking quickly but stepping carefully in the accumulating dusk, her feet accustomed by now to stealth.

Smoke was rising from the ridge of granite that reared up from the streambank. Walker's dragon-kiln. Of course, she thought. She should have known. Though how could she? She had never smelled that fire from a distance, she'd always been right there beside him, feeding the first flames.

At the thought, she felt a wrenching, something torn from its place. It was a ritual they performed together, the firing of a warrior. The kiln on the ridge was used for nothing else. The cycle was unpredictable – sometimes years between the figures, once several in quick succession – but the pattern of creation was always the same. Walker would retreat into his work and stay there for weeks, preoccupied, sullen, impatient with her, a mood she'd weather easily, knowing what it would produce. Then one day, she'd sense a change in him. She'd ask if it was ready and he'd invite her to come see, the conversation never varying, their words part of the process, too. They'd walk together to the studio, and when she was settled in his chair, he'd unwind the white sheet from the vaguely human shape, peel back the swathes of plastic, one layer at a time, her excitement growing with every veil that he lifted, until the last was pulled away and he'd come to stand beside her, the figure bared before them, damp and glistening.

Even later, when she'd grown accustomed to his style, to the curl of scorched tissue, to the absence of limbs, even then, when she knew enough to prepare herself for what she would see, still she'd be shaken by the starkness of the form, by the human soul she'd sense within the tortured pose. Inside the kiln, the clay would harden, darken to a bruise, and the figure would alter, become impervious, remote, monumental. A warrior. She'd feel in it Walker's power, which was thrilling, but unsettling, too, and she'd return in her mind to the unveiling, to when the clay was soft and moist, the colour of flushed skin. The figure seemed more human to her then, and she could love it, no matter what it had become.

The kiln was on the other side of the ridge, a tunnel of brick that clung to the granite slope, its mouth nuzzled among the boulders on the ground. From where she stood, all she could see was the chimney that extended from the uplift of stone, and rising from it, a thread of smoke.

She'd held herself apart, and he'd carried on without her, sealing a new figure inside the dragon, the transformation already begun.

But what, she asked herself, had she expected? He'd always been a single-minded man. When they would walk the bush together, he'd never see the things she pointed out, the rare wood-land mushrooms, the wild ginger and leeks. He'd keep his eyes raised to the trees, identifying species, isolating specimens – a *Quercus macrocarpa* he hadn't tested yet, a cedar that would yield a certain greenish glaze. He could calculate with an accountant's accuracy each tree's contribution to his art. The number of thermal units in its fibres. The tinting traits of its ash. He loved a solitary tree especially, moved by the fuel and the glaze it could become, but also by the spread of its branches, the peculiar twist of its limbs. If she ventured to say how sad it looked, a lone oak in a field, a marooned sailor, a lost son, he'd launch into one of his lectures. Isolation is the essence of art, he'd say. It's what an artist does. Disconnects an image from the chaos so that nothing will ever seem the same again.

Sometimes she'd wonder if that was all there was to it — what about love? she'd think, or compassion? What about the things that drew people together instead of forcing them to stand alone? — but the questions were always fleeting, and she'd let the force of his vision sweep them aside.

She circled the ridge along the moat of fuelwood, withdrawing into the trees as she approached the kiln. Walker was squatting in front, feeding a small fire with sticks that he pulled from the heap of tinder at his back. He was facing her, leaning so close over the flames that the light shafted upward, gouging dark furrows into his cheeks.

And suddenly, she was twelve, pushing open the door to the little room off the kitchen, everything in disarray, the books, the shelves, chair, and table, all piled against the window, her father hunched in one corner, the aquarium in his arms, the long shadows in his cheeks flexing as he stared down into the light. Then he turned to her, his mouth open in a silent shriek, and she ran from him, screaming for her mother. She'd sat rigid in her room, listening for the ambulance, and this time, waiting her aunt, her small red suitcase packed and squared neatly on the bed beside her. All through the summer she'd stayed on the farm she'd been haunted by that image of her father hunched over the light, so that when she returned, months later, and crept back into the room, she was terrified she'd see him, still cowering in the corner.

But the room had been restored to the way it had always been — books lined up on the shelves, the table squared in the centre, the chair at its customary angle in front of tightly drawn drapes – as if nothing had happened, she'd imagined it all. Then he was right there behind her, his voice sharp in her ear, you don't belong here, get out, his body bent away from hers, his face averted as she passed, as if he was sickened just by the sight of her.

All through her adolescence, she'd replay those scenes, waiting for the shriek, the rebuke, the turning away. She had thought the memories would dissipate if she leaked them out bit by bit, but there they were, undiminished, a dark shadow on a cheek provoking an anguish so familiar it felt almost soothing.

She pulled her gaze away and followed the spine of the kiln up the granite slope. At the top of the ridge would be Walker's encampment. His down sleeping bag. The old army chest stamped AMMUNITION where he kept his food – cheese, rye bread, summer sausage, a bag of green tea, a small bottle of sake. A cooler of drinking water off to one side. An alarm clock, his knife, an enamelware mug. Everything laid out square and precise.

She didn't have to see it to know. She'd been through these preparations half a dozen times before, his routine intricate as a dance. The kind a shaman might perform, she'd thought the first time she watched him, each step simple in itself but accomplished with such devotion that it had seemed to her a privilege to be allowed to be there. That feeling had stayed with her, long after the rituals had lost their mystery, long after the process had become second nature to her, too, and she was moving through the dance beside him, though he never seemed to see how well she'd learned her part, always giving her the same instructions, telling her what to do.

You have to keep the flame constant. Stoke too slow and the clay will sag. Too fast and the tendons will burst.

I know, she'd say, don't I always do it right?

But he would explain it to her anyway, how each element, the wood, the air, the clay, the fire, each one had its own expression, it was up to him to bring it out. Lightning streaks in the glaze, wayward blooms in the clay — he took credit for it all. And working there beside him, she accepted what he'd said, that his control was so complete it allowed even for the unexpected.

Though it looked different to her now, from her perspective among the trees.

Even the dragon firing itself. She remembered how enthused she'd been when he described how the kiln had evolved in Japan, all the potters in a village filling the chamber with their pots and working together to feed the flames. But Walker had scaled down the design, devised special systems. I don't want people around, getting in the way, he'd said, and she'd taken the comment as praise for how unobtrusively she worked. She'd studied the texts and learned the principles so she would know what came next, splitting tinder, mixing mud, bringing the bricks just when he needed them, knowing enough to stay quiet while he calculated how to front the figure to the flame, how to set the walls to direct the heat, creating the eddies that swirled back the glazing ash.

You work so hard, Renata said to her once. It's none of my business, but it doesn't seem to me he appreciates it much.

Well he does, she had replied, more sharply than she intended. Besides, he'd do the same for me.

Though he never had, she thought now. He'd done what she'd asked and he'd done what he wanted. But never what she needed. Not on his own.

As though he could sense the way his every move had been recast, Walker stood and stretched, shifting his shoulders, shaking the stiffness from his legs. He looked around, as if there were something he'd forgotten, then he headed up the granite slope, strolling along the flank of the kiln, pausing now and then to inspect the fresh skin of mud he'd smoothed over the bricks, laying a hand on it, tenderly, like a father gauging the warmth in the flushed cheek of his child.

And it came back to her what he'd said: It never occurred to me the baby would come early. The phone just kept ringing, so I figured you were out. I came as soon as Abe called.

She had nodded at the time, but now she asked herself, didn't he know she never would have missed his call? Shouldn't he have done something to make certain she was all right? Had it bothered him at all, leaving her alone like that?

The smoke was billowing from the chimney now, filling up the sky. Firing the dragon had always taken the two of them, spelling each other off, one falling to the stone to sleep while the other took up the work, which lasted through a night and a day, sometimes into another night. They'd both be spent at the end of it, barely able to lift their heads to eat or drink, capable of nothing during the week it took the kiln to cool down but lolling on the ridge, sleeping in the sun, sometimes making love, too drained to speak.

Now he was doing it alone.

She settled among the cedars and watched. Watched as he napped between the first stokings, setting his alarm to keep the rhythm of the burn. Once the fire was at full throttle, there would be no rest, not a moment's respite.

She watched as the smoke from the chimney blackened and his face grew ruddy from exertion and the heat, the logs shoved into the fire-hole an armload at a time, wood sucked to ash the instant it hit the flame. Once the sun was high, he threw off his shirt, let the wood lacerate his skin, but as the light faded, the biting insects forced him to cover himself again, the cloth staining dark with his sweat.

Still, she sat on her mat of ferns and watched. Watched as she had in her parents' house, sitting cross-legged on her bed, the door to the hallway scarcely open, just enough to see her mother passing back and forth to her father's bed, always something in her hand, a book, a hot drink, a cold compress, whatever her mother decided would be good for him. She would wait and watch until she'd hear her mother's voice on the phone, low and complaining, the tone reserved for her friends. Then she'd slip into her father's room and stand beside his bed, willing his eyes to open so she could ask him what he really wanted and she would bring it to him, whatever it was, anything to see him sit up and smile, but he just lay there, only once looking up at her, his eyes pleading, like a child asking permission.

The roar of combustion deepened. Red flames leapt from the chimney, matching the blaze of the setting sun. The body of the kiln heaved. Fissures opened along its spine. Tongues of fire darted at the gathering darkness, orange, then white. Then the flame from the chimney grew weary and hunkered down, too exhausted to find the sky, but still Walker pushed more fuel into the dragon's mouth.

She sat watching the chimney flame, assessing its colour, waiting for it to rise again, tall and assertive, waiting for it to whiten. She knew the signs as well as he. She imagined the figure inside its crucible, each element in the clay heating to the brink of collapse, to the cusp of melting like magma, but held back and in that split-second pause, turning to stone, the flesh hardened bit by bit over those hundreds of degrees, the surface bathed in the vapours released from the wood – every inhalation of every leaf, every mineral leached from the soil or pulled with rain from the sky, every drought, every sunless, dripping spring, every tearing winter wind, all that a tree had endured and recorded in its cells etched in glassy hues on the warrior's skin.

Then she noticed that Walker had stopped. He stood half-way between the kiln and the low mound of firewood, his arms

sagging under their load, his legs almost buckling. She leaned
forward, keen to catch every falter and pitch of his collapse, to
know his limit.

He lifted his eyes to the sky above the ridge and she looked
up, too. The grey smoke was whitening. His back straightened.
He threw off the load of wood and went back for more. And so
he carried on, maintaining the temperature at its peak while she
lay on the ferns, squinting through the tangle of brush. As the
horizon paled, he uncorked the bottle of sake and sprinkled it
over a last splinter of kindling, then he kissed it, and slid it into
the fire, a final offering.

It was done. She didn't need to watch him cap the chimney
and mud over the mouth-hole and the draft ports, sealing in the
vapours. She knew he'd stay on the ridge until the air inside the
kiln had cooled, until the ash and the suffocating smoke had been
drawn into whatever skin on the figure was still bare. He would
wait the days, the hours, the exact minutes until the chimney
could be opened, the fire-mouth unsealed, then he'd burrow into
the tunnel, cooled to the warmth of his own blood, and brush
aside the ash that would be banked against the walls, drifted
across the warrior like the dust of a thousand years.

She left, then, pushing back through the woods, weak with
hunger and something else — a smouldering fury. Alone in their
bed, she felt too agitated to sleep. When her eyes finally closed,
her dreams were bitter, restless meanderings and she woke with
the notion seared more deeply into her thoughts, that there was

no place for her, he'd made no place for her, she'd made no place for herself.

Days later, when he opened the kiln, the sun was just about to set. By the time he eased the figure out, all she could see in the odd, angled light was the rough outline of a woman, bulbous in proportion. Shame flushed through her. The contours were those of the Venus of Madawaska he'd made that autumn afternoon as she posed by the fire.

He lifted the torso gently in his arms and carried it up the ridge, mounting it on the pedestal he'd set at the top, then he bent to the cloth that she knew would be laid out on the stone, bits of coloured glass and metal lined up, ready to be set into the finished clay. He worked by moonlight and the embers of his fire rising into the sky. The light flickering over the surface revealed nothing, though she stood fixed among the cedars, straining to see.

She waited until the sky began to lighten and Walker lay collapsed on his sleeping bag before she crept up the ridge. She moved forward slowly, watching the rise and fall of his chest to make certain he remained asleep. His body looked small and wasted, curled in its cocoon, and she felt an urge to lie down beside him, but the figure drew her. It faced out over the trees, its pedestal moved so close to the lip of the stone that all she could see was a profile, a silhouette against the brightening sky. She made her way down the ridge and circled through the woods until she could see the form above her, rising from the granite.

A pale radiance played across the surface, glinting off the saw chain that lay like a confession across the headless clavicle. Beads of crimson resin spilled from the breasts. The rounded belly was split wide, sliced from pubis to breastbone, a jagged incision wedged open by two disembodied hands, one pulling at the softly rounded form inside, the other clenched and plunging, forcing it back in.

She let out a cry. But Walker was already staggering from his bed, hands clasped together, elbows locked, the blow coming from the side, and she stumbled out of the way as the figure reeled and fell tumbling over the edge, smashing onto the bank behind her as she ran, fragments scattering across the mud, splashing into the stream.

Alyson would never mention to Walker what she had seen on the ridge.

After the trembling stopped and the shock of it passed, after she'd managed to assure herself that the figure had nothing to do with her, that it was a product of his artistic vision, still she was left with the feeling that something inside her had shattered, too, the pieces so alarmingly sharp that she didn't dare try to fit them together, though she carried them with her, thinking there might come a time when she would be able to make some sense of them.

Weeks later, when she happened upon the shards of fired clay in the shadow of the ridge, she wasn't thinking of Walker at all. She was thinking of Margaret MacBayne, of the place she'd read about in the back of the book — *the hidden Garden I made in the meadow beyond the Cedars, at the farthest edge of Harry's land* — wondering where it could be, following the lead of the stream through the woods. The bank was slippery where Walker had dug into it, and so she was moving carefully, conscious of her footing. Otherwise she might have stumbled on the ragged bits of pottery strewn among the stones, larger pieces littering the bank ahead, and in the stream, under the veil of rushing water, curves that looked like a woman's, though she no longer thought of them as hers.

She made a wide arc around the debris and continued west along the stream past the cedar swamp. On the other side was a grassy meadow, a small clearing in the woods raised here and there with hummocks that had always looked to her like old beaver lodges in a dried-up pond. In the ten years she'd lived in the north, she'd seen how streams could jump their banks and slowly drain, cattails sprouting and decomposing, wildflowers taking root, then shrubby trees, conifers, stripling maples, the forest determined in its sovereignty. Though perhaps, just this once, she thought, it might allow a woman her garden.

She pushed through the tall grasses, through the blackbirds and sparrows that whirred up startled from their nests. She kept her eyes on the vegetation at her feet, looking for what, she wasn't sure. Not neat rows of herbs, certainly. The garden Margaret planted would have long since disappeared. But it was possible that some persistent root or tendril, some errant seeds had survived to make a scattered planting of their own.

Black-eyed Susans, blue speedwell, daisies, Queen Anne's lace. The wildflowers caught her eye first, then the coarse leaves once used as herbs. Nettle, lamb's-quarters, plantain. Some were native, and some had been brought by the first settlers, the plants spreading faster than the farmers until they'd colonized every roadside and field. She'd made a point of learning the distinction, walking the woods and meadows with a field guide in one hand, pioneer reminiscences in the other. She'd had the idea she would get a special book and sketch every species that grew on their land, but she had not started soon enough, the forest bursting into bloom just when there was so much else to do, and then it seemed she would never catch up, so she didn't bother to begin. Which was too bad, she was thinking as she moved across the meadow, for if she had followed her inclination, she might have already seen what she was looking for, bending into the grasses, peering through the snarl of stems — something distinctive, a plant peculiar to that place.

From then on, she spent most of her day there, leaning into the grasses, her father's watch swaying on its chain. She'd taken to wearing it again, a reminder to be back in her gardens at the house by the time Walker was out of bed, for they had resumed their old routines. Her heart was no longer in it, but still, she kept to the established order of things, the evening meal they shared, the hours they spent together before they each went to their work. She'd read once that the gestures of the body can act as a catalyst for certain states of mind, so that by sitting up straight and smiling a person who is unhappy will feel better almost at once. She thought perhaps it was working, for she seemed to move more easily through the days, though when she returned to the house, she could feel the alteration where the pattern, once broken, had been fitted back in place, the features of her face too rigidly aligned, her lips drawn thin, her gaze veering off at odd angles whenever Walker was in the room.

It was only on her own in the meadow that her muscles loosened, massaged by the sudden warmth of June and the meanders of her search. She wandered knoll to knoll, her skirt swishing in the grass, the soft fabric a consolation against her legs. She was thinking it wouldn't matter if she ever found what she was looking for, she could go on like that forever, wandering until the point of the search was lost. And then one day, in a hollow at the edge of the meadow, she drew apart the grasses and saw a reddish stalk, the leaves a bit like celery, the flowers more like dill, chartreuse umbels just about to open.

Lovage. It was a poor, frail specimen, but she knew it right away. She'd seen it growing behind Renata's compost, shooting up ten feet or more before it had to be hacked down just to keep it contained. The plant was so unruly in its habit that she'd never dared to grow it, even though it was supposed to be a tonic for women, one of the amulet herbs once worn between the breasts, an inducement to good fortune. And there it was, poking up through the sod. She fell to her knees, tearing at the grass that choked it, praising the ruddy stalk for its vigour, its stubborn perseverance.

As soon as she spotted the lovage, other plants came into view. Some reddish mint by the stream. On the opposite side of the meadow, a low bush of tormentil. At the crest of the hummocks, hyssop and lemon balm. In a boggy spot by the cedars, a low mat of mother-of-thyme. A stem of sweetbrier rose entwined in the collapsed rail fence at the boundary of their land. And scattered here and there, what she thought must be field pansies, the old heart's-ease.

She tore strips from the bottom of her skirt and tied them to the shafts of grasses near each plant. The ragged ribbons flickered behind her as she hurried back along the stream, worrying that the wind would unravel her hasty knots or that the crows and blackbirds would tug them loose to line their nests, and she'd never find the herbs again.

That evening, she made small talk with Walker in the way she'd taught herself to do, filling up their time together with inconsequential matters, taking care not to let the meadow tumble out, for fear he'd give it another meaning, a crazy woman alone in a field tearing her skirt to shreds. They sat in their places, moving food from their plates to their mouths, taking turns with the condiments, their hands extending cautiously into the common space between them.

Then he said, I've had enough.

She thought he meant, enough of the way things were with them, and she was taken aback by the bluntness of his words. She had assumed she would be the one to say it, if either of them did, and she knew she never would. The sentence sounded too dramatic, too direct for the two of them. It belonged in a movie or in a book, where characters confronted each other and said what was in their hearts. In real life, important things were held inside. You carried on.

He didn't wait for a response. I made you enough garden planters for the summer, he was saying, but when they're gone, that's it. I've closed up the studio.

So. While she was searching in the meadow, he'd been shaping the last of the clay, packing his tools in boxes, something he'd done countless times before, growing discouraged, giving up. And she thought: it was because of the smashed figure. It had been too much, even for him.

But he was saying something else.

He'd taken a job with Sauvage, working in the gravel pit. He told her about the shed where he'd sit all day, tallying the loads the trucks hauled, a separate column in the ledger for each grade of gravel – armour stone, clear stone, round stone, pea gravel, crusher run of all dimensions, stone dust, screenings, sharp sand, river stone. While she thought he was building pots, he'd been studying in his studio, learning to identify the trucks he named off for her, single axle, tandem axle, tri-axle dumpers, belly dumps and pups, live-bottoms and stone slingers, ten-yard, eighteen-yard, twenty-two-yard loads. If he ever got a driver's licence, maybe he'd find something else, but for now, he'd walk to the job in the pit, taking the bush road through the woods. I start tomorrow, he said.

So, she thought with a confusing sense of disappointment and relief. Not the end, after all.

She didn't set out to recreate what she would come to think of as Margaret MacBayne's garden. One day she was still looking for proof that the herbs she'd found were the scattered relics of that old planting, and the next she was digging up the grass, clearing a swath beside the lovage, loosening the soil in a rectangle just big enough for those few rescued plants. Though the bed was small, the work was hard, for the grass was densely matted in the earth.

Sometimes, when she paused to rest, if the wind was blowing just right, she'd hear the grinding gears of a truck moving out of the pit, and she'd think of Walker, see him crouched in the stone archway of that door the day they met, terrified by the traffic, his hand gripping his chest. The same hand that carved the shape inside a clay woman's belly. The hand that made it monstrous. That swept through the morning sky, raining shards down on her. And what began as melting sympathy would harden, becoming dry and brittle, and she'd wait until it was like sand blowing from a distance, something she could turn her back on, and only then would she resume her work.

She gave herself over to the herbs she'd discovered. She dug the lovage up first, bathing it in the stream, gently palpating the roots until she had freed them of every clot of dark earth, every strand of meadow grass. The tenderness of her ministrations opened a well of sadness in her, and she recalled bending over her baby, cleaning the blood and filaments of mucous from her skin, swathing her in flannelette, watching as her eyelids closed, her tiny fingers stretching as her body settled into sleep. Though she wept at the memory, she felt a certain solace, too, and she made a habit of it, then, lingering each day on one particular or another, the damp wisps of amber hair, the kiss of tiny lips on her breast, living a lifetime in every detail, so that she went about her work feeling heartsore but not unhappy.

The plants she moved took root again. The leaves brightened. Fresh growth appeared. Perhaps it was the sight of that vibrant green against the bare, tended earth, or the familiar motions of her hands in the soil, but it wasn't long before she felt an urge to return to the gardens she'd abandoned by the house.

A litter of weeds had sprung up through the mulch. Even the hardy sage and oregano were all but obscured by the growth that had run wild during that cool, moist spring. In some ways, though, the weather had worked in her favour. If she'd planted at her usual time, at the end of May, she would have lost her seedlings to a killing frost in early June, but, as it was, neglect had put her as far ahead as diligence. There was a lesson in that, she thought, as she began to clear away the mess.

Within weeks the household gardens were thriving again, though they were nothing like the plans she'd drawn in the ripe days of her pregnancy. Everything from that time had been closed up and stored away, the ideas kept in quarantine as if infected with a virus that could be contracted simply by revisiting a thought. Only the seedlings had survived, rescued by Renata from the greenhouse. When Alyson phoned, it was Abe who brought them back. Renata had been called home, he said, an illness in the family.

Alyson felt a moment's guilt, then relief that her seclusion would go unnoticed, for her days were full again, her time divided between the meadow and the gardens by the house. The ache she allowed herself to feel as she moved among Margaret's herbs, scaled over as she worked near the house. There was a ruthlessness about her there, a hardness to her heart that she might have found alarming if she had thought it affected anything but the insects that preyed on her plants. Once it would have worried her as she soaped down the nasturtiums, sending thousands of aphids to a slippery death, what their place in the cosmos might be. But she no longer gave it a thought. She took delight in finding ways to dispatch her garden's enemies, squeezing their round little bodies, snipping longer ones in two, smearing caterpillars between two stones, crushing larvae in the folds of their nursery leaves.

But in the meadow, she was still the person she had always known herself to be. She would wake early and slip from the quilts, race out into the birdsong, stopping at the cabin to collect the old cookbook, then she'd hurry on to the little herb bed, arriving just before the sun rose. She'd wait until she saw a sliver of gold above the trees, then kick off her boots and step onto the bare soil, flexing her toes in the cool earth, feeling it rub against her arch, and she'd stand there among the plants she had rescued until the last of her rat's-claw dreams drained away.

She'd start each day with a reading. Just a paragraph, a sentence or two, the selections growing shorter until a phrase or sometimes a word was sufficient to inspire her imaginings. She'd lie back in the grass and see Margaret in the distance, foraging for mushrooms, or her brothers choosing rowan trees at the verge of the woods.

When the sun reached a certain height – caught between two tall Scots pines – she'd walk back to the house, returning the book to its hiding place on her way. She felt revived by what she conjured, by the strength and resilience of the young woman. And she recalled how she'd been sustained by the horticultural studies she had thrown herself into after her father's death. All through that agonizing autumn, she'd travelled the paths through the city's ravines, wrestling with the particulars of plant taxonomy, morphology, anatomy, physiology, absorbing herself in the rise of moisture through a stalk, in the slow pirouette of leaves turning to the sun, in the way a stem grows, not pushing straight ahead but scribing a spiral through the air, a process called nutation. In both instances, she thought, it was the language that drew her in — tropism, guttation, inflorescence, saddlebacks and chicots, cataplasm, cathartic, crone — but it was the stories that kept her there long enough to heal.

By the time Walker left for work, she'd be back in her gardens by the house, patrolling the paths, her eyes scrutinizing the rows. She'd notice that the carrots were ready for thinning, the radishes wanted pulling, and she'd see up ahead that the lettuces needed weeding, it was time to seed another bed of cilantro. Her thoughts would thicken with all that had to be done, the work appearing before her like so many brightly coloured beads to be ordered, slid into position in her day. And her body, so recently one with the cool, damp soil, would coil with the energy that would propel her through those tasks and she'd welcome it, having been without desire or determination for all those unspeakable months.

She'd straighten as Walker called his goodbye, watching as he disappeared up the path into the bush, then she'd turn toward the shed, gathering her trowel and snips, her cotton gloves, her weeding tools and seeds, and carrying them back to the gardens in the wicker basket Walker bought her at a fall fair where a spirited old man had set the basket on its side and jumped up and down on the interwoven twigs, proving to her how strong it was, how much it could withstand.

You can't keep to yourself forever, Renata was saying, and she was thinking, why not?

But her friend would not be distracted.

Do it as a favour to the rest of us. We miss you.

It was the thought of all those open arms, falling into them, that swayed her, although driving up to Bear Mountain for the midsummer party, she imagined them differently, the women clustered at the end of the road, their arms crossed or held slack, waiting, murmuring, what a shame she lost the baby, as though she'd been careless and misplaced it, didn't deserve to have it even if it could be found.

But only Renata rushed up to greet her.

I'm going to steal this beautiful woman, she said to Walker. You've been hogging her long enough. And she leaned into Alyson, kissing her and whispering, Let's go somewhere quiet.

Alyson followed, grateful for the narrow path that required her to walk behind, alone. The sight of so many people made her dizzy. A kaleidoscope of human bodies incessantly shifting, breaking apart, forming again around the bonfire, the food table, the tubs of beer. Men throwing Frisbees, playing hacky-sack. Someone strumming a guitar, tuning a violin. Yae rubbing citronella on guests as they arrived. People spreading out across the yard, spilling into the lake, the air charged with a buzzing sound, like white noise, she was thinking, though it didn't seem white to her.

Renata kept up a steady monologue as she led the way to the flat stones tucked out of sight above the lake, never breaking the ribbon of words that Alyson knew was meant to bind her there, to the place they'd met, wrapping her in their friendship as if nothing had changed, as if she didn't remember the plan they had made six months before, when they'd looked ahead to the summer, to sitting on those very stones, their children on their knees. The madonnas of Bear Mountain, they'd laughed, though her motherhood had felt sacred to her then, everlasting.

She drew in a breath and pulled it deep into her lungs, thinking of Margaret MacBayne, the enduring herbs. But no sooner did she ease her muscles back to where they belonged than her limbs drew themselves together again, legs crossing, spine curving, arms circling her knees, her body folding into itself, enclosing her heart in a basin of bone, as if it were likely to split open.

Renata was telling her about her mother, the sudden stroke she'd had, how worried they'd all been, though the hardy old soul was already walking, scrawling messages on her little chalkboard, telling everyone she was fine.

Renata leaned forward. And how are you doing? I'm sorry I had to leave you like that.

That's okay. Don't worry. I'm good now, she said, letting her gaze drift past Renata toward the moon. She'd never seen it so full, she thought. It seemed ripe to bursting, hanging there above the water, draining its thick light over the swimmers below. Darkness had a way of smoothing out contours, flattening perspective, but the moonlight that night raised into high relief every convolution of the human form. It made her think of something Walker once said, after he'd talked the Faculty of Medicine into letting him study dissection with the student doctors. He'd come rushing into the bookstore where she worked, going on about the inter- lace of arteries, tendons, and muscles, the cat's cradle of organs, the way bones articulated in their sockets, exhilarated by how all the parts fit together to make a curve, a crevice, a fold, and he'd grabbed her hands, looking straight into her eyes, something he almost never did, saying, I've found a landscape I can lose myself in. And looking at the swimmers, she thought she understood.

Just the women were in the water, a few already far out in the lake, waving to those who paddled near the rocks or sat dangling their legs. The only one she recognized was Yae, not by her face, but by her hair, a drape of dark silk down her back. The woman leaned forward to scoop water in her hands and the veil parted, exposing her buttocks, narrow as a man's, moon-shadows catch- ing at the ridges of vertebrae, sculpting her spine.

Yae was turning to call up to someone on the rocks above the lake. Alyson craned her neck to look and saw Walker stepping back among the trees. At the sight of him, something inside her clamped shut, as if beneath her woman's skin lay a beetle's shell, shiny and black, snapping to, sheathing her vulnerable parts. Though at the same time, she felt a softening, a desire to spread the shell open. And the confusion of feelings must have shown on her face, for Renata was reaching out to her, grasping her arm.

Alyson, answer me, what's wrong?

Look, I'm sorry, she said, shaking Renata off and heading toward the path. I'm just not ready for this.

Safe inside the van, the two of them alone on the vacant road, she let the softening take its course. She forgot Walker's complicity, thought of him solely as a comrade, a fellow survivor of a disaster they had narrowly escaped, not unscathed, but not fatally damaged either. No permanent scars beyond the dull ache of her heart. They didn't speak, but the way he'd put his arm around her and guided her back to the van, the way he'd buckled her into the passenger seat and taken the wheel himself, the way he brought her hand to his thigh and capped it with his own, asking nothing of her, especially that, made her long for their old love, lopsided with hope and a faith, she thought, that might be justified after all.

That night, they made love. When he slid her nightgown up her thighs, she relaxed her legs, allowed her knees to fall open. She turned to face him, relieved to let herself be comforted at last, craving the touch of his body along the full length of hers, a gentle pressure shoulder to toe, hands and fingers coming later, their love consoling, slow and cautious, both of them willing to let the moment ripen. But he was already pushing into her, and she wanted to call out, wait!, but it was too late, he was plunging inside her, and though she resisted, the thought overwhelmed her that what had grown tender was wilting, wadding deep, compressing to a weight that she would carry inside her forever.

Faith. In her mother's mouth, the word acquired a certain taint. Faith was something to be salted away against future need, drawn on sparingly. Another sort of accounting. When your life gets hard, her mother told her, faith will make up the difference.

Her aunt had offered her another image. Faith is like a shrub in bloom, she said. The more you pick the flowers, the faster they come. Catherine had warned her of the dormant times, long months when it would seem that faith had withered and died. But it will revive, she assured her, hugging her close that last night on the farm. One day you'll see a small, bright spot, and before you know it, the world will seem a lovely place again.

But nothing had come of the faint glimmer she'd seen as she drove home with Walker from the party. He'd fallen asleep without a word, and though she'd lain awake half the night, having conversations with him in her head, by morning she'd settled back into the silence she forged for herself the day she burst into the kitchen and Walker had turned on her that look of his, wanting more from her than she knew how to give. For months, she'd been trying to work her way out, but there she was again, alone inside herself.

Her mood turned restless, her outlook bleak. When she pressed her toes into the bare soil of the herb bed in the meadow, she felt no release. On that morning, for the first time, Margaret kept her distance, a shadowy woman among the trees.

It was time for the summer harvest, and for a while, she kept up with the work. She trimmed back the oregano and thyme,

pinched the flower stalks off the basil, sowed new beds of coriander, arugula, and fall fennel, though often, she would begin a
task, become distracted, and start another that she'd abandon,
nothing keeping her attention for long, so that the cut herbs
withered where she heaped them on the terrace walls and seeds
sprouted in the packages left out in the rain. She felt an empti-
ness opening up inside her, and with it came a craving, for what
she couldn't tell. One day the thought came to her that if she
could just find a hairpin or a button, some small token to carry
with her, secreted in her clothes, in her fist, she might be able to
hold the bolstering example of Margaret MacBayne close.

Before the notion could slip away or crumble, she gathered
the rake, a pick, and a shovel from the shed and loaded them
into the wheelbarrow along with a ball of twine, a bundle of stakes,
and headed into the woods. The undergrowth had reclaimed the
clearing she'd made around the cabin, snaking up the logs,
sprawling over the pile of stones. She urged herself into the work,
pulling out the wild blackberry, the stinging nettle, the snakeroot, retracing the path to the stream, raking the bank where she
thought the graveyard would likely have been.

When she'd laid bare the ground within the fallen walls
again, she hammered in the wooden stakes and stretched the
twine between, marking the soil into squares. Then she started
shovelling. She excavated each square in turn, digging down a
foot, breaking up the clods with the heel of her boot, pitching
the crumbled earth into the air, determined that nothing

would escape her, not a splinter, not a nail. The work was oddly calming. It took the edge off her agitation and moulded it into expectation, her heart lifting each time she thought she glimpsed a rim of china or heard the high-pitched ring of steel on forged iron.

There was something wilful about soil, she thought, the way it made things disappear. More like water than stone. Always on the move, pushing rocks up to the surface, dragging anything left lying about down into the depths.

A dropped comb, a forgotten pie pan set out for the rain to lift a stubborn crust, they'd be buried now, but how deep? The archeologists who excavated the ruins of Troy had laid bare one city wall, then another, and another, until they'd unearthed the crumpled ramparts of nine ancient cities, one on top of the other, the earth constantly flowing in, covering up.

She had witnessed the same slow accretion in her gardens. Each spring she would heap a three-foot mulch of rotted hay around her plants, and by September the soil would be bare again, every bit of organic matter absorbed, the level of the ground rising higher every year until now, after a decade, it was mounded like raised beds. In Japan, garden designers took this into account, anticipating even the lichen that would dissolve the rocks to soil, preparing for the moment, three hundred years hence, when the garden they conceived would reach perfection.

It was bad enough, she thought, pitching down her shovel in despair, that wood rotted, buildings collapsed, that relics were swept away or buried, but the landscape itself was shifting, hills flattening, lakes filling in, each becoming the other.

If that was the case, what hope was there for her?

She no longer trusted herself. She'd always been so sensible, but something had come undone.

She tried to stopper her thoughts, stopper her mouth. She would think she had done it, kept it all inside, then Walker would come through the door and she'd find herself muttering deprecations, accusations, vituperations under her breath. She'd glance at him, thinking that surely he must have heard, but his head would be bent over a magazine or over his plate. She'd feel the anger pounce on her then, fierce and full-blooded, from where it lay in wait, hidden on the beams overhead or behind the woodstove or under her bed, ready to leap at any minute, take her in its grip, the way she had gripped the nightgown her mother sent for her birthday, infuriated by the fabric, rampant with grinning cherubs, the feeling of the cloth yielding in her hands so deeply satisfying that she hoped the tearing would never end, though when it did, she felt sick with the thought of what she had done, of what she might do.

She bound herself more tightly then, removed herself farther, to a safer distance. She refused the messages from Dorothy, who called to say the elderberries were ripe, and from Réal, who had something to show her, and from Renata, who asked again and again to come to visit. When she spoke to Walker, she took care with her words, not wanting him to know how altered she was, in case that hollowed-out feeling would one day crack open and she'd fill up with herself again, take her place in their life, the gardener and the potter, going on as always.

# MARGARET

*1 8 6 6 - 1 8 6 9*

The years slip by like a stream.

Margaret thinks often of her mother's adage, what is full can be emptied and what seems empty once was full. Her mother intended it as a warning against conjecture and conceit, but the phrase fits perfectly with how Margaret sees her forest now, filled with Zahgahseega's faerie folk, all but empty of her tribe, forever empty of her darling Ewan, emptying quickly of trees, filling up with all manner of people on the move.

Hardly a winter's day passes now without the echo of a distant axe to accompany her clicking needles. And hardly a month goes by without a stranger at her door. The first was a young mapmaker who claimed to be walking every road and uncut line from Georgian Bay to the Ottawa River, comparing what he observed with his own eyes against the jagged lines and notes marked on the sheaf of maps protruding from his pack. He spent a day on her river rock, sketching her cabin and its dooryard drifted with snow. In exchange for a plate of stew, he gave her one of his drawings, which she pinned to the wall over the crack in the logs where she hides her mother's cookery book.

Once, Harry came, taking a detour from the Opeongo Road as he walked south to Renfrew with his young son and a frail, listless wife whose shallow breaths pressed her brother too quickly on his way, leaving Margaret with a fearsome loneliness such as she hadn't known since her first winter alone. Her spirits flagged for days until she came across the old tin whistle she used to play, remembering how Harry would dance, twirling in front of her, her fingers flickering over the slender reed, spinning out the tunes that kept him singing, and she played all the jigs and reels, feeling him there in the cabin again.

Later that same year, there was Holy Marks, an itinerant in rags who offered for a dollar to enter in the family Bible the names of her loved ones buried in the graves by the river. The letters he showed her were the most beautiful she had ever seen, but she closed the door on him abruptly, unwilling to let him witness her tears. There were parties of hunters and sightseers who paddled her river, occasionally a pedlar of tin pots and cloth, and once a travelling naturalist, who called himself a collector of curiosities, though he seemed ripe for collecting himself, with his orange homespun trowsers, a jacket to his knees, and a red jelly-bag cap perched on his head, the wide leather belt strapped around his waist hung with the oddest assortment of tools she had ever seen, and in his hand, a gun taller than the man by half.

Margaret has become something of a curiosity herself. With Ewan buried in the ground, she took up his clothing, pressing her skin against his outline, making it hers. What began as a comfort is now her habit – a bright flannel shirt, grey lumberman's trowsers patched until hardly a scrap shows of his mother's worsted cloth, and on the coldest days, his old blanket coat tied with the scarlet sash that was a gift from Peter Constant. When her boots wore through, she took to wearing *mukaseens* laced to the knee, and in winter, mitts that Zahgahseega made for her from the hide of a moose. In summer she smears her skin with bear grease against the insects, and she leaves her hair long and loose to curl down her back, catching twigs and flying beetles as she strides through the forest, gathering wild herbs.

The empty places in her heart she fills with the plants she gleans and the ones she sows in the meadow, brewing the petals, leaves, and roots into infusions and decoctions, tinctures, extracts, and fomentations, refining their properties, noting the efficacy of each in the back of her mother's book. Sage to make a gargle to strengthen a strained voice, marsh mallows for a demulcent tea, lemon balm to provoke a sweat. Centaury to cleanse the kidneys. Sweet fennel and thyme as antiseptics for every sort of scrape and burn. Comfrey to wrap a bruise. Chamomile for colicky pains caused by wind around the navel. Wintersweet to counter deep-hearted, melancholic sighs.

Through the summers she tolerates her brothers' presence, restored by the long, sweet months when they are gone. She sees the way they look at her when they think she is busy with the pots by the fire. She sees the glances they exchange when they think her head is bowed.

They judge her peculiar, and she counts them beneath her notice.

In the tenth spring, the brothers return from the camp earlier than is their custom. Their arrival catches Margaret unprepared, though they don't seem to notice the unfamiliar arrangement of the furnishings in the cabin. They are too preoccupied with their own affairs to wonder at the way she bustles about, shifting chairs, shoving baskets and bottles under the table, setting out saucers for their pipes, digging in the barrel for a slab of venison to put on to boil. Their meal is finished and the three of them are settled by the fire before Margaret learns what weighs so heavily on their minds – the lumber business is failing, sawlogs are piled high, their winter work is at an end, they say, for as far into the future as anyone can predict.

They clear a pause for her response, but she says nothing, for she has taken to refusing such unspoken invitations, a form of retribution none the less sweet for all that it is unknown to them. She keeps her features smooth until they resume their conversation, then she pulls her knitting into her lap, grateful for the steadying rhythm of wool over polished wood and for a pattern sufficiently difficult to justify the crease of anxious concentration that spreads across her forehead.

It is only when she is lying under her quilts, listening to her brothers sleep, that she feels her own breaths shorten, feels the muscles of her belly contract as if she has eaten something sour, impossible to digest. The wall that looms beside her bed seems about to tumble down on her. She resists the impression for as long as she can, then she tugs her plaid tight around her and creeps on tiptoe out the door.

She paces up and down the clearing, river to forest, cabin to barn. She thinks of going to the garden, the moon is full enough to light the way, but she doesn't dare for fear her brothers will waken and find her missing, come searching after her. That is the thing that tugs at her belly, always the men to consider now, every independence won by stealth.

But stealth is something she knows, a skill she honed as a child on the braes. She recalls the nights she sneaked out of the stone cottage to track nightjars as they churred through the moonlight to their eggs laid bare on the stones, and she stops her pacing, fixes her eyes on the cabin, her ears keen to every sound. With measured steps, she backs slowly into the woods, slipping deep

among the trees, retreating into the darkness until the fumes of
the hearth fire give way and she smells nothing but the night fragrance of the earth.

She waits amid the pines and elms and maples as in the
company of dear friends. When she feels herself again, she steals
back to her bed, where she falls asleep at once, though her dreams
are restless, strewn about with obstacles that hinder her passage
as she wanders a maze where the possibilities are endless but
there are few escapes.

William and Robert take up their farm chores as they do every
spring. To Margaret, the days seem to go on much as before.
There are differences, but she does not judge them significant.

In the time between planting and harvest, the brothers work
close to home. No new fields are cleared. Instead, they extend a
verandah at the front of the cabin. They cut the grease-paper out
of the windows and purchase glass to install in its place. They
spend two weeks widening the lane from the clearing to the line
cut through the forest where they expect the side road will be
opened one day soon. These improvements give the place an air
of prosperity, though stones and stumps still clog the fields and
the yield of winter wheat, barley-corn, and root vegetables is
hardly yet sufficient to carry the three of them through a winter.

When Margaret overhears them discussing a fence to mark

the boundary of their land, she worries they'll take the cedar rails from the stand near her meadow, stumbling upon her *weegawum* and the garden she has kept hidden so well from them. In the end, they cut them from trees closer to the road, but though her nervous trepidation lessens, her mind is never free of the fear that her secret will be known.

She grows cautious in her movements, timing her visits to the garden to coincide with customary excursions into the woods to gather leeks for a spring soup, or blueberries for a cobbler, slippery jacks, milkcaps, and blewits to dry for winter stews, making certain to tell her brothers where she is going and why, though she wonders that they don't comment on her sudden fondness for every sort of woodland mushroom.

She often catches William studying her out of the corner of his eye, and more than once, he remarks on the frequency of her absences. His observations so unsettle her that in midsummer, when the herbs need her constant attention, she waits until her brothers sleep, then she slips out of the cabin to harvest the leaves by moonlight, hanging them to dry on thin poles mounted wall to wall inside her *weegawum*. Every night, she spends in the meadow, even when there is little to do but wander the paths, brushing the low bushes with her fingers, releasing healing fragrances to the air. Occasionally the brothers come upon her napping during the day, and then she makes a show of her complaints — sleeplessness, something she ate, the screech owl whose eerie call kept her anxious through the night. But the truth is, she can't bear to leave the garden before the sun begins to rise, her love of the place deepening the more it is circumscribed.

As if sensing the changes in the routines of the clearing, Zahgahseega stays away. Margaret no longer hears her greetings drifting through the woods, although she often stops to listen, thinking she hears in a dove's coo-coo her friend's soft voice, for she craves the conversations, the stories they shared.

Then one day, while William and Robert are far down the lane, Zahgahseega steps into the clearing. The forest is on fire, she says. The places where she made her camps are open fields now. Her people are being settled onto land that has been surveyed and fenced.

She lays in Margaret's hands an owlskin bag worked with quills in the shape of a leaf. She'll veer to the north, she says, disappear among the trees.

*Where my brothers employed Addition, Multiplication — more land, more logs, more wheat — I found use only for Subtraction, one Parting after another, Loss upon Loss upon Loss. In the end, it becomes Habit, how you calculate your Lot in the World.*

Not until the nights grow longer than the days and the weather begins to cool does Margaret fully grasp the consequences of her brothers' continued presence. Soon, the three of them will spend whole days huddled together before the fire, weeks when blizzards rage so wild that even journeys to the barn or the privy will require strict adherence to the worn path. Her footsteps through the snow will tell the tale of her visits to the garden, the hand-fasting oak, the graveyard by the river.

Nothing will be hers. Not the food they eat, for she will prepare the joints they prefer, instead of the delicate soups with which she has learned to sustain herself. Not the arrangement of the room, for everything will stay as it is, positioned for their comfort and convenience. The air will always smell of their labouring bodies, of their pipes and purchased tobacco, not of the fragrant herbs she likes to puff in the evenings or the fomentations and decoctions that occupy her through the coldest season.

It is time, she decides, to press forward her plan to make her own way in the world.

She finds her chance in late August when William and Robert leave for Renfrew to purchase the winter supplies. They won't be back, they say, for a week. As soon as they are gone, Margaret gathers her harvest from the *weegawum* and carries it into the house. She works swiftly, wrapping leaves and flower heads, bits of bark and slivered root in the small squares of muslin she found among her mother's things, saving them for no reason other than that they had belonged to her.

On the last morning, she clears away the empty baskets and arranges the muslin twists in neat rows across the table. In front of each, she stands a card that she letters in maple-bark ink.

*Oak Bark: Gargle decoction for Sore Throat. Apply to Sores on Man or Beast.*

*Parsley: Drink freely of infusion for Dropsy, painful urine. Bruised leaves applied as fomentation cure the bites and stings of insects.*

*Pipsissewa: Sip tea to relieve the Rheumatism.*

*Wild Geranium: Strong infusion for Ague, the curing of the Flux. For children, boil in milk, give by teaspoon.*

*Wissakaypuckkay: Take infusion for Headache, disorders of the Nerves.*

On a slat from a crate she finds upturned in the piggery, she paints in letters so large it seems immodest, MARGARET MACBAYNE — SIMPLES FOR ALL AFFLICTIONS, then she props her sign amongst the herbs, and steps back to admire her display, imagining it on the counters of the general stores in Sebastapol, Harriet's Corners, Hopefield, Newfoundout, all the settlements her brothers have told her are springing up along the Opeongo Road. She imagines the mothers with sick children, fathers and husbands desperate to stay healthy to clear their fields within the allotted time, women struggling to carry on though their joints ache and their bodies weep strange fluids. She imagines them making their way along the side road, cleared wide and smooth, past her brothers' tall houses, each with a wife on the doorstep and a clutch of children in the yard, past their neat, prosperous homesteads to her place among the trees. The sick, the anxious, the down-hearted, the lonely: she will heal them all.

There is to be no ship's canal. No Bell's Line. Not the grand thoroughfare the Crown agent promised, opening up the wilderness from west to east.

This is the news the brothers carry back with them from Renfrew, conveying the first of it to Margaret as they lower themselves into the chairs she set on the verandah in anticipation of their return, planning to welcome them with mugs of sumac cider, allowing them to refresh themselves from their journey before she ushers them inside, before she leads them to her secret garden, shows them her *weegawum* hung with drying plants. She is thinking how astonished they will be at her ingenuity, how they will praise her enterprise, thankful to be released at last from the burden of their spinster sister, happy to raise a cabin for her on the land that was her dowry — she imagines it all as she waits for them to finish, though she is listening to them, too, for there is more.

No side road will be cut to join their clearing to the Opeongo. The land is too rough. Too many roads have already been opened into land unfit for tilling, that is how the postmaster put it, and the decision is his to make.

A road or a path, it hardly matters to Margaret, though she observes her brothers are undone by the changes they report, for they are flushed and glance often at each other, as if to verify what they've learned. In the village, they found only a handful of new settlers where before crowds were clamouring for land. Men who struggled to clear their twelve acres were giving up and moving out, defeated by the winters, the meagre harvests, the voracious insects, the resistant, abundant stone. Bush lots were being abandoned up and down the Opeongo, the road to their prosperity now a path to ruin.

They take turns with the conversation, handing it back and forth between them with such skill that it is some time before she understands that this is a display they have prepared on their own.

Territories in the west are being opened up for settlement, Robert says, describing with enthusiasm the fertile land, flat as the sea and as barren of trees.

Then William takes it up. The new land has none of the hardships of our current location, he says. No matter how diligently we labour at this holding, it will never yield much more than a harvest of stones.

We chose poorly, Robert admits.

And William agrees. For the price of our lots in the Madawaska, he says, we can buy a piece of prairie half the size of Fife.

*My* brothers, seeing no future here, posted our Land for Sale.
They took positions with a Timber merchant cutting farther North.
They signed me on as Cook.

I won't do it! she exclaims.

But their arguments are prepared. And suddenly, she sees it
all — the verandah, the window glass, the extended trip into
Renfrew — as part of their grand, dislocating scheme. Even her
hot reply.

It is her duty, they say. Just as it is theirs to carry forward their
father's dream to prosper in this new country. It is what their
mother would want, the family together wherever they may be.

Though she wails, they keep their voices level, repeating what
they'd heard their father say in Pittenweem: better women should
weep than bearded men.

At that, she calms herself.

Do as you please with your two lots, she says at last, I'll not
sell my land.

It is so clear in her mind she could draw it for them as a map.
Robert will be won over and against William she'll hold her
ground, ready for his rage, his cold insistence, ready for anything
but the quizzical look he lifts to her now.

Your land?

She reminds him of the dowry, Harry's land deeded to her,
and as she does, she feels that chill again, the one that caused her

to reach for Ewan's hand. It ripples down her arms, up her neck, over her scalp, as if her skin were splitting open, peeling back, for the land was Ewan's, he is saying, never hers. A woman cannot own property, it must be held in trust for her by a father, a husband, a brother, a man who has the right to sell, just as they have done, to an emigrant from Aberdeen, one George Christopher Pollock, who takes possession of their clearing and its three hundred acres at the end of the month.

She doesn't run far. She stops at the mountain ash, the one she begged her brothers to spare, the one from which she plucked the berries that hung over her mother's birthing bed. She lets go the tails of her shirt and the twists of muslin she scooped from the table tumble and scatter over the ground. She scrabbles through the packages, picking out borage to give her strength and lavender for energy, foxglove to stimulate her heart, mother-of-thyme to dispel her anguish, make her brave. She nibbles on the dry leaves, going over what her brothers said, going over it again until she catches it — a certain nervousness, a shifting look to William's eye, overshadowed in the moment by the authority of his voice, but there it is, planted in her memory, a slender impression that weighs more heavily than all his words.

She creeps up to a side window, the new glass thin as air, releasing all her brothers' words to her. The papers have not been signed, they haven't yet been drawn up, the brothers must return to Renfrew to make good the sale, not on the morrow, but on the day after that. Then their voices lower, as if they sense her crouching by the sill. The sentences drift out in fragments. . . . Uncertain of the law . . . what's best . . . no choice for her.

The plan comes to her whole. She'll find her way to Harry, he'll sign his lot to her. William and Robert will not prevent her going, she has the means to make certain of that.

She stands and moves toward the door, preparing her face, contrite though not submissive, reluctantly willing to do as they suggest. Perhaps, by the end of the day, some faint enthusiasm for their project. They will never guess she knows the truth. Their satisfaction at having their way will cloud their eyes and dull their brains, and it will never occur to them to wonder what a woman might do when she is betrayed.

# A L Y S O N

*1 9 9 1 - 1 9 9 2*

W hat is sufficient to grieve a death?

Give it time, the doctor said, Renata said, but how much time? Six months? Six years? Sixty? As long as the person was alive? And how to make that calculation? From the split second of conception? The moment of birth? And if you've had a hand in it, the living *and* the dying, how long then?

Alyson sat in the grass by the herb bed in the meadow, mired in questions she barely knew to ask. Where once she'd craved motion, now she sat in a stupor, barely breathing, her muscles numb. She felt stuck in the middle of something weighty and boundless, as if this grief had gathered to it every grief she'd ever known, the soil spread before her like a sea that, if she kept very still, would rise and drift over her, no ledge to reach for to pull herself out.

The torpor held her, unrelenting, through what was left of the summer and on into fall. It seemed an achievement just to make her way to the meadow and sit staring through the day. The rest of the time, she stayed in the house. Mostly she slept, long dreamless sleeps, as if exhausted by the labour of keeping so still.

She would never understand what it was, exactly, that roused her. One morning, she arrived to find the meadow bathed in a chill mist. When it cleared, the herbs she'd rescued hung wilted and blackened. Such a small loss, set against the others, yet it drew her, and she knelt in the bed, trimming off the damaged leaves, warming the plants with her breath, unwilling to let them go. She blamed herself. She'd bared the soil around the first plant she'd found, expanding the bed for the others, not considering the contour of the land, the way it would trap the first frigid autumn air.

Margaret MacBayne would never have planted there, she thought.

She stood and looked around, assessing the meadow through the other woman's eyes, searching for a gentle incline that would drain early frosts, a wall of forest to temper harsh westerly winds, water that would flow through the longest summer drought. And it appeared to her, then. A faint but definite image in the shape of a perfect square on the slope by the stream, in the lee of the sheltering elms. Margaret's garden.

She could do little that late in the season but trace the outline of what she'd seen and remove the grass within its boundaries, peeling the sod back like skin. Tentatively at first; then, with returning strength, she worked the soil, reviving it, kneading in leaves from the woods and rotting matter from the stream, grateful to be moving, to be thinking again.

The space was large, the base dimensions of a house. When she saw it that way, it occurred to her there should be rooms. She raked the ground smooth and staked two wide paths across it, one horizontal, the other vertical, dividing the soil into four smaller, equal squares. The design was less a conscious choice than a whim, yet looking at it she thought she couldn't have conceived of any better. For weren't there four seasons, four cardinal directions, the four elements of air, water, earth, and fire?

Where the paths crossed at the centre, she made a recess in the ground for a wooden seed flat and placed the old cookery book inside, wanting it near. She covered the flat against the weather with a sheet of pressed tin and set the chair from the ruined cabin on top. Then she scoured the woods for reddening stems of wild dogwood, inserting them in an overlapping pattern around the edge of the dark soil, weaving the twigs together to form a dense, enclosing wall that even from a short distance gave the appearance of a stand of thickly ravelled shrubbery.

By the time she finished, it was late October and frost was sealing off the ground. She spent the last weeks of decent weather hastily putting her household gardens to bed. She'd neglected the summer harvest, let the savory go to seed, the basil turn bitter, the chamomile dry to dust, all the herbs ruined in one way or another, so that there was little to hang from the beams in the kitchen, nothing at all to offer at the Christmas sales.

She expected it to bother her, but it didn't. Looking up at the meagre bundles of oregano and thyme, it suddenly came to her that she'd been wasting herself on garnishes – herbs to dress up a dinner plate or decorate a patio, to mix into a sachet, a bowl of potpourri. How much more satisfying it would be to cultivate a garden of curatives, she thought. And she smiled to herself, imagining the shock of her customers, all those eager weekend decorator-chefs, when they found her sage ground into a gargle instead of arranged in an artful pot.

She felt buoyed again by possibility. When the cold weather forced her inside, she brought the book in, too, making a false bottom in the box where she stored her seeds, certain Walker would never happen across it there. She thought Margaret's story might inspire her in choosing which healing herbs to plant even though none had been mentioned by name. But one day, thumbing through the old book, she noticed again the cryptic lists. She'd never bothered to decipher the long columns of cramped writing that filled the pages reserved for cookery notes, assuming they were nothing but recipes, but now she fixed on the odd shorthand of figures and letters, curious. She brought the magnifying glass she used to sort her smallest seeds and squinted through the lens, scarcely able to believe what she read.

They *were* recipes, though not for the stews and soups she'd supposed. For powders and poultices. Salves and ointments.

Infusions. Decoctions. Tinctures and oils. Detailed instructions for the harvest, preparation, and therapeutic application of a gardenful of herbs. The simples of Margaret MacBayne.

She set the magnifying glass down, waiting for the erratic beating of her heart to calm.

Some of the plant names were unintelligible, phonetic renderings of what she took to be native terms, but of those she could read, almost all were familiar. She'd been growing them for years.

It was the directions for their use that made them seem so strange. Marigold flowers, gathered in full bloom and pounded to a pulp that was enclosed in new linen and pressed, the juice mixed with alcohol to cleanse and close a wound. Comfrey root, dug in the spring and ground to a mass that was smoothed around a broken limb to dry as a healing cast. The leaves of rue, laid fresh among quilts as a discouragement to vermin or boiled to a decoction to expel an unwanted child. Strange prescriptions, she thought. Strange and dire.

The notes were incomplete. When she transcribed them, filling out the abbreviations and expanding the points to sentences, still there was much she didn't understand. What were witches' thimbles? And gillyflowers? By saffron, did the woman mean the stamens of crocus, or did the name refer, in her time, to some other plant? The herb itself was never described, only its habit and use, so there was no way to know which of several gentians or cranesbills Margaret had grown, and surely, she thought, their healing powers would each be different.

She scoured her books for information on settlers' gardens, on the plants they grew, the seeds they brought with them, what they purchased once they arrived. She reread the diaries she'd collected, the lumbermen's accounts and the reminiscences of men and women who had made their homes in the wilderness and of those who had travelled through. She suppressed the urge to skip across the words, to jump in her excitement from one book to the next, reading slowly, moving methodically through the texts, determined not to miss the faintest reference to what was growing in a dooryard or between the stumps, what was crumbled into a tea to bank a fever or laid as a poultice on blistered feet.

It was concurrences she was watching for. Verifications. Evidence to support and augment what she'd found in Margaret MacBayne's lists. She prepared a chart, recording each herb, its Latin name and common names, the cultivars that were grown, its application in the sickroom, the part collected – leaf, stem, flower, root – and how it should be stored, as well as a neat cluster of hieroglyphs at the end of each entry to indicate the soil, the moisture, and the light it preferred, the zone to which it was hardy, the month it would bloom.

Her energy was suddenly boundless, as if those weeks sitting downcast in her chair had been a kind of chrysalis from which she'd emerged like an imago, in perfect form. When she'd gleaned what she could from her own store of books, she drove to the libraries in the villages around, searching in basements and backrooms, through racks of old, discarded books, looking for encyclopedias and histories of herbs, old gardening manuals and botanical treatises, medical pamphlets and books of mother's remedies, dictionaries and grammars of the lost language of flowers and herbs. She begged the librarians to break the rules, to let her see what was hidden, take home more than was allowed, and she thought later it must have been the look of her, a certain wildness about her clothes, her tangled hair, her eyes, that made the women pity her, stamping all the books she wanted, never asking why.

She considered stopping at Renata's to go through the boxes of back-to-the-land manuals her parents had sent her from their bookstore, for she was certain she'd find something useful there. But a visit would have required so much explanation – why she'd stayed away, what prompted her to come – that she never did.

In mid-December, when the ground froze solid and the gravel pit closed for the winter, she stowed away her books, unable to work with him constantly in the house, thinking of Margaret MacBayne, the accommodations she'd made when her brothers returned.

But Walker noticed.

Why did you do that? he asked the first morning as he lingered by the stove. You don't have to stop what you're doing, just because I'm home.

She should have told him then. About Margaret and her brothers. About the garden in the meadow, the collapsed cabin by the stream. But she held back, just as she had the day she burst into the kitchen, though it seemed different to her now, the conversations between them grown so stunted, so diminished that she felt her words stayed not by a look or what she thought he'd want, but by something damaged, something missing inside her.

It wasn't anything, she replied. Just some gardening books.

And he nodded, as if he understood. It's been a bad year, he said.

She wondered what he was thinking of – the blackened harvest, the summer of silence, the anguish of that spring, their solitary winter.

Almost *exactly* a year, she said. A year since you told me you were leaving.

She'd intended it as a recollection, a place to begin, but she saw how he recoiled. She started to apologize, to say it wasn't what she meant, though it was, so she let it be.

He got up and put his teacup in the sink. Then he spread newspapers on the counter, brought in his chainsaw, and started to dismantle the machine, loosening the bolts, removing the arm, lifting off the chain. She turned away, toward the window, wondering how on earth they would bear it, a winter together in that little house.

That year, the ground stayed bare until well after Christmas. The experts predicted wild storms, extreme shifts in the weather, but they were wrong. The snow, when it came, layered steadily in regular siftings. The mercury slid, hunkered low, then rose again in measured increments, laddering toward a spring in which the melt was so gradual that even the basements that always flooded stayed dry.

Early in January, Walker took a job renovating Yae's house, closing in her deck to make a painting studio that would over-look the lake. Her collages of handmade paper, torn and brushed with watercolour inks, were suddenly in demand, she explained, the first morning she came to pick Walker up for work.

Otherwise I couldn't afford this guy, she said, poking at Walker's arm. I hope you don't mind me borrowing him for a while. I promise to have him back every night in time for supper.

It's fine, really. Keep him as long as you want, Alyson said, playing along, though she meant it, too, for nothing would make her happier, she thought, than to spend those winter days alone, cloistered with her books.

It took her most of January to source the seeds for the new garden. On the first of February, she laid out her sketchbooks and pencils, but then she put them away again, unable to conjure anything but what she'd already envisioned – a fragrant hedge around each square, the herbs inside shafting upward like rangy bouquets.

Lavender, broom, hyssop, and artemisia. It was the particular traits of the hedging plants she chose that in the end suggested a way to group the plants on Margaret's list. Within the lavender enclosure, the cleansing herbs, the antiseptics, the diaphoretics that brought on a sweat, and those that siphoned sickness from the body. In the bed bounded by Scotch broom, she would plant the healing herbs that staunched the flow of blood, drew wounds closed, shrank swellings in joints and tissues, paled the discoloration of bruises, knitted broken bones. The hyssop would contain the soothing herbs, the relaxants and carminatives, herbs that allayed pain, cheered the heart, and lifted the spirits. And where the artemisia grew, she'd arrange the tonic herbs, the stimulants and alteratives that worked upon the body as a whole.

She spent long days considering the proper bed for each plant, for most had more than one use. The actual arrangement of the beds she would leave until the spring when she was working in the ground. In every way, the garden would be unlike any she'd ever grown. A planting without design. The harvests would be staggered through all three seasons, sometimes the leaves removed, sometimes the flowers, sometimes an entire plant dug up for its root, but never a mass shearing, a wholesale clearing of a bed. One species or another would always be leafing out or coming into bloom, so that just as the woods remained full from May to September regardless of the cycles of individual plants, so she imagined Margaret MacBayne's garden – always changing, yet steadfastly itself.

When Walker returned in the evenings, she dealt with him kindly, grateful for the long hours he was away. He'd sit with the books he brought home from Yae's, books on ceramics and the *Shinto* religion, on *haniwa*, the ancient burial sculpture of Japan.

She noted the titles with curiosity — *Object as Insight, Spirit Stones, Representations of Sacred Geography* — though when she asked him about what he was reading, his answers were curt so she left him alone. Still, she felt encouraged, thinking it was just as she'd suspected, he hadn't given up the clay for good.

In March, when the work at Yae's was finished and the gravel pit opened again, she saw even less of him. When he was home, he rarely spoke, which was not unusual. He ate, as he always had, quickly, without a word, his head bent to his plate. And he lived to work, although not in his studio. That was different. When he left to walk the bush road to the pit, as well as, see you later, he would sometimes add, don't wait supper, I may go out for a drink. On those nights, it might have been the beer or the company he kept, for he would come to bed hard and demanding, pushing her head between his legs, turning her over to take her from behind or pulling her on top, squeezing her breasts so hard she'd cry out, thrusting himself inside her like a boy who couldn't wait, his lovemaking urgent, the way he ate.

She noticed these things, but she didn't take them to heart. She had been with him long enough to know that one day, without warning, the configuration of their life would alter, and he would be back in his studio again.

It seemed to her that everything she'd ever read, everything she'd ever heard or thought had been leading always to that second spring. All the years of digging in the soil, sniffing the air for frost, attending to the push and pull of the moon, the effect of one species on another. In February, although it meant waiting an extra week, she delayed sowing her seeds until the moon was waxing. When they sprouted, she played music for the plants and bought extra lights to artificially lengthen their day, calibrating the brightness precisely to mimic the advancing spring.

On the markers that identified the seedlings, she noted the application of each herb, so that as she moved among the plants, watering and feeding them, transplanting them to larger pots, she could teach herself their uses. Yarrow was an anti-hemorrhagic, everlasting an astringent, mullein an emollient and an expectorant for coughs and colds. Sweet fennel and thyme were antiseptic. Lemon balm, a febrifuge. Foxglove was a diuretic, good for the heart. Elecampane, safflower, and hollyhock were anti-tussives, healing to the lungs. St. Johnswort was for the bladder, horehound for the bowels, sweet basil for the stomach, tansy for the womb. She repeated the names and their applications until she could stand among her seed flats and recite them from memory. Sage for the throat, speedwell for the liver, hyssop for sore muscles, sweet marjoram for the joints, lovage for the skin, columbine for the nerves, and gillyflowers – which she'd always grown as pinks – for whatever cast a person down-at-heart.

Of all the herbs listed in the old book, only one was missing from her plantings – sorrel. Walker had named the baby Sorrel, she didn't know why. She'd never grown the herb. It was invasive and the leaves were said to be bitter, even when picked very young. I wasn't thinking of the plant, he said when she told him. I just liked the name.

She thought it sounded like sorrow.

All through the trailing end of winter, she heard it in her head as a softly building tone, a two-note chant, a round, a knell. By the first day of spring, it was a steady keening, impossible to ignore, though she tried, filling her days with work, brewing herself a tea of valerian before she went to bed, hoping to induce sleep.

On the thirty-first of March, she moved the seedlings to the greenhouse, intent on honouring her baby's birth in some way other than with tears. But they came anyway, washing through her with their shreds of bitter memories, torn loose by the wailing in her head, and though she tried to hold to the image of her newly swaddled child, it was the icy rain that caught her up, the cannonshot of splitting trees, the soiled nightgown tugged over her head, blinding her, the baby lost.

And she lived it all again, the grief, the anger welling up as if no time had passed. When Walker called for her through the darkness, she stayed in the greenhouse, huddled between the benches, watching the stars, which on that black, moonless night looked like pinholes in the glass.


She set the hedges in the ground first, not knowing how else to begin. She'd started them from softwood cuttings taken in the fall from shrubs growing near the house, so that by the time she placed the lavender, broom, hyssop, and artemisia in their borders around the beds, they were large enough to produce an encouraging, embracing effect.

Next, she moved the herbs she'd rescued. The maturity of those plants gave the beds an instant air of permanence, but it was the ease with which those eight survivors divided naturally and equally among the four beds that cheered her most, for it suggested that the arrangement she'd come to was one that Margaret MacBayne might have used.

It felt strange to proceed without a plan. Wrong, in fact. But she resisted her impulse for order and carried on, planting the seedlings from the greenhouse more or less at random within the appropriate squares, giving herself up to the hidden pattern of things – to her instincts and to what she'd come to think of as Margaret's guiding hand.

For what else could it have been?

One day, late in the spring, she sat at the centre of the garden and surveyed the four squares. The plants were just beginning to fill out, their leaves jostling against one another, though none was yet so tall or broad as to obscure the others from view. Books lay scattered at her feet. She'd made it a habit to bring a knapsack from the house, so that when her work was done she could settle in the chair for an hour or two to study the herbs she'd been tending.

Not only how they healed the body, for that seemed simple

enough, a question of formulae and dosages. And not only their effect on matters of the heart, though she was intrigued by how a common plant could settle a worried disposition or excite flagging spirits. But more than that, she was entranced by how in their habits and traits, plants were once thought to convey meaning. The shape of a flower, the tang of a leaf, or how a plant grew – lush and sprawling or upright with a single meagre bloom, exact in its requirements or thriving in any soil, any light – had each been ascribed with a virtue, a failing, some human desire. Taken together, these particulars became a form of expression, a vernacular that Margaret would surely have known, and one that she herself was learning, the meanings coming to her slowly, piecemeal. Coriander for hidden worth, milkweed for hope in misery. Cornflower for hope in love. The vocabulary accumulating in the way a language does, until individual words no longer need translation, for the whole is understood.

So it was that on a clear day in mid-June she looked out across the garden and saw not an arrangement of cleansing and healing, soothing and tonic herbs, but one bed that signified single-mindedness, another childbirth and sorrow, while in the third she recognized lost love in every leaf.

She got up from her chair and moved closer to the plants, eager for what she had hoped from the beginning she would find there. A final chapter, written not in criss-crossed lines but secreted in the lists she'd deciphered and grown. She scrutinized the beds, taut with anticipation, waiting for whatever it was to make itself known. Then she saw it, an odd greening of the soil, and she bent low over the lavender, shoving aside the yarrow and sage, until she could clearly make it out — sprouts arrowing up through the earth like a stain seeping to the surface, sorrel sowing itself wild among the cleansing herbs.

She sat back on her heels, astonished.

Not Margaret's story, then. Her own.

It didn't come to her all at once. That day, she noticed how the sage and everlasting, planted as astringents, twined their stems around each other, grief allayed in memory. And in the healing bed, the nettles brushing up against the artemisia — cruel absence — made her think of that bed as Walker's, though it would be well into midsummer before she noticed that the solitary milkweed had been all but overwhelmed by the cornflower's profuse blooms.

It was the fourth bed, the tonic bed, that remained a mystery to her longest. At first she thought it must have something to do with Margaret, for at the centre was valerian, a herb with such a repertoire of cures that in the language of herbs and flowers it signified an accommodating disposition. Often, she would pause by that bed, searching for the hidden message she was still convinced she'd find, though when she did, it was not at all what she expected.

It was the branching stem that drew her attention to the low shrub of rue, growing at the foot of the mints. Its stem bifurcated neatly into two wands of yellow flowers, each a perfect reflection of the other, which called to mind the dual nature of the plant, for it was known as both the herb of repentance, herb of grace.

And she thought then of the game of snakes and ladders that Catherine had played with her for hours on rainy days at the farm. The board was old. It had belonged to her father's mother when she was a girl, Catherine said. Its squares were painted with miniature scenes labelled in a fine, upright script, so that when Alyson rolled the dice, her piece would slide down the snakes from Dishonesty to Punishment, from Betrayal to Regret or, if she were lucky, climb the ladders from Patience to Attainment, from Confession to Forgiveness, from Sympathy to Love.

She forgave her mother first and then herself.

When the memories came, she opened herself, gave them room to fill out, all the players with their parts. She viewed them with intense interest, as if she'd never seen them before, as if the scenes had been composed by someone else.

There was her mother, standing at the door, barring it, begging her not to leave, telling her she would regret it, moving in with a man she hardly knew, pleading with her to reconsider, she was still so young. The tone of the tirade desperate, she thought now though she had never seen it, how terrified her mother was for her, for herself.

She'd had her mind made up for weeks, ferrying her favourite books and clothes, piece by piece to Walker's room until, on the morning that she told her parents she was leaving, she had only a small suitcase in her hand. And so she left, giving hardly a thought to either one. Saying nothing to her father, who sat silent on the couch, staring blankly at the wall. Pushing past her mother, who was shouting, You can't do this, I won't allow it, leave now and you can forget about coming here again. But she'd stormed out, escaping to Walker on the sidewalk, yelling back, You can't run my life, *I'm* not crazy in the head.

Then, three months later, that awful pounding on the basement door of the rooming-house where she lived with Walker, her mother accusing at first, I tried to call, where have you been? Then, Oh my god, Alyson, he's gone.

She had lasted through the viewing, through the funeral, through the tears and condolences of her mother's friends. Through all the lies, too, everyone saying it was such a terrible accident, though she knew better. And she'd felt it building, an imperative to tell the truth, or so it seemed to her then. Her mother should have known. Should have seen it coming and never left. Made certain her father was never left alone.

When she thought she couldn't contain herself a moment longer, she'd fled to the kitchen, where she stood at the window, clutching the curtains closed, unable to bear the sight of the concrete patio, its burden of crackling leaves. She felt a hand on her shoulder then, and she turned, glaring, so certain of her own judgment that when her mother said, You should come in, people are asking for you, she'd shot back with words that could never be retrieved – Why? So I can watch you pretend that you had nothing to do with this?

After that, they rarely saw each other, rarely spoke. What words passed between them were weighted with recrimination, and shame. When she and Walker moved to the country, she'd felt relieved, the distance making it easier to let her communications dwindle to a sparse sentence or two above a signature on birthdays and again at Christmas, the cards chosen carefully for the indifference of the message. All the while, her mother's letters lengthened, becoming chatty, full of her cruises, her little Pekinese, the wooden deck built where the patio had been. Never what she was waiting for, never anything about what had gone wrong between them. Reading those letters, she'd wonder who her mother was, how the woman had come to be so easy with the world. Sometimes, inexplicably, she'd feel a yearning to see her again, but then her fury would sweep in and she'd crumple the page, pitch it into the fire. In all those years, never forgetting, never forgiving her mother. In all those years, feeling within her mother's words the unspoken blame.

And yet, recalling the scene in the kitchen, she found she could no longer muster the anger that had fuelled her at the time. For a moment she missed the hard comfort of her anguish and almost reached for it, the succor of a pain kept fresh. Her father. The baby. But there was no nourishment in self-pity or reproach.

What happened simply did. Beyond the bitterness and the blame was only loss, and she couldn't go on like that forever. Sooner or later, she would have to let it go.

She imagined her father, then, as if for the first time. Taking his decision. Toes bare against the slate shingles, pushing off from the roof, his legs lifting into the air, his lean body arching, leaping off and flying. The only time I was truly happy, he always said, was when I was in the air.

# MARGARET

*August 1869*

Where? Which path?

Margaret has seen them in the forest a hundred times, more. She pulls a branch off a dying pine and sweeps at the ground as if they might be hiding there, in the leaf litter, although she knows better. She pushes through the cedars. Were they near the bog? No, on drier ground, she thinks. In the open woods, under the maples or the elms.

Hastening back across the meadow, she steps carelessly on scattered milkcaps. Any other day, these are what she'd be after, scooping them by the handful into the basin of her skirts, chopping them into the stew, stringing what was left to dry for the winter. But no, it is the one Zahgahseega taught her to avoid that she searches for now.

All the mushrooms that spawn in the woods rise to mock her. Pale puffballs and chalky blewits, decaying witch's caps and velvet shanks, elfin saddles and men-on-horseback, lawyer's wigs and waxy caps and slippery jacks, and the ones for which she has no name, pale wisps like faerie hair that sprout from rotting leaves, flat growths on fallen logs, flat as stools for wrisks and *Pukwudj Ininees*.

She sinks to her knees when she spots it, a rusty cap flaked with white. If she cannot find the other, this fly agaric may do. She scrabbles at the rotting leaves, loosens the fruit at its base, lifts it carefully into her pocket, then sitting back on her haunches, she spies another, and another, and she moves around the ragged circle, plucking the deadly faerie ring.

Five, seven, how many will she need? Her Indian friend showed her the proper measure for driving vermin from a bed, for driving a man wild with lascivious dreams, but how many to induce what she desires for her brothers? A deep and lingering sleep.

She hurries further into the trees, scuffing at the ground in search of more faerie rings, more spotted orange fruit, or best of all, the pure white mushroom that is certain to deliver her brothers to her.

It never occurred to her she might not find it. She left this, the easy part, till last, prepared the stew and the antidote first, setting her traps in the night, collecting the limp bodies of six brown hares before the sun was fully risen. She cleaned them by the river, pulling out the stomachs, scooping out the brains, tossing the carcasses into the woods, all but two, slick and pink, that she carried into the cabin just as her brothers stirred, greeting them with a promise of stew, cautious in her demeanour, giving nothing away.

How like newborns the rabbits seemed, the limbs so human in proportion as she cut through them, so like a child's. Bile rose in her throat, but she persisted, breaking the spine with her hands, severing one part from another, dredging them in salted flour, frying them golden in drippings with onions from the garden, a sprinkling of herbs, setting the stew on the stove to simmer, making it tender, irresistible.

*The stomachs of Three hares, the brains of Seven — this, my friend told me, was the Antidote to the poison Mushroom.*

She had only six, would that matter?

She held this thought and others at a distance as she sharpened her knife, the stroke of steel on stone a comfort. She stretched each stringy mass of stomach on the table and minced it fine, spooned the paste into a bowl and set to work on the brains, chopping them to a pudding, the coiled grey matter offering little resistance to the blade of her knife, which rose and fell in a steady rhythm.

Scrabbling through the forest in the long light of late afternoon, she almost gives up. She thinks of the sugar soaking crimson in the blue crockery bowl, and her resolve falters. But in the same instant, her gaze falls upon an opening in the trees, on a spread of early-fallen leaves, on a solitary white mushroom with a veil that hangs in shreds like a decaying bridal shroud.

*It was not until the Sky began to lighten that my Brothers felt the ill effects of our evening Meal. They clutched their Bellies, their Foreheads bathed in sweat. In their Delirium, they did not notice I crept away. Now I wait for them to Sleep.*

Margaret passes the hours of her brothers' agony with words written small upon the page, margin to margin, then she turns the book on its side and lays fresh sentences crosswise over the first. There is room for one last line, but she can think of nothing more to say.

She closes the book and creeps cautiously toward the cabin, pausing by the door to listen. There is no sound from within, only the wind worrying the branches above her head. The brothers lie sprawled, their limbs flung across quilts wrung tight with their thrashing. Quickly, she slips the book into its soft leather bag and wraps it in a square of clean flannel, then she returns it to its hiding place, pushing it deep between the logs, stuffing the gap with rags and bits of loose chinking, propping the mapmaker's drawing in front.

She pulls the blankets up over her brothers, tucking them in for their long night, then she lifts Ewan's coat from its peg by the door. The deeds to the MacBayne land are in the owlskin bag worked with the red-quill leaf that she crosses over her chest like a shield.

She pauses on the threshold, looking back, then latches the door behind her, and touching the lintel for luck, she walks out into the whirlwind of leaves.

# ALYSON

*August 1992*

A lyson was putting the letter to her mother in the mailbox when she saw Réal's red pickup coming up the road, so she waited, the August sun a hot compress on her skin, feeling the satisfaction of having set one thing right, at least, thinking that tomorrow she'd call Renata, suggest a visit, make amends.

When she handed over the letter, Réal slipped the truck out of gear, as he often did, although on that day it seemed to mark the event, something he wouldn't have done if she'd handed him an envelope addressed to the telephone company or the bank. He reached to the dashboard, pulled his tobacco and papers onto his lap, and while he rolled his cigarette, they chatted, exchanging opinions on the sweetness of the corn and the likelihood of rain, Réal filling in the gaps with gossip.

I saw Sauvage this morning at the township office, he said, leaning out the window to exhale along the flank of the truck.

The smoke swirled over the bright metal like mist against a rising sun, and she thought, red sun in the morning, barely listening to what he was saying, something about a road, how it would cut five miles off the trucking route.

She squinted up at him. What are you talking about?

Henri Sauvage. The pit back there. He jerked his thumb toward the trees and raised his voice as if the problem were her hearing or her sense of direction. Says he's buying a piece of your land.

Her throat felt suddenly tight, too dry.

What do you mean? she finally managed.

Saw him applying for a permit to put in a road.

She shook her head, knowing it wasn't possible, though she couldn't make her jaw move. She felt foolish standing there, the truck so high she couldn't see into it properly, Réal looking down at her strangely, then he was handing her a bundle of mail, telling her that the piece he'd called about, the one about *la vieille fille*, was folded in with the newspaper, she couldn't miss it. She nodded, and he put the truck into gear, though his foot hovered on the brake. There was something else.

The way Sauvage told it, you two drove a hard bargain. I figured maybe you'd be taking off, moving out.

Perhaps Walker would make a joke of it — old Réal massaging the story, turning it inside out and backwards, creating something out of nothing. She worked through that scenario as she walked up the lane, hearing Walker's sharp laugh, his reassuring, surely you know me better than that?

The question stopped her, spun her back to the beginning. She tried to imagine it again some other way but, in the end, she had to admit it. There must be some truth to what Réal had said. The land might not be sold, but discussions had taken place. Sauvage had made enquiries. Walker hadn't turned him down.

Just the thought of it infuriated her. A steady traffic of trucks from the pit to the county road, loaded with their harvest of stone and earth. The woods turned into a thoroughfare. What was Walker thinking? He'd been so adamant when they were looking for land. It had to be isolated, he insisted. Absolutely quiet. Together they'd drawn up the list of what they couldn't live without. His clay. Her gardens. Wood enough for the kilns. Wild spaces to wander. A place that would be theirs alone. Now, suddenly, he was willing to let gravel trucks drive through it? It didn't make sense.

Maybe Réal got it wrong, she thought. Sauvage bought someone else's land.

She tried not to worry as she worked through the afternoon, but she could feel the questions circling in the back of her mind. Now and then they'd break through and she'd think again, could he do such a thing? Had he changed so much?

At four o'clock, she put a chicken in to roast and laid the table with the sky-blue cloth. She was about to set out their usual dishes, when she thought, no, and reached to the back of the cupboard for the plates he'd made to celebrate their first year on the land – raku the colour of freshly plowed earth rimmed in the pale, unguarded green of early spring. She found serviettes to match, and a pair of darker green candles. From the terraces by the house, planted now with a tumble of wildflowers, she picked a stem of white campanula, for constancy, and set it in the centre of the table in a slender glass.

She had decided she would say nothing, not a word about what she'd heard until they were finished eating. But then the sight of him, coming through the door, frowning at the table, assessing what she'd done, just the sight of him was enough to disperse all of her intentions.

We have to talk, she said abruptly, struggling to keep her voice level. I saw Réal.

And? Walker bent to untie his boots.

He told me Sauvage was buying a piece of our land.

Walker paused, then he straightened and turned on her that look of his, that glare he used to push her away. She knew for certain, then. What Réal had said was true. A surge of anger rose inside her and she didn't hold it back, she just stood there, letting it dissipate like vapour, so that when she found her voice again, it was cold, the edge tempered.

And when exactly were you going to let me know?

I was waiting until Sauvage was sure he could get a permit. He's supposed to find out tomorrow. I was planning on telling you then.

It was his tone she found so galling. And the way he stood there, almost nonchalant, as if he weren't giving up the very things they'd set their hearts on, the things they'd held to all those years.

Besides, he continued, what Réal said isn't true. Sauvage isn't really buying the land, he just wants to lease a right-of-way. And only for a few years. He's got a big contract south of here and cutting through our farm saves a lot of time. When that job's done, the pit will pretty much be finished. I thought that would make you happy.

But he'll be making a road.

Not where we have to see it.

It might as well be right through the yard, as far as I'm concerned, she snapped back. She couldn't believe he was still defending the idea. Couldn't he see that those trucks would change everything? Wherever they walked, they'd feel a rumble under their feet as if the earth itself was trembling. No amount of money was worth that. I don't understand what's happened to you, she said. We used to feel the same about this.

She grabbed the cooler he brought home from the pit and carried it to the sink, pulling out the empty water bottles and food containers, setting them down hard, lining them up on the counter as if they were points in her argument.

She turned. That was the real reason you didn't tell me, wasn't it? You knew I'd never agree. And you were right. I won't. I don't want any damn road, I don't care how little land it takes.

Well what *do* you want then? Because I'm not counting gravel trucks for the rest of my life. Did you think I'd given up on the clay? Or don't you think about anything but yourself?

That made her stop, but he kept going, his voice rising as he paced a taut square between the door, the table. She stood by the counter, waiting it out, trying to resist the feeling that it was she who'd done something wrong. He had his reasons, he went on, though she hadn't bothered to ask, had she? But it didn't matter. He'd given Sauvage his word, and he wasn't going back on that, not for her, not for anybody.

I'm doing this, he shouted. I have every right. And he slammed out the door, grabbing her keys as he went, gunning the van down the lane in a shower of stones.


By the time she reached the barn, she was running. She shoved open the door to the studio, pushed Walker's wingback chair out of the way, and ripped up the loose floorboard, then she groped between the joists for the strongbox, pulled it up, threw open the lid.

Her birth certificate. The insurance policies on the house, the van. Her father's will that left her the down payment for the property. Underneath it all, the deed.

She riffled through the legal papers, searching for a signature, trying to reconstruct events, her at the bank, arranging the mortgage, encouraging Walker to do his part, dropping him at the lawyer's. Maybe he had signed the deed himself, she thought, and she'd never got around to signing, too. If so, he could do whatever he wanted with the farm, lease the land, sell it. She could feel the panic rising as she ran her finger down each page, and there it was, the proof she needed, not one name, but two. *Walker Freeman. Alyson Thomson.*

She tucked the document under her arm and shoved the rest of the papers back into the box.

No, you don't have the right, she said, addressing the empty studio. This is something we'll decide together.

She never would have seen it if she hadn't jammed the strongbox so furiously back into the hole that a corner caught on the wood, snagging something else, too, dragging it out into the light as she wrenched the box free.

She fished the thing out by one corner, pinching it between two fingers – an old plastic folder, worn and cloudy with age, the dimensions odd, long and narrow, too large for a wallet, a case for a map, perhaps, or insurance documents.

Her first instinct was to fling it back, something she wasn't meant to see.

But it was too late. The folder was cracking open in her hands. Inside were ragged pieces torn from a newspaper. At the back a single sheet of grey, official-looking paper, doubled and doubled again, so small it fit in her palm.

She opened it slowly, the creases all but worn through, as if it had been unfolded a hundred times or more. She laid it on her lap, smoothing out the ridges, leaning over to read.

It was a birth certificate.

*Terry David Hiltz.*

*Date of Birth: The fifth of June.*

Walker's birthday.

A thrill ran through her. This is it, she thought, what he'd kept from her all those years.

Terry Hiltz.

She said it again, out loud. Terry Hiltz. The name made her think of mountains, the earth. Why had he changed it? And why hide this name from her?

She read on, thinking the answer must be there, within her reach.

*Place of birth: Canaan, Vermont*

*Year of Birth: 1950.*

She sat back on her heels. He'd told her he was born in 1960, in New Brunswick. Only the date of birth was the same. Maybe it wasn't him, after all.

She scattered the clippings in her lap and searched through them until she spotted the corner of a photograph, a school picture, dark and blurred. She knew him in an instant. A younger, slimmer Walker, the same bank of sandy hair sloped across the forehead. The eyes that, even then, refused to look.

Underneath the photo, a caption: *Terry Hiltz, still missing.*

The headline was torn off. She flicked her eyes down the columns of newsprint. It was a piece about a house fire, an old place so far out in the country it had burned to the ground before anyone saw the smoke. She scanned the article quickly . . . *started around midnight . . . everyone asleep . . . no survivors . . .* finding what she was looking for at the end.

> *The body of the youngest son, Terry, 15, was not found among the ruins. Authorities continue to search. As of yet, no cause for the blaze has been determined, although it appears to have begun in the cellar of the house.*

And it came to her — all the fires he'd lit in the yard behind the rooming house, just experiments, he'd said, digging a pit and loading it with broken crates and chair backs, offcuts salvaged from construction sites, a match always ready in his pocket, candles burning on the floor, so many fears but not that. She was the one who had worried. *Aren't you afraid it'll get out of control?* she'd asked early on a morning when the flames licked the sky, and he'd turned on her that look of his. As if he thought she knew.

She put her hand to her neck, drew the collar of her shirt closed, the room suddenly grown cold.

There was more.

*FIRE CLAIMS SEVEN, YOUNGEST SON SOUGHT*

Three brothers, a sister, parents, a grandfather, an uncle. The reports spared no detail. Bodies strewn in odd poses. Clutching at a window ledge. Head thrown back. A locket melded to a rib. Legs severed by falling beams. Skin curling off the bone.

My god, she thought. Not warriors. A family.

His family.

Not a gallery. A shrine.

She read all the bits of newsprint, then read them again, the blood in her temples pounding so hard she could no longer think, though she felt it like a certainty – this was the source of the darkness in Walker. What she'd been waiting for all those years, watching so carefully, calling herself foolish and faithless to doubt he was anything but what he seemed to be, a ceramist, self-absorbed but brilliant. All the time knowing there was some-thing else, it could only be called knowing, though she couldn't have said that it was there, hidden under the floorboards of the barn, nor could she have described how it would look, an old plastic folder, yellowed as if steeped in smoke for years. Nor could she have guessed what it contained. Though now that she had seen it, what was she supposed to do?


It was evening by the time she finally got to her feet. She felt as though she'd suffered a blow, knocking all that she'd thought about her life askew, her memories, her perceptions and vision, even her balance affected, so that she had to steady herself as she pushed open the barn door and stepped out.

Even the yard looked different, the slanting rays of the setting sun highlighting contours and facets she'd never noticed before. A perilous lean to the spruces by the house. A subtle undercut on the granite bluff. A rhythm in the eaves from barn to shed to greenhouse, all in perfect alignment, as if each building had slipped into the one behind it. The whole world poised to collapse in on itself.

The lane was empty. Walker was still gone. But he'd be home soon, she thought. He always was. She was sure of that much about him, at least. The quick blast of his temper. The self-reproach that never lapsed into apology no matter how long it lingered, keeping him deep within himself, and she'd have to spend hours, sometimes days, luring him back from wherever it was he retreated to. And she thought: I know that now, too.

She leaned against the kitchen door, closing it behind her, overcome by the thought of those figures, the image of the severed limbs, the scorched skin. He'd recreated each one of them, every shred of burned tissue, as if he'd seen them all. Though he couldn't have, she thought. He must have run, kept running across the border. Was still running.

The pieces fit themselves together. She hardly had to think, only lean against that wooden door and let them surface. The driver's licence he'd never tried for, the jobs that always paid cash, his insistence that she do the banking, buy the van, get the mortgage. He had signed the deed but she remembered now, the lawyer laughing, you're supposed to show me a birth certificate or something, but I guess we all know who we are, right? Once, years before, she had suggested they get married, and he'd said no, absolutely not, a piece of paper wouldn't make him love her more, and she'd been touched, and a little ashamed that she hadn't seen it that way herself.

She pushed herself away from the door, suddenly angry. She swept up the plates, the cutlery, intending to put it all away, then she flung them down again, and grabbing the four corners of the cloth, she lifted the whole thing off the table, bundled it up and pitched it into the corner, wanting it out of her sight.

Had he ever told her the truth? Would he tell her now, if she asked?

And if he did, what would it be? That he set the fire?

No, she thought, brought up short by the question, by the image, again, of those bodies.

An accident, maybe. Teenage boys did stupid things. Renata had told her once about the blowtorch her brother rigged up when he was fourteen, a can of spray paint strapped to the muzzle of a rifle he'd carved out of a two-by-four, a hole for a match at the tip and a trigger that pressed the nozzle open. The flame had shot out six feet, searing the paint off the basement wall.

A careless, thoughtless act. That was something she could understand. But why go missing? Then it came to her what he'd told her, that he'd run away from home. Maybe he'd already left when the fire broke out, she thought. He would have been afraid to go back, thinking he'd be accused, unable to face what he would find — his family, the house, his whole life gone.

She moved to the window, still clutching what she'd found, feeling the weight of it. What he'd kept from her. What he'd had to carry all those years.

She peered down the lane, watching for him, wondering, her mind an agony of questions. She thought of that day, so close to the beginning, when she had begged him to tell her who he really was, and he'd knelt on the grass in front of her.

What you see is what you get, he'd said, stretching his arms wide.

The gesture stung her now. He could have told her then, they could have concealed the truth together, but he'd left her alone, set the silence of his past between them.

She stared out at the dusk, at the empty road. She'd been duped. By him. And by herself. For if indeed she had sensed something, she could have persisted, kept at him until he'd told her everything.

She rested her forehead against the coolness of the window. She tried to imagine it — their life with his secret revealed. Every moment of that night accounted for. Even then, she thought, she never would have let it go. She knew herself that well. She would have seen evidence of the fire's effect and what he had or hadn't done in everything he did. She would have tried to ferret out every detail, for her own sake and his, pulling at him, frustrated by his resistance. The same struggle they'd always had. The secret just a line he'd drawn, a way of keeping to himself. His deepest feelings reserved for the clay.

If she said nothing about the folder, they could go on as before. Except she'd know, and how could she live with that?

The folder, lawyer's papers slipped from her hand, pages fanning to the floor. She bent to pick them up, setting the plastic folder on the table, scanning the words on the deed at random, out of habit, grasping at the distraction, at the legal language that reduced every circumstance to a precise ordering of the facts.

Glancing through the pages, through the formal description of the property, the surveyor's report, the title search, she was surprised she'd never looked at them before, never thought to pull them out when she first found the ruins of Margaret MacBayne's cabin. For they had something to tell her, she could sense it, alert at last to the signs and signals that had been hovering all along.

> *The farm consists of three lots originally registered to three broth-*
> *ers, William, Robert, and Harry MacBayne of Pittenweem, Scotland,*
> *in the fall of 1859. Harry's lot was transferred to William in 1865,*
> *Robert's in 1871. All three lots were bequeathed to Margaret*
> *MacBayne, their sister, on the event of William's death at the age of 85*
> *on August 25, 1919.*

So, there had been no murder.

The story she'd spun around those criss-crossing sentences — it was nothing but a fiction, her own wild invention.

When a calyx splits, cracked open by the wind, the sun, or some invisible pressure, a blossom opens swiftly. That was how the revelations came, one hard upon the other.

She would never know what made her look for Réal's clipping just then. Something he'd said as he handed her the mail.

Had it only been that afternoon?

She found the clipping inside the weekly newspaper, a note scrawled across the top,

*La vieille fille* —

RENFREW TIMES-RECORDER          *Friday, June 19th, 1992*

## The Mystery of Lost Nation

By Jamie MacCallum

HOPEFIELD— Fifty years ago this week, the residents of the upper Opeongo called off their search for Margaret MacBayne, an elderly spinster who went missing sometime in the spring of 1942.

Few today remember the woman, who was said to be the oldest person living in the township. She was famous as a local recluse, and some called her a witch, although this reporter could find no evidence to support the claim.

According to George Pollock, Jr., a former neighbour who has taken up local history as a hobby in his retirement, the MacBaynes were among the area's first settlers. "Not much here then but rocks and trees," he said, when asked what the MacBaynes would have found when they emigrated to Canada.

According to a survey map of the county in Mr. Pollock's possession, three MacBaynes, Harry, Robert, and William, bought adjacent 100-acre lots near Hopefield, in the region known locally as Lost Nation. Margaret MacBayne is not mentioned. Mr. Pollock speculates that she may have been a sister or perhaps a daughter born in Scotland to William, the eldest brother and the only one to stay in the area. According to Mr. Pollock, many settlers moved on after a few years because the land was poor for farming. He has found records of a Robert MacBayne who owned several sections of land in southern Saskatchewan, and a Harry MacBayne who ran a fishing lodge in Algonquin Park. Neither married or had children.

Mr. Pollock's wife, Vera, was in the search party that combed the woods for Miss MacBayne. "I was just seventeen. George was gone to the war. All the young men were, so it was just us girls out looking." The exact circumstances of her disappearance were never established. It was assumed she collapsed from a heart attack or stroke. "We didn't like to think of her lying there alone in the bush, but we never found a thing. We had to give it up."

After Miss MacBayne disappeared, the property was abandoned and fell into ruin. Many said it was haunted. To this day, the fate of Margaret MacBayne remains a mystery.

Not a young heroine bent on revenge. An old woman who endured.

The sound of tires on the gravel, then Walker was there, in the kitchen, urging himself toward her in low, apologetic tones.

I had a plan, he was saying. I was going to surprise you, wait until the deal was signed, then buy a bottle of champagne, lay it all out. I'd go back to work in the studio. No pots, just the figures. I'd give it a year. I made sure Sauvage was paying enough for that. We'd contact the galleries, get an exhibition. I thought you'd help. You're good at that sort of thing. If it didn't work, well, at least I would have tried. Either way, after a year, we could try again for a baby, if that's what you wanted. I was thinking of both of us.

She searched his face as he talked, checking for lines at the edges of his mouth, his eyes. He didn't look as old as he was. His skin was as smooth as hers.

He tried to catch her eye, but she shifted her gaze, and there it was, on the table, sitting out in plain view. At any second, he would turn his head and see it. And he'd tell her another story. One she would believe. For she could feel it like an ache between her ribs, that longing for familiar ground.

No, please, she said, raising up her hand as if to stop him. Not now.

And with that, she moved past him, out the door, into the night, where a slender moon was rising, the closing bracket of a long parenthetical remark. She headed toward it, up the path, into the woods. When the trees closed around her, she paused, the light sieving through the branches too faint to mark the trail. She slipped off her shoes and let her feet find the way, the earth smooth and cool beneath her soles. At the slightest brush of leaf or stem, she veered, feeling for bare soil again, moving forward at the pace of touch.

It was only when she tripped, her arms flinging out to break her fall, her head jerking up, that she saw it, a pale, rounded radiance, not far off the ground, some distance through the trees. She picked herself up and advanced slowly along the path, watching the light, a strange eerie glow that all at once brought to mind their first night on the farm, when Walker had nudged her awake and she'd pulled on her down jacket, trailing after him into the woods to where the slope was steepest, no sound but the crush of snow under their boots. The light then had been so colourless it seemed to come to her through gauze or from a sun slipped too far away. She'd had to squint to see him, already speeding down the slope on the flattened packing box he'd brought, weaving past rocks and trees, calling up to her from the bottom, and though what she'd wanted more than anything was just to stand there until the landscape came clear to her on its own, she had lowered herself onto the cardboard and pushed off with her hands, sledding by moonlight, careering into the darkness, hating every minute of it, hoping for the best.

She stopped. The light stayed to one side. If it was Walker, he was keeping pace with her, though she wondered what he was carrying that would shine with such a greenish hue.

She moved forward again, holding her breath, listening for his step. A slow wind moved through the treetops, coming at her from a distance, stirring the leaves as it passed. Something skittered across the ground. A nightjar shrieked.

He must have seen the folder. Why else would he follow her now?

She called out.

The light held steady in the silence.

She'd left it there on the table, a simple, unthinking gesture, but maybe this was what she'd intended, after all.

She leaned into the underbrush, staring, not sure what it was she hoped to see. She focused on the light and, slowly, the contours of a wide, slanting stump emerged, the cut face of it shimmering as if the heartwood still smouldered with an ancient flame.

Foxfire, witch's bloom, will-o'-the-wisp, corpse's light. The scientific name was barren by comparison, though precise in its description. Bioluminescence. The light produced by life, by mushrooms feeding on rotting flesh, neither wood nor fungi visible, the boundaries of matter dissolved in that singular light.

There was no one in the woods but her.

She carried on, pausing when she left the shadow of the trees to slip on her shoes again.

Night had almost fully fallen, though she could still see across the meadow. Night in the north was never as dark as she'd once thought it would be, sitting on the doorstep of their rooming house in the city. She'd pictured a blackness, then, so blinding that it would obliterate the landscape, but beyond the glow of street lights was the light of the sky itself, hiding nothing, only softening the edges of things, tempering every colour to some subtle shade of grey.

She moved through the grasses toward the hedge of dogwood, toward the break in the woven stems that would indicate one of the paths that crossed through the garden. She'd taken this route more times than she could count, but it had always been in the daylight and the landscape seemed unfamiliar now, reshaped by shadow.

The garden was transformed. She stood, staring at the four squares, at the leaves and flowers coalescing in the gloom, all the fragrances mingling in the air, tantalizing, only the whitest blooms still visible — dame's rocket, sage, pearly everlasting.

A different story altogether.

It would shift again when the sun rose, become something else in the spring. Alter with the years in spite of her, in ways of its own determining.

Nothing fixed, nothing certain.

Once she would have pushed such a thought from her mind, cast about for something rooted to take its place, but now she let herself see the truth in it. The possibility.

She moved into the garden, walking the periphery, touching the edges of the plants, marvelling at how the shapes and colours metamorphosed in the night, her fingers on a stem appearing lean and purposeful, the capable hand of her aunt. When she came to the chair at the centre, she settled into it, conscious of the book concealed in the ground beneath her, thinking of Margaret MacBayne, the old woman, the young woman, too. And the brothers, waking from their sleep, frantic at their sister's absence, never suspecting what she'd done, so that by the time she'd found her way back to the cabin, something must have softened in William and he agreed to stay, moving the log barn, building the little house, sheathing it with pressed tin.

Soon, she thought, she would return to the house and Walker would say what he had to say. She would let him remain undisclosed, if that was what he wanted. But she had things to tell him, too. A world of things. And from all their words, she would take what she needed, what she needed to make sense of what had happened, of who they'd been, of wherever it was that they found themselves now. Of where she might go from here.

For the moment, though, she would stay, watching the pale flowers brighten like stars as the darkness deepened. The night air cooled, taking on substance. She felt it as a fabric draped loosely over her body, over the garden, the trees, the house. Every breath she took rustled leaves in the canopy, shifted doors in their frames. As the breeze died down, earth-scents rose to take its place.

# ACKNOWLEDGEMENTS

*The Holding* was inspired in part by my great-great-grandmother, Margaret Cornfoot, who emigrated from Pittenweem, Scotland, to make a home in the Canadian bush, and by her forbear, Jannet Cornfoot, who died on the beach at Pittenweem, January 30, 1705, the last Scottish woman stoned to death as a witch. Although the depiction of Jannet Cornfoot's death corresponds to the historical record, the rest of Margaret's story is imagined.

The incident of the chopping contest was loosely based on a report in Samuel Thompson's memoir, *Reminiscences of a Canadian Pioneer 1833-1883*. I am grateful to all the diarists and memoirists who left such a rich encyclopedia of stories of the settling of this country, and especially to the many scholars who have made a study of early gardens, herbs, and their uses, most particularly Eileen Woodhead, whose *Early Canadian Gardening: an 1827 Nursery Catalogue* proved invaluable in recreating Margaret MacBayne's garden.

The native tales that Alyson imagines Margaret and her Indian friend sharing are adapted from those collected by Anna Jameson after her travels to the Ojibwa nation in 1836-37 and published in *Winter Studies and Summer Rambles in Canada*, and also from the *Algic Researches* published by Indian Agent Henry Rowe Schoolcraft, a keen student of native customs and language who kept detailed records of hundreds of interviews with natives between 1822 and 1841. My appreciation to Ojibwa scholar Basil Johnston for his consultations. As much as possible, I have retained the archaic spellings used in books that Alyson might have had easy access to. Any errors are my own.

Several people have been instrumental in the development of the novel, principally, Karen Landman, professor of plant design at the University of Guelph, a woman of calm and gracious intelligence who was more generous with her time and knowledge than any friend has a right to expect.

I also owe a debt of gratitude to ceramist Steve Irvine for his scrupulous reading of the text, as well as to plant historian Patricia MacDonald and her colleagues at the University of Edinburgh, to restorationist Richard Moll for his expertise in the preservation of paper, and to cultural historian and writer Joan Finnigan MacKenzie, without whom the stories of the Opeongo would have been buried with those who lived them. My appreciation, too, to Emily Conger for the use of the log cabin in the woods where much of Margaret's story was imagined. To Lori Richards, my admiration for the visual sensibility she so willingly shares, and especially, my thanks for the title.

To my sisters, my children, and my friends, particularly my dearest friend, Diane Schoemperlen, my deepest thanks. To my husband, Wayne Grady, words just aren't enough.

My profound appreciation to my editor, Ellen Seligman, who has with astonishing skill and patience brought this book from my desk to its readers. Also to her assistant, the ever-gracious Anita Chong, for all her help; to Kong Njo, for his sensitive and elegant design; and to copy editor Jenny Bradshaw for her perspicacity. To Bella Pomer, my agent, my enduring gratitude for her devoted support.

The four years of writing *The Holding* were punctuated with the loss of several people dear to me. To them, I dedicate this book – Matt Cohen, Al and Zoe Grady, Michael Keeling, Robert Simonds, Ellen Stafford, Zal Yanovsky.